NOAH'S
GARDEN

NOAH'S GARDEN

Rosemarie E. Bishop

Library of Congress Number: 00-190569
ISBN #:   Hardcover   0-7388-1838-0
        Softcover   0-7388-1839-9

This book was printed in the United States of America.

To order additional copies of this book, contact:
Xlibris Corporation
1-888-7-XLIBRIS
www.Xlibris.com
Orders@Xlibris.com

CONTENTS

*This story is dedicated to my nieces and nephews, and in order,
as my grandmother, Sophie Lagowski, always said,
"Ladies before gentlemen; age before beauty."
Renee, Jamie, Mariah, Candice, Madison, Emily,
Christopher, Brennan, and Nicholas.*

I want to thank the children in my life who inspire me on a pure level and my friends, especially Michelle Grucela, Mindy Riley, Suzanne LeBlanc, and Debbie Simbalist, who stand behind me no matter what. I want to thank Suzanne for her help in creating the cover of this book and the "soul sisters" for their friendship and assistance in showing my spirit a higher level in which to soar. I wish to thank my original editor, my mother, Elaine Mandy, for her wisdom and vision in all my projects and my father, Stephen Mandy, for his unending support even in my worst times. And I'd like to thank them both for the picture of their property in Friendship, NY which is on the cover of this book because it is a true expression of the paths we must choose, then follow. I want to thank my in-laws, Patricia and Raymond Bishop, for extending my family with love and accepting me without question. And so much thanks to Alison & Steve Bishop, Diane & Dennis Miller, and Kathy & David Mandy for the godchildren that give my soul a very special place. Most of all, though, I want to thank my husband, Christopher, for his willingness to grow, to learn, and to never stop getting better as a person, a husband, and a friend. It is his love and open heart that proves there is hope for everyone who is willing to really try.

"We are all masters in our own evolution."
Deanne Beaudoin - Reiki Master

CHAPTER 1

Jewell ran as fast as her padded feet could push her through the moonlit backyards that bordered where she lived. She'd been tied up for hours without a thought and now it was exhilarating to finally be free. She ran through the woods behind all the newly built houses, past the last one on the street that was still under construction and straight ahead without looking back, not even once. The wind blew hard and furious, but she didn't care. It felt good, refreshing, free. Her long, black and brown hair flew wildly around her as she raced into the trees that had grown for centuries beyond where her neighborhood now stood. The rest of those beautiful trees had been cut down to make room for all the families that kept moving in.

She crossed the freshly paved country road that wound its way through the wooded land on the other side and away from the young neighborhood she had just left. The pavement was hard on her feet, but the brief discomfort didn't matter. She could go where she wanted now, do what she wanted, and no one could stop her. No one would even find her. She was determined to make absolutely sure of that as she ran so fast that everything appeared to fly by.

On the other side of the road she entered a larger wooded area. It felt good to be on soft, moist ground again and it made her run faster. She ran through the trees and over the railroad tracks as if her life depended on it, nearly tripping when she landed on the sharp decline on the other side, but she caught her footing and continued into the meadow that was her favorite place in the summertime. The meadow was cold and wet now that it was autumn, but that didn't slow her down.

When she was on the other side she lost her balance for the second time and plunged into a deep, thick, mud puddle. She reached out for the edge in order to find something solid to step on and felt a rock brush against the bottom of her foot. Using it for stability, she quickly crawled out and shook off the mud, then looked around to get her bearings on which direction she was going to head next. For a moment she wondered if this might not be such a good idea after all, but the huge horse farm where the angry rottweiler lived caught her eye, and without a second thought she was headed straight for it. It only took seconds before the big, black dog was hot on her trail for making all the noise in the yard, but the farm was fenced on this side of the property, so the old canine could not get to her. All he could do was chase her down along the inside of the gate.

Jewell was safe.

As she ran past the farm she could feel her leg muscles begin to tire, but she pushed herself to keep going. She was home free, now with nothing but trees for miles and miles. They would allow her escape to continue as easy as it had been so far and it was the trees that would keep her safe once their denseness grew and became the forest with its thick expanse of foliage she had so admired. She looked around to get her bearings and saw that she didn't have much farther to go before she reached the place she'd never been to, so she pushed herself forward even though she was breathing heavy now.

When she was deep in the woods she slowed a bit. Far ahead she could see a grassy clearing and the forest that stood on the other side. That was where she wanted to go. She had been this far before, to the edge of the forest with its large, thick growth of trees and underbrush that she could barely see into, but it had been off limits in the past. Not this time, though. Now she was free to go where she wanted, and into that forest was exactly what she had in mind for no reason other than the fact that she'd never been allowed to go there before. She stood for a few moments, panting hard, trying to catch her breath, yet anxious to get where she had always dreamed of going. She waited until her breathing slowed before she took one last look behind her, thought about her family, remembered the chains, then took off at full speed.

Jewell ran through the rest of the woods, across the grass, and straight into the forest. It was a new place for her, a place where she had never been before. The mysterious, intriguing forest that she had only seen from the outside held her spellbound whenever she stood at its edge. She would stare into its dark mass of green and brown, think she saw things moving, but she could never tell what they were. She'd always wanted to step into the endless trees, investigate, maybe chase a thing or two, but she'd never been allowed.

Now, she was here! Now, she was inside the very place she had wondered about for so long. She could see nothing but trees in front and to either side of her.

Trees and neverending darkness. She looked around, suddenly alarmed. This was not quite what she had expected. It was too dark in here and Jewell was frightened.

Jewell's pace slowed as she continued to try to find her way. It hadn't seemed to be like this when she was on the outside looking in, so dark and uncomfortable. Why hadn't she noticed it before? Now that she was inside the forest she could hardly see a thing, but she could hear noises all around her. Her fear brought her to an abrupt halt in the middle of nowhere. She was cold and wet, covered with mud that still dripped from her hair. Her legs were sore and trembling from having taxed their endurance as she tried to get here as fast as she could. She was breathing so hard her lungs ached. The cold, damp air she inhaled made her chest feel as if it were freezing inside of her body and there was nothing she could do to warm up. Being in the forest didn't seem like such a good idea, anymore. She wasn't having fun. Her former curiosity had quickly been overshadowed by the abrupt onset of fear and she was surprised that she only wanted to be home when all her life she'd wanted to be anywhere but home.

She turned around to look behind her, expecting to see her

own footprints so she could follow them back out the way she had come in and get out of this cold, dark place. But she could not see a thing. She looked frantically from side to side and all around her, but she didn't have a clue which direction she'd actually come from. Her fear and desperation got the best of her and she began to cry.

She was lost, terribly frightened, and so exhausted she could hardly think straight. Her muscles were throbbing, her chest burned from breathing in the cold air. There was nothing else she could do except to stay put until morning when the sun would shed some light on her whereabouts. But for now, it was hopeless and she knew it.

Jewell sat down in the cold, wet leaves that were strewn everywhere beneath the dark canopy of trees. She cried endlessly in heart wrenching sobs and in soft whimpers until she finally laid down and cried herself to sleep.

CHAPTER 2

Jewell awoke to the melodious sound of humming close by. She felt snug and warm the way she did when she was in her own bed at home.

Home. Was she really home?

Maybe she was never lost. Maybe it was simply an awful dream.

She heard the noises coming from her stomach as it rolled over inside her. Breakfast was a welcome thought.

Jewell stretched her body fully before opening her eyes to the day, but what she saw confused her. She looked around, saw the trees and brush now that the sun had risen, felt the leaves and moss beneath her fur, smelt the fresh earth, and the memories of the previous night came flooding back. She wasn't home at all.

Disappointed, she took a deep breath, then laid her head back down on the ground. She could see the foliage more clearly than before, but there was nothing normal, nothing familiar about any of it. These trees seemed to shimmer and sparkle as if they were covered with droplets of rain that reflected the sun's rays, but they weren't wet at all. Even the leaves beneath where she lay were dry. It was a different world compared to what she saw last night. This morning the forest actually looked . . . pretty.

Still, the sad truth remained. She was lost.

"So it wasn't a dream," Jewell said out loud.

"No," a comforting voice said from behind her. "You really are still here."

Jewell's head spun wildly around, shifting her entire body with it. Right beside her lay a beautiful doe with soft brown eyes, a comforting smile, and a sweet aroma of springtime all around her. Jewell jumped to her feet, surprised. "Who are you?" she asked.

The deer also stood up slowly and stretched her limbs. Then she bowed her head toward Jewell and her gentle voice spoke once more. "I am Daffonia," she said. "I kept you warm and dried you off while you slept. I was afraid you might get sick from the dampness that was in your hair." Daffonia looked at Jewell with an almost motherly expression on her face, but said nothing while she watched Jewell inspect her.

Jewell walked around Daffonia in a cautious manner. She'd seen deer before, chased them, too, but no deer ever smelled like flowers. "I'm Jewell," she said, sitting down on the carpet of leaves. She wasn't afraid now that the sun's light had given definition to the forest. "What kind of name is Daffonia, anyway?" she asked.

"A very old one," the doe said. "What kind of name is Jewell?" She took a few steps toward a nearby bush that was full of blueberries.

Jewell watched as Daffonia began to nibble on the fruit that grew on the little bush. Every few seconds she looked sideways at her, as if expecting an answer.

Jewell was hungry, and she guessed Daffonia knew it. As much as she wanted to walk right over to the bush and see just how those round blue things tasted, she didn't want to reveal any kind of weakness. She did not want Daffonia to know she was driving her crazy by eating in front of her like this. Jewell let out a soft, frustrated whine as she stared at Daffonia, then at the berries once more before deciding to answer the deer's question.

"I guess Jewell is a fairly young name," she said. "I really don't know."

"Well, how old are you?" Daffonia asked. She continued to enjoy her morning meal, but watched Jewell carefully.

"Thirty five." Jewell tossed her nose in the air in a precocious manner.

"Thirty five?" Daffonia's voice had an evident air of disbelief. "You certainly don't act like it. Tell me the truth, Jewell. How old are you, really?"

Jewell turned slowly toward the deer and did her best to maintain a direct gaze into Daffonia's eyes as she spoke. "I am thirty five!" she said, almost demanding that Daffonia believe her. But as she watched Daffonia's expression soften into one of understanding, Jewell knew she was caught in her little, white lie. "In a dog's life, that is," she added, looking away. "In human years, I'm only five." She shrugged. "At least that's what my friends told me."

Daffonia raised her head and smiled. "Ahh, now that sounds more like it," she said. She reached down and picked a mouthful of blueberries from the bush, then walked over to Jewell, and dropped the berries at her feet. Then she turned around and lay down on the ground. "Eat them," she said to Jewell. "They're very good."

Jewell looked at the blue things lying on the ground, sniffed them for a few seconds, then decided she'd rather have the food she was accustomed to.

"They're better for you than what you've been eating until now," Daffonia said, seeming to have read Jewell's mind. "At least try them. If you really don't like them, there are many more kinds of food in this forest. Sooner or later we'll find something that agrees with you."

Jewell looked uncertainly at the deer who lay calmly by the blueberry bush nibbling at its fruit here and there. Then she looked at the berries once more. The grumbling in her empty pit of a stomach made the decision for her. Jewell reached down, gingerly picked up a single berry, and carefully rolled it around on her tongue for a few seconds, trying to get up the nerve to crush it in her mouth. It was the simple accident of her right fang nicking the unsuspecting blueberry at just the right angle that finally let a small spurt of juice ooze across Jewell's tongue. The fresh picked berries had a sweet, clean taste. "Mmmmmm," she said. "That's very good."

"I thought you might enjoy it," Daffonia said.

Jewell gobbled up the rest of the berries that lay at her feet. "Are there a lot of these berries around here?" she asked.

Daffonia nodded. "Anywhere you see a patch of sun on a little, rocky hillside, you'll find these berries," she said. "But there are many other kinds of berries in this forest, as well as many other kinds of fruit."

Jewell jumped up and ran toward Daffonia. "What about meat?"

Daffonia cringed visibly.

"I'm sorry," Jewell said, thinking she had frightened the deer with her playful antics. "I wasn't going to jump on you or anything."

"No, it wasn't that," Daffonia said. She slowly rose to her feet. "No one who lives in this forest ever eats meat."

Jewell stood still and looked at the kind doe as if she were purple. "Why not?" she asked. "Meat is delicious! My family always gives me meat."

Again, Daffonia cringed though with a more tolerant air about her this time as she walked to Jewell's side. "Because my dear, Jewell," she began, "meat comes from animals."

"What?" Jewell asked, surprised.

"That's right," Daffonia replied. "Animals like me or even like you. After all, meat is meat as far as we're concerned. Why one of my best friends in all the world is a cow. I'd no sooner eat my best friend than I would eat myself. Humans are barbarians in that regard."

Jewell didn't know what to say, but she was thoroughly disgusted.

"Don't you agree?" Daffonia asked.

Jewell shrugged. "I guess so," she said. "When you look at it that way I suppose I have to agree with you. How awful! I never knew."

"Of course you didn't," Daffonia said in a soft tone. "How could you? You're just a dog, after all."

Jewell frowned. "What does that have to do with anything?" she asked. "I may be a dog, but I'm not a stupid dog."

Daffonia smiled. "No, you're not stupid," she said to Jewell. "It's not your fault that you didn't know what meat was. Your

human family, who you love and trust unquestioningly, was feeding it to you. What reason could you have had to even wonder
about it? To humans, and to many animals, it means nothing."

Jewell slowly tilted her head as she looked at Daffonia, trying
to figure out what the deer was getting at. But eventually it made
perfect sense to her. She wasn't stupid at all. It was the humans
who had been stupid.

"Does meat come from people, too?" Jewell asked Daffonia.

"It sure does," the deer answered. "In fact, in some places in
the world, people actually eat each other."

"Yech!!" Jewell said almost spitting. "That's gross!"

Daffonia took a few steps deeper into the forest. "Isn't it,
though?"

"Hey, where are you going?"

"The same place you're going." Daffonia continued to walk
away slowly.

"Where's that?" Jewell asked.

"To Noah's Garden," the deer answered.

Jewell ran to Daffonia's side as fast as she could from fear that
her new friend might disappear. She didn't want to be left alone in
a place that was completely foreign to her.

"Don't worry," Daffonia said, nearly laughing. "I'm not about
to abandon you."

"Why don't I just go home and come back to see you another
time?" Jewell asked. She was beginning to get a little nervous.

"Because you can't," Daffonia said. "You ran into the forest in
search of something. This is a very special forest, Jewell. You cannot just come and go as you please here until you have obtained
what you came for in the first place."

"Why not?" Jewell asked. "Why can't I come back every so
often just to visit?"

"Would you come back?" Daffonia asked.

"Sure I would," Jewell said, but she wasn't really sure herself if
she would or not. Especially after how frightened she was last night
and her inability to find her way out.

"You can visit other forests, Jewell." Daffonia continued her stroll deeper into the trees. "But this one is special. This one holds many secrets that are here for everyone and anyone who cares to look for them. But until you fully understand the magic of this place, you cannot be allowed to leave just to tell stories about it to your friends. This forest is different and personal to each soul that enters it."

"What's it called?" Jewell asked. She looked at the tree tops in awe as they sparkled like glitter.

"Why Noah's Forest, of course," Daffonia said, smiling.

"Noah's Forest?" Jewell asked. "Then what is Noah's Garden?"

Daffonia stopped walking, looked at Jewell, and smiled. "Noah's Garden is at the heart of this forest," she said. "That is where you'll be when you reach the end of this journey."

"Will it take long?" Jewell asked. She was frightened at the thought of going further, and she was beginning to miss her neighborhood and friends.

"It might seem that way at times," Daffonia said. "But when it's all over, you won't think it was long at all."

Daffonia continued her leisurely gait while Jewell stood still, uncertain whether or not to follow Daffonia or try to find her own way out.

"Are you coming, Jewell?" Daffonia's voice seemed to echo through time itself as she walked farther and farther away.

Jewell watched her grow smaller with each step. She still didn't know what to do, but when Daffonia was nearly a dot, and all Jewell could see of her was the whiteness of her tail, she panicked, afraid to be alone and lost. She started to run after her as fast as she could. "Don't leave me, Daffonia," she yelled. "Don't leave me alone! I'm coming with you Daffonia!"

In an instant, she completely lost sight of the friendly deer. Out of sheer and utter dread, Jewell stopped dead in her tracks and froze in place. She looked around, moving only her eyeballs to see what she could see. The rest of her body had become paralyzed from fear. Once again in such a short amount of time she was lost and alone. Why did she question herself for even a moment? Why didn't she just follow Daffonia right from the start? What was she afraid of? She wasn't too happy back home either, so why was she in such a hurry to go back there?

"Because it's familiar," said Daffonia. She walked out of a thicket of trees next to where Jewell stood. "Only because it's familiar."

"Daffonia?" Jewell said, excited. "Oh, I'm so glad to see you."

"That's nice to know," Daffonia said, bowing her head in a gracious manner. "Now I'm familiar to you."

Jewell thought for a moment, then looked at Daffonia and smiled. "That's right," she said. "You're familiar."

"Then you should not feel lonely anymore," Daffonia said smiling. "And I won't feel lonely either, because you're familiar to me, too."

Jewel raised her eyebrows and tilted her head. "I am?"

"You are," Daffonia said with a nod of her head. She nudged the side of Jewell's head with her nose. "Now, are you ready to walk with me?"

Jewell looked tentatively at Daffonia for only a split second before she smiled at the deer and turned to face toward the heart of the forest.

"The other way," Daffonia whispered.

"What?" Jewell asked.

"The other way," Daffonia repeated. "Turn around. Your headed the wrong way."

Jewell looked at the deer, embarrassed, and shrugged her shoulders. "OK. How about if I just follow you?"

"That'll be good for starters," Daffonia said. "Then we'll walk together."

Jewell smiled. "I like that."

"Good, then let's go," Daffonia said, taking the first step toward the next leg of their journey.

CHAPTER 3

Jewell and Daffonia walked for a short time in silence. All around them the trees continued to sparkle as if covered with glitter or gem stones. Every few seconds Jewell saw a small but vivid splash of color mixed in with the illusion of wet leaves and wondered where these colors were coming from. She had never seen such a sight before and it amazed her.

"So, what were you running away from last night?" Daffonia asked her.

Jewell hesitated a moment while she thought about the question. It had been a spur-of-the-moment decision for her to run away even though she had thought about doing it many times. But she wasn't sure she wanted to tell Daffonia the whole story.

"Oh, I wasn't really running from anything in particular," she said.

"I see." Daffonia looked around the forest as if she were seeing it for the first time. "Well, you were in an awful hurry to go somewhere."

Jewel stuck her nose in the air and looked away. "I just wanted to get away," she said. "I wanted to see and do new things."

"Mmmmm." Daffonia nodded, then changed the subject. "There's a patch of berries up ahead," she said. "If you're still hungry, you're welcome to join me for a little snack. We could both use the extra energy for our morning walk. You never know when we'll find these berries again and I'd hate to end up starving simply because I didn't eat when I had the chance."

Jewell turned to look at her and frowned. "Don't you know your way around the forest?" she asked in a sarcastic manner.

Daffonia shook her head. "Not always."

Jewell was surprised. "How can that be?" she asked. "Haven't you lived here long enough to know your way around?"

"Oh, I've lived here for a very long time," Daffonia said. "But I only come out to the forest when someone new arrives. Every journey back to the garden is different than the time before."

Jewell felt an uneasiness creep into her thoughts. "Why is that?" she asked.

Daffonia looked at her and smiled. "Because the journey belongs to the newcomer, in this case, you," she said. "This is your adventure, Jewell, not mine."

"What do you mean?" Jewell asked. She knew her voice was shaky, but she couldn't help it.

"Relax," Daffonia said, smiling as they approached a patch of red berries that grew close to the ground. "I'll do my best to explain while we stop here for a snack."

"Suddenly, I'm not so hungry." Jewell sat next to the patch of red berries and watched her new friend begin to nibble on them.

Daffonia walked over to her and gently pushed her in the ribs. "Oh, go ahead and eat," she said. "You really do need the nourishment."

Jewell looked at her through the corner of her eyes, then stood up and inched her way toward yet another new culinary experience. She looked at Daffonia twice before she picked the first strawberry from the little stem. These berries tasted sweeter, with no outer skins to get stuck between her teeth. She liked them.

"You see," Daffonia said, "every creature that lives within the bounds of the forest actually spends their time in the garden. We almost never venture into the forest unless we have to."

Jewell swallowed her first mouthful of berries. "Why not?" she asked.

"Because everything we need is in the garden."

"But it's so pretty and sparkly here in the forest." Jewell looked around at the trees once more and saw a flash of deep golden light blink four times, then disappear.

"Yes," Daffonia agreed, "but the garden is beyond compare in beauty. Once you've been there, you would have no desire to be anywhere else."

"Then why leave at all?" Jewell asked.

"Because you were headed this way," Daffonia answered. "Someone had to be there to greet you as you entered the forest. Look at the state you were in when you realized you were lost."

"That's because it was so dark," Jewell said. For a moment she relived her fear of the night before. "I couldn't see anything and I was . . I was . . scared."

Daffonia gave her a sympathetic look and smiled. "I know, Honey" she said. "That's why I got to you as fast as I could."

"Well, it wasn't fast enough!" Jewell snapped. "If you were really supposed to greet me, you would've been right there when I ran in. I would have never been so afraid if you were there."

Daffonia nodded. "That's true," she said, "and I'm truly sorry that I couldn't be there at the exact moment you entered the forest. The truth is, I wasn't supposed to be."

Jewell flashed her an angry look with a frown that caused deep furrows above her eyes. "What do you mean?" she asked, growing angrier by the minute. "Do you mean that you left me all alone, as frightened as I was, on purpose?"

Daffonia glanced away and sighed deeply before answering. "Yes," she said, hanging her head.

"Well, that's some kind of greeting," Jewell said, spitting out the berry she had just begun to chew. "I don't think I like you or this place very much, just now."

"I understand," Daffonia said softly.

"Then why did you do that to me?" Jewell demanded. "What kind of place is this, anyway?"

Daffonia lifted her head proudly, then pranced over to a plant that was so full of berries its stems hung all the way to the ground. She picked a mouthful of nine berries and dropped them on the ground at Jewell's feet. Without saying a word, the deer backed up and returned to her original place before answering. "The forest is a learning place," Daffonia said. "It isn't open to every-one. It isn't seen by everyone, either. It's only seen by those who are looking for something that they lack within themselves. Only those of Abba's creatures who need the forest are able to enter or to even see it."

Jewell's face softened and she cocked her head to the side. "Who's Abba?" she asked. "You say 'Abba's creatures', but I belong to my family. I don't know anyone named Abba."

"Abba created everything," Daffonia said. "And He takes care of everything He created."

"Well, he doesn't take care of me." Jewell turned away. "My family takes care of me."

"Do you take care of them in return?" Daffonia asked.

"I don't have to," Jewell answered. "They take care of me and they take care of themselves, too."

"Then what do you do?" Daffonia asked.

Jewell looked at her and smiled from ear to ear. "I run around the neighborhood and play with other dogs," she said. "There's a great, smelly swamp in the woods behind the houses that we run in and chase frogs and birds and all kinds of little things. Some-times we tear up all the garbage in the whole neighborhood and eat all the scraps of food and play with everything else. We go visit the other dogs that are always tied up and try to get them loose so they can run with us. It's a great time."

"So you're something of a leader," Daffonia said.

Jewell stopped talking and looked surprised. She hadn't thought of it that way before, but now that it was mentioned she liked the idea that she was the leader. It made her feel important. "Yeah," she said proudly. "I'm the leader."

"Don't any of you get into trouble?" Daffonia asked.

"Well, yeah," Jewell said. "Some of us do. Our families get mad at us sometimes." Jewell thought of her family and the rope that tied her to the post every time she got caught. She was quiet for a moment, then shrugged. "But, so what?" she said. "At least we have a good time."

"Well, that sounds like quite a lot of fun," Daffonia said.
"It is."

"Then what is it that you're not happy with?"

"Well, that part is fun," Jewell answered, "but sometimes I'm tied up and I don't like that. Sometimes I have to be on a leash when I want to go to other places, like into this forest. But I'm never allowed. That's why I ran away, so I could do all the things and go to all the places I was never allowed to before."

"Why do you think you weren't allowed to?" Daffonia asked.

"Because they were being unfair to me," Jewell complained. "I thought about running away lots of times before, too."

"Then what took you so long to finally do it?" Daffonia asked.

"I don't know. I finally did, though, because they were trying to teach me tricks and stuff," Jewell said. "Things like sit, drop, and stay. That's the one I refused to do. 'Stay!' they'd tell me, and really expect me to sit in one place until they said I could move. No way!"

Daffonia looked at her knowingly with a superior look that infuriated Jewell. "I'm surprised you didn't bring any of your friends with you," she said. "What with all the fun you have together, I would have thought you'd bring them here, too."

Jewell thought about that. The truth was, she hadn't even thought of bringing anyone with her. Once she saw the chance to run away she just started running. She never looked back and she never thought about her friends in the neighborhood. Suddenly, she was no longer angry with Daffonia's attitude. Instead, she felt bad, but she was not about to let Daffonia know it. "This is my adventure," Jewell said. "I'm not sure I want to share it with anyone."

"You're sharing it with me," Daffonia said, smiling.

"That's only 'cause you're already here," Jewell said.

Daffonia nodded. "Well, that's true," she said. "Still, it seems that you wouldn't have been so frightened last night if you'd had a friend with you."

Once again, Jewell stopped to think about Daffonia's words. She was making a lot of sense. But Jewell was determined that she was smarter than anyone else. "I'm brave enough to go out on my own," she said. "I don't need anyone else."

Daffonia glanced over at Jewell and shook her head. "Are you glad you ran away, now?"

Jewell looked around the forest again, catching a flash of pink light this time. "Yes, I am," she said. "I like it here."

She lay down by the pile of berries Daffonia had brought her and began to eat them in earnest. She enjoyed their sweet, earthy taste.

"That's good," Daffonia said. "It's important you like it here."

"Well, I do," Jewell said between swallows of strawberry juice. "But I still don't understand why you had to let me come in here all alone and be afraid."

"Were you happy to see me when you woke up?" Daffonia asked her.

"I sure was," Jewell answered, her tough exterior shattered for a moment.

"That's why," Daffonia said. "If you hadn't known fear, then you wouldn't know the relief you feel when the fear is gone."

Jewell looked at her and squinted her eyes. "So?"

"Did you like being afraid?" Daffonia asked.

"Not like that, I didn't."

"Would you try to avoid being frightened like that if you could?" Daffonia asked.

"Of course, I would," Jewell said, nosing around the berry patch for more juicy berries. She was trying to act like she was growing bored with the conversation.

"How would you do that?" Daffonia asked.

"Well, I wouldn't go running aimlessly into . . ." Jewell stopped sniffing through the berry patch and looked up at her new friend. From the corner of her eye she saw a small patch of yellow high up in the trees and gracefully floating from one sunny spot to another. She looked back down at Daffonia. "Why did you say that this is a learning place?" she asked.

"Because you learn things as you travel toward the garden,"

Daffonia said, giving her a questioning look. "What makes you ask?"

Jewell looked up again, trying to find the beautiful, yellow butterfly, but it seemed to have disappeared. "What else am I going to learn besides why I shouldn't run around aimlessly?" Jewell asked, still keeping watch for the graceful flying flower. "Whatever you want to learn. Whatever you need to learn," Daffonia said. "I really don't know for sure. I'm simply here to keep you company as you travel toward the garden. It's up to you which way our path goes." Daffonia stood still and stared at Jewell for a moment. "What are you looking for?"

Jewell shrugged. "I saw a yellow butterfly way up there," she said, pointing her nose toward the tree tops.

"Oh, that was Tempo," Daffonia said, smiling. "She'll be following us through our journey."

"Why?"

"Just to keep track of where we are."

Jewell frowned. "Won't she come visit? Isn't she nice?"

"Tempo is a little shy," Daffonia said. "But more important, it's too shady down here for a butterfly. They only like to be in the sun."

Jewell looked up, but was unable to see where Tempo had gone. "Still I'd like to meet her sometime."

"I'm sure you will," Daffonia said.

Jewell gave up searching for the small patch of yellow wings and turned her attention back to Daffonia. "What if I want to go straight to the garden?" she asked.

Daffonia shook her head. "Only those who are complete inside themselves can actually enter the garden."

"Are there a lot of animals in the garden?" Jewell asked. She was excited at the possibility of meeting new playmates to terrorize neighborhoods with.

"There are many different creatures there," Daffonia said. "Even people live there."

"Does anyone ever leave the garden and go back out where they came from?"

"Sure they do," Daffonia said. "Anyone who wants to can leave here once they've found what they came for. Most end up staying though."

Jewell hesitated, an unpleasant image of a crowded place in the forest full of creatures standing shoulder to shoulder crept into her mind. "Is there enough room for everyone?" she asked.

"There is as much room as is needed," Daffonia answered, gently pawing the ground. "The garden will never be too small for everyone who lives there."

"Why not?"

"Because it's a magic place, just like the forest is magic," Daffonia said. "Abba made it that way."

Just then a flash of sky blue light caught her eye. "What are all those flashes of color I keep seeing?" Jewell asked.

Daffonia let out a quick giggle. "The Eyes of the Forest," she said. "They don't just exist in here. They're in the Outside Place as well, where you came from."

Jewell shook her head in disbelief. "I've never seen them until now."

"That's because of all the pollution in the Outside Place," Daffonia said. "There are quite a few things that have been ruined out there because of it. The colors in the spectrum of light can't be seen clearly because of all the nasty things that float around in the air. The pollution dulls them."

"What a shame," Jewell said, looking around now for a glimpse of the Eyes. "I could sit in one place and watch them all day."

"In time you'll come to know them well," Daffonia said. "They see everything that happens everywhere in the world. But for now, eat up as much as you can so we can be on our way."

Jewell did as Daffonia suggested to her, sniffing out every last berry she could find in the patch. When the two travellers were no longer able to find even a single strawberry left anywhere, they decided to move on.

"Which way?" Jewell asked, belching out loud.

Daffonia looked around the forest, but did not give a direction for them to travel. "What do you think?" she asked.

Jewell carefully studied their surroundings. She knew it was a serious decision if she was going to get out of here soon. "This way," she said, feeling proud of herself for leading the way.

"That's a very good choice," Daffonia said, smiling as she quickly followed Jewell's lead. "A very good choice indeed."

CHAPTER 4

To her right Jewell saw a group of trees that she was sure she'd already seen. In fact, she knew she'd seen them a few times. The three white birch trees growing out of the ground in the same way with that little maple tree trying to crowd in between all of them couldn't happen the same way more than once, maybe twice. But one of the birch trees was unmistakable because it was missing four of its bottom branches all in the same place. It was as if Jewell had run through this exact spot many times in her life, but she knew that was impossible.

"We've been walking for hours," Jewell said. "But I'd swear I keep seeing the same trees over and over again."

Daffonia glanced around. "They do seem to look alike after awhile," she said. "But relax, Jewell. I've been through this before with other newcomers. We'll get there eventually."

"I hope so," Jewell said, feeling discouraged. "I'm even getting used to the Eyes. They're not as exciting as they were at first."

Daffonia stopped and sniffed the air. "Most things are that way," she said. "When something is new it holds our interest, intrigues us. But as with most things, we get used to them sooner or later. Eventually, things that used to hold a huge appeal don't mean that much to us."

Jewell nodded in agreement. "I know what you mean," she said. "When my family first brought me home with them everything I saw excited me, but once I got used to the people and the woods and the neighborhood, I got bored."

Daffonia turned to her and appeared to be thinking before she spoke. "Is that why you run around causing so much trouble now?" she asked.

Jewell looked up, somewhat embarrassed. "Well, I haven't really given it much thought," she said, "but I suppose that could be the reason." She lowered her head so that her shoulders felt hunched. "I know I get bored with things easy."

Daffonia smiled. A soft, understanding look was on her face. "That's probably because you don't know your purpose." She looked up and sniffed the air once more.

"I'm not sure what you mean," Jewell said, puzzled. "And what are you sniffing around for?"

"Food," Daffonia said. "It looks like the sun will be setting soon. If we can find anything close by, we should probably eat. If you remember, I told you it's difficult to know when the next berry patch will come up."

Jewell felt a rumble in her stomach. "I remember."

"Let's walk a little further," Daffonia suggested. "I'll keep my senses alert for something edible in the area."

"Oh, I like that idea." Jewell felt a second rumble roll through her insides. She turned to Daffonia to ask what else might be available for them to eat when she noticed something very strange up ahead. "What is that big black thing over there?"

"Where?" Daffonia asked, looking around as if she didn't see anything out of the ordinary.

"Right here." Jewell began to run straight toward it.

"No!" Daffonia yelled.

Jewell stopped, then turned around. "What's the matter?" she asked. "I was just trying to show you what I was talking about."

"I know," the doe said, letting out a sigh of relief. "But the forest holds many secrets, Jewell. You have to be careful in here. Everything in the forest is not pretty and sparkly. There are some nasty parts in it, too."

"Oh, come on," Jewell said. "We've been walking all day long and we haven't seen anything but trees and berries. How dangerous can it be here? I know every inch of the woods back home. There's not a single animal that can scare me. And I've seen them all."

"No one has seen everything, Jewell. Please. Let's go this way." Daffonia nodded in the opposite direction from where the dark area was. "I smelled something sweet coming from over that way just before you started to run. Let's get something to eat. I heard your stomach growling."

"We can eat later," Jewell said. "I want to explore that area that's all black. It looks like the entrance to a cave, maybe." Jewell looked behind her toward the Black Place. "Come on, Daffonia," she said. "Come with me. It'll be fun."

Daffonia hesitated, looking from Jewell to the blackness that lay just behind her. "It's not a good idea."

"Why? Have you been there already?" Jewell asked.

"No," Daffonia answered. "But I've seen it before."

"Then let's find out what it is," Jewell said. "Haven't you ever wondered?"

"No," Daffonia replied. "And neither should you. Can't you feel that it's not a good place?"

"No," Jewell said. "I feel goose-pimply and excited. I want to go there and see what it's all about."

"Jewell," Daffonia said, almost pleading now. "I'm telling you, it's not wise to go there. Some things are better left alone."

"Now you sound like my family," Jewell said, disappointed.

"Maybe your family is simply trying to protect you when they tell you, 'No,'" Daffonia said. "That's what those who love you will do. They'll try to stop you from hurting yourself."

Jewell looked at Daffonia, then back at the black expanse that seemed to grow with each second that ticked by. "Well, I'm going." In the blink of an eye, she was off and running straight for the center of the blackness that stood amidst the beauty of the forest.

"JEEWWWEELLLL!!" Daffonia yelled.

Jewell heard her calling, but chose to ignore her. Instead, she ran forward as fast as she could toward the blackness. It briefly occurred to her that she was running aimlessly again, but she brushed the thought away as quickly as it entered her mind. She

knew where she was going just as she had known where she was
going the day before. She was headed straight into what looked to
her like the entrance to a cave and she couldn't wait to get there.

The very moment Jewell crossed the line between the forest
and the blackness she felt a dramatic change all around her. The
air became stiffling like a humid summer day when it's too sticky
to move in comfort or easily breathe. The other thing she noticed
was that she couldn't see a thing. Not even an outline or an edge.
The blackness was complete, total. The only thing that helped her
keep her balance was the feel of the ground beneath her feet as she
continued to run. Even that was no longer soft and cool like the
floor of the forest had been. The ground beneath her was as hard as
the pavement she had crossed the day before, and dry enough for
her to kick up hot dust behind her as she ran. Jewell could smell
the dry earth. It had a rancidness in it that she did not like.

Why am I still running? she thought to herself, then began to
slow. I can't even see where I'm going.

But it was too late. Even as her decision to stop and look around
dawned on her, Jewell ran straight into a thicket of dried, dead
thorn bushes. In fact, she went into them so fast that when they
stopped her, their thorns remained embedded in her skin, causing
her to cry out in pain. "AAARRRRRROOOOOO!!" Her high
pitched wail echoed through the thick air. She bucked and turned
trying to free herself from the inch long thorns, but all she managed to do was force herself into the ones on her other side.
"AAARRRRRROOOOOO!!"   she   wailed   again.
"AAARRRRROOOOOO!!"

Every time she moved she felt more thorns enter through her
fur and pierce her skin. She tried to remain still, but the pain
surrounded her and she began to whimper.

Suddenly, the earth seemed to tremble. She stood still, listening. From the distance, she could make out the sounds of something breaking branches. Whatever it was, it was big enough to
make the ground shake as it travelled over its surface.

Jewell was frantic. She tried to think of a way to free herself.

Her eyes were just beginning to adjust to the pitch dark, but all she could see was how large the thicket of thorn bushes actually was and how far into them she had managed to travel. It looked to be at least twice as long as her own body from where she entered the thicket to where she was stuck. On both sides and in front of her the dead bushes seemed to go on forever with no end to them in any direction. She felt the ground shake and lifted her head, stretching her neck as far as she could. What she saw terrified her. The creature that was making all the noise in the distance and moving the ground beneath her was more like the shadow of something huge and dark. Jewell could not make out any features whatsoever, no eyes, no mouth, no outlines of arms or legs. Just a huge, black mass that frightened her, not just because of its size or appearance, but because she could feel the thing's anger. It looked at her with severe evil intentions toward her in its eyes and she knew she had to do something fast.

She bent over to gnaw on one of the branches with thorns that were stuck in her right side, but the very moment she bit into the dead branch, she yelped in pain and surprise as a thorn poked right through the roof of her mouth and another punctured her tongue. "Yipe!" Jewell blurted, immediately tasting the blood that ran from her new wounds. She was panting heavily from fear, but taking in very little of the thick, sticky oxygen. The ground continued to shake as she looked toward the huge shape, the Monster Shadow as she'd started to think of it.

"JEEEEWWWWEEEELLLLLLL!"

Jewell perked up, her ears suddenly erect as more thorns pierced her skin.

"JEEEEWWWWEEEELLLLLLL!"

She looked around, again. The sound of her name came from behind her.

It was Daffonia! It had to be.

"JEEEEWWWWEEEELLLLLLLL!"

"Daffonia! Is that you?"

"Jewell? Where are you? I can't see a thing. It's too dark here."

Jewell could barely make out Daffonia's delicate shape cautiously moving toward her. From the opposite direction, deeper into the black abyss, the evil, dark shape had grown and was closer now. The earth trembled and shook harder than before. The sounds of breaking branches as the Monster Shadow made its way toward them grew louder with each passing second.

"Over here, Daffy," Jewell called. She was barely able to see Daffonia's head perk up and look in her direction. "Keep coming," she called. "I'm stuck in a thicket of thorn bushes. Be careful."

"I can't see you," Daffonia called back. "And I can hardly breathe."

"You're looking right at me," Jewell said. "Just walk straight ahead. But be careful not to get caught in these thorns like I am."

"I'm coming," Daffonia said. "My eyes are starting to focus better. I can almost see you."

"Hurry," Jewell called back. "I've got thorns stuck in every part of me."

"Try chewing through them." Daffonia was moving quicker.

"I did that and cut my mouth up pretty bad," Jewell said. "I don't know what else to do."

Daffonia reached the thicket and came to a halt just a short distance from Jewell. "Why is the ground shaking so much?" she asked.

"Something's coming," Jewell said. "Something big and nasty."

Daffonia inspected the prickly shrubs. "Oh, Jewell," she whined. "What did you do? Look at the situation you got us in? How are we ever going to get you out of there?"

It seemed hopeless. What was worse, she felt the first tugs of weakness from her steady loss of blood, but she knew she was firmly stuck and there was nothing she could do. She looked at the big shape and realized the trouble they were in, but there was no reason for Daffonia to be harmed. She wasn't stuck like Jewell and the Monster Shadow was close now.

"Oh, Jewell," Daffonia wailed. "What are we going to do?"

"Run back," Jewell said. "You can make it out of here."

"I can't leave you," Daffonia cried. "I'm responsible for you. I can't just run away like you do."

"I'm sorry, Daffy," Jewell said. "I really am, but there's no way to get out of this thicket. Even if that thing doesn't kill me I'll bleed to death right here. It doesn't matter. Just go."

Daffonia looked at Jewell, then at the living expanse of black evil that loomed over them from a few hundred yards away. "I can't!" she yelled at Jewell. "Now stay still while I try to dig these dead bushes up from the roots."

"There's no time!" Jewell insisted. "Just go!"

Daffonia ignored her and began to paw at the ground in earnest, digging as close to the roots of the thorn bushes as she could get. She yelped every few seconds as the thorns pierced the skin around her face when she came down hard with her hooves, too close to the thorny branches. Still, she persisted. Over and over again, slamming hard into the dry, putrid earth, driving her whole body in the direction of the roots, Daffonia worked to dismantle the sharp barracade that surrounded Jewell. The moving ground beneath her threw her launching attacks off target more than once, but she kept at it while Jewell watched, frightened and bleeding. Finally, sweaty and breathing hard, Daffonia hit the roots of the first bush, breaking through the outer strands. They both felt it move. "I'm going to try to rip this bush out at the roots," she said. "It's spread is at least as wide as your body is long, but it won't be enough to clear the way completely. There are more bushes tangled with it."

Jewell turned to her in time to see Daffonia look past her and straight at the Monster Shadow as it loomed large and dangerous.

"How far away is it?" Jewell asked, too drained of energy to be frightened by this time.

"Not very," Daffonia said. "Once I get this bush moved, you're going to have to run through whatever is left of the thicket. There's not enough time left to try to dig out another one."

"I don't . . know if . . I can," Jewell said, panting from exhaustion. "I used up all . . my strength trying . . to get out before . . you arrived. I'm so sore . . I can't feel anything, anymore."

"That's good," Daffonia said. "Then you won't feel the thorns when you have to push through the few feet that will be left."

"Daffonia."

"Be quiet," Daffonia said. "There's no time. I'm going in under this bush to pull it out. Be ready to run as soon as you see it move away from the rest."

"I can't." Jewell breathed heavy.

"Yes, you can," Daffonia said. "Now be watchful."

Daffonia took a deep breath and dove under the thorn bush just as Jewell turned to argue further, but Jewell was getting very tired, very fast. *I can't even lay down to go to sleep*, she thought to herself and whimpered.

"It's moving," Daffonia called amid her struggles with the dead roots. "Get ready."

"I can't," Jewell said softly to herself. She looked at Daffonia and was startled to see such a huge mass of thorn bushes move right out of the way, taking with it all the dead branches from surrounding bushes that had died intertwined with its own. Jewell looked back into the dark just in time to see the Monster Shadow begin its last few steps toward them.

"RUN!!" Daffonia yelled as she backed up.

The intensity and volume of Daffonia's voice caught Jewell completely off guard. Instinctively, she took off, running right through the remaining foot or two of thorn bushes without feeling a thing.

"RUN!!" Daffonia yelled again from behind Jewell, nipping her in the buttocks to keep her going.

"Yipe!" Jewell yelped, but kept moving, her muscles raw and numb from the thorns that remained embedded in her skin.

"Look!" Daffonia said as they ran. "Up ahead! There's a dot of green light. Run for it!"

Without saying a word, Jewell headed for the green light with Daffonia only inches behind her. The ground was shaking so fierce it threatened to pull her legs out from under her.

The green light grew larger and Jewell could see it was actually the entrance to the forest. It gave her hope. But the Monster Shadow was close behind now, casting its own blackness across the entrance.

"Can you . . still . . see it?" Jewell asked, panting. Suddenly, she lost her footing and stumbled.

"Just barely," Daffonia answered. She nipped Jewell in the buttocks one more time to get her back on her feet.

"Stop that!" Jewell said. "I'll get there."

"Run faster!" Daffonia orderd. "It's gaining on us."

The immenseness of the Monster Shadow had completely darkened the entrance to the forest and they realized just how close the thing was to them.

"Now what?" Jewell asked. She continued to run nearly stumbling with each step. Her body ached from exhaustion.

"Don't give up!" Daffonia yelled. "Just keep going."

"Toward what?" Jewell said. "I can't ss . . ."

At that moment, a flash of brilliant, spring green light appeared before them, lighting up their escape route to the forest which they could clearly see was now only a few strides away.

"It's one of the Eyes!" Daffonia yelled. Her voice was jubilant. "Run for it!!"

Jewell made her final dash and expended all of her remaining strength to make it to the forest entrance and beyond.

CHAPTER 5

Jewell stumbled as soon as she felt her feet touch the soft, cool ground of the forest. She rolled end-over-end twice before she settled in a cushioning bed of ivy and looked up in time to see a large protrusion extend from the Black Place where she and Daffonia had just escaped. The Monster Shadow seemed to be reaching around for them, trying to get out of its own world to continue its chase. It reached toward her as if it could see exactly where she was. She tried to roll away, but the pain from the thorns that were still embedded in her skin stopped her. She could feel the heat of its anger as it came within inches of her face, then froze. She heard the sounds of hooves racing through the forest, saw the shiny, white horn pierce the Monster Shadow straight through from one side of its arm to the other. She heard a howl coming from the Dark Place as she watched the protraction retreat. Jewell looked to her left, breathing easier now that the threat was gone, and saw the most beautiful, white horse she had ever seen. This one was so different than the horses that walked down the street where she lived with people on their backs. The horse before her was glistening white and wore a gold chain around its neck with a huge, purple stone attached to it. She looked into its deep, blue eyes and saw it smile. "Thank you," she said.

The horse bowed, smiling, and Jewell saw the horn for the second time. The horse looked at her. "You're welcome," she said in the most melodious voice Jewell had ever heard.

Jewell looked around. "Daffonia?" she called, but the deer was nowhere to be found. Jewell tried to stand up so she could search for her, but the thorns that were still embedded in her skin began to ache and throb, again with each movement.

"I'm right here," Daffonia called. She bounded out from be-hind a small clump of young tamaracks. "Are you alright?"

Jewell turned toward her friend's voice, startled and concerned by what she saw. Daffonia's face was covered with blood from the thorns that had cut into her when she worked to dig out the prickly bushes by the roots. "Daffonia," Jewell called, breathing heavy. Again, she tried to stand up. "You look awful. Your face is all bloody."

Daffonia smiled. "Aw, it's nothing," she said. "It looks worse than it is." She walked over to Jewell, looking back briefly at the Black Place. "You're the one who needs some attention," she said. "How do you feel?"

Jewell looked around for her new friend but noticed that the white horse was gone without a sound. She lay back in the bed of ivy and groaned. "Like one big burr," she said, exhausted and sleepy. "How am I going to get all of these thorns out of my skin?"

"Don't you worry, Jewell," an unfamiliar voice said in her ear.

Jewell whipped her head around to locate the source of the voice, but did not see anyone except Daffonia. "What was that?" she asked.

Daffonia laughed. "Lay back and relax," she said. "It's the Eye that led us out of that awful place."

Jewell remembered the flash of spring green light that had shown them the entrance back to the forest. She turned to her right and saw a tiny sparkle of the same green light flittering out from behind her head. Now that she was so close to it Jewell could see that it had wings. When it turned around to face her, she could also make out the form of a very tiny person, much like the family that took care of her. Only this little person was the same shade of green from head to toe, and from wing tip to wing tip. She looked at Daffonia. "What is it?" she asked.

"Don't ask me," Daffonia said. "Ask him yourself."

Jewell turned to face the little creature, feeling the thorns in her sides more pronounced than ever. "What are you?"

"I'm Sprig," the little green light answered. "I'm one of the

Eyes of Noah's Forest. That was a mighty close call you had there. Thank heavens, Amethyest showed up."

"Was that her name?" Jewell asked, feeling more at ease. She lay back in the cool ivy that was beginning to relieve some of the throbbing heat caused by the thorns. "I never had a chance to meet her. She was gone before I knew it." She turned her head toward Sprig. "Nice to meet you," she said, wincing in pain. "And thank you for helping us get out of there."

"That's what I'm here for," Sprig said. "Now let's see about your damage."

Jewell watched Sprig fly over to one of the thorns that was almost as big as him. After he was done surveying a few of them, Sprig flew a foot straight up, then stopped, and seemed to sit down in mid-air. "This calls for some major repairs," he said. "But it's do-able. We're going to fix you up in no time."

Daffonia took a few steps forward. "While you take care of Jewell, I'm going to hunt up some of those berries I smelled just before this happened."

"Excellent idea," Sprig said. "You're both going to need some food to heal you up and get you back on your way." He fluttered up to Jewell's face, took a tiny step out of the air, and walked right onto the tip of her nose. He weighed no more than a butterfly. She could hardly feel him.

"While Daffonia gathers up some food, I'm going to call in the troops to get these thorns out of you, and start closing up those wounds," he said. "We'll have you back to normal in no time."

He placed the two middle fingers from his right hand in his mouth, and let out a whistle so loud Jewell's whole body jerked at the shriek that pierced her ear drums. "Don't do that!" she yelled at Sprig. "It hurts my ears!"

"Oh, that's right," Sprig said. "You dogs have such sensitive hearing, even in the Outside Place where sound doesn't travel nearly as far as it does in the forest. Your ears must really bother you here."

"They do," Jewell said, lying back slowly.

"Well, I'm very sorry about that," Sprig said, nodding his head.

"Relax. I won't have to do that again. It always works the first time."

Jewell glanced at her wounded side. "What do you mean?" she asked.

"You'll see." Sprig stood confidently on the tip of Jewell's nose, arms crossed in front of him and looked around the forest. In less than a minute, bright flashes of light came from all over and converged on her. Jewell looked on in awe. She had never seen such a beautiful show of color in all her life. There were different shades of red, pink, yellow, blue, green, orange, and even purple lights sparkling all around her. And every one of them was just like Sprig. They were tiny people like her family, but with wings, and each one a different, sparkling color, shimmering as if they were sprinkled with glitter. Together, they worked to remove each and every thorn from her body. Hundreds of thorns were pulled and discarded into a sack that the Eyes of the Forest had brought with them and placed on the ground next to her. Every time a thorn was removed, Sprig placed his hands over the hole that it had made, and somehow made the pain go away. Only the intense exhaustion seemed to linger and grow stronger as the Eyes of the Forest worked to repair her wounds.

When the last thorn was pulled from her skin, and the last pain removed, she threw her head back on the bed of thick ivy and breathed a sigh of relief that it was over.

"How do you feel now?" Sprig asked, standing on the end of her nose once more.

"Much better," Jewell said, "but so tired. How can I ever thank you?"

"Simple," Sprig said, placing his hands on his hips. "Don't ever do anything so foolish again. You almost cost both of your lives because of your pig-headedness."

"Don't worry," Jewell said. She lifted her head and saw hundreds of Eyes of the Forest standing in mid-air, their auras blinking in a multitude of colors as their wings fluttered back and forth too fast to see. It was a beautiful and soothing sight. "Thank you all," Jewell said. "I won't do anything like that again."

"That's good to hear," Daffonia said. She approached with four more Eyes who were carrying a sack similar to the one used to hold the thorns. It looked like it was made of liquid silver, so fluid were its movements as it glided through the air.

When she reached Jewell and stopped, the four Eyes who were with her fluttered to the ground. Two of them let go of their sides of the sack and allowed its contents to spill out onto the ground.

"Berries!" Jewell said. "I never thought I'd be so happy to see berries in my life."

"Just relax, my friend," Sprig said, a stern look on his face. "You need to replenish your strength. You and Daffonia have a long way to go yet. Now lie back."

Jewell did as she was told. While she watched, the four Eyes who had accompanied Daffonia back from the berry patch each picked up a berry and flittered over to her. The first Eye, a pale lavendar one, placed the berry in Jewell's mouth, then flew back for another. The next Eye, a deep yellow one, placed her berry in Jewell's mouth, then flew back for another. The next two Eyes, a dark crimson one and a bright peach colored one, each did the same.

"They'll feed you so that you don't use your energy up unnecessarily," Sprig said. "But don't get to used to this attention. This is only to help you heal. You didn't come to Noah's Forest to get yourself killed. At least I hope not."

"No, I didn't," Jewell said. "I came here to play." She cast a sheepish look in Daffonia's direction, then looked at the ground. "Well, I thought that's what I was coming here for."

Sprig laughed as he nestled in the fur of Jewell's neck. "While you eat, I'm going to catch a nap," he said. "It's been a long day for all of us."

"Thanks again," Jewell said, but Sprig was already falling fast asleep. She looked around and noticed that all of the Eyes who had removed her thorns were gone. She wondered where they went.

"How do you feel now?" Daffonia asked, interrupting Jewell's thoughts.

Jewell turned toward her while Daffonia lay down on the other side of the pile of berries and began to nibble on them. The four Eyes that had returned with her were still systematically bringing the berries from the pile on the ground to Jewell.

"Oh, so much better," Jewell said between swallows. "But very tired."

"Me, too," Daffonia said.

Jewell moved her head just enough to look better at Daffonia while they talked. She could see the cuts all over the deer's face and neck. There were even a few scrapes on her shoulders. Suddenly, Jewell felt a deep regret such as she had never known. "I'm sorry, Daffonia," she said. "I should have learned last night, but I didn't."

"Some people take forever to learn a good lesson," Daffonia said, munching on a berry. "Unfortunately, most of us don't really learn until it hurts us in some way."

"I guess," Jewell said, filled with remorse. "It's just that I never ran into that kind of danger before. I always thought I was invincible."

"Ah, Jewell," Daffonia said. "No one is invincible. Keep in mind that just because it has never happened to you does not mean it never will."

"I'm starting to see that, now," Jewell said. "I'm really so sorry I got you into such a mess."

"That's alright," Daffonia replied. "Let's just be thankful we got out of it alive. The few wounds we have will heal and we'll forget all about this nastiness."

"I don't think I'll ever forget this," Jewell said. "It was just too terrible to forget."

"Maybe you really have learned this lesson then," Daffonia said. "There's just one more thing, Jewell."

"What's that?"

Daffonia gave her a stern look and frowned. "Don't you ever call me Daffy, again."

"I won't," Jewell said, laughing. "I promise you, I won't."

"Good," Daffonia said. "Now eat your fill. We'll rest right here until morning and give our bodies a chance to heal a bit."

"Are you sure you want to sleep here with that black thing so close by?" Jewell asked.

Daffonia looked at the blackness. It was beginning to blend in with the rest of the forest as the setting sun darkened their surroundings. "I can see your point," Daffonia said. "But I don't think you should move yet."

"I'm not sure I'll be able to sleep right here," Jewell said, glancing over at it once more.

Daffonia appeared thoughtful for a moment, then shook her head. "I don't know what to do, then."

"Might I make a suggestion?" the tiny lavendar Eye asked, stopping in mid-air above the pile of berries.

Startled, both Jewell and Daffonia looked at the little Eye in sync. They had both gotten so used to the silence of the four Eyes it caught them off guard to hear the tiny voice.

"Sure," Daffonia said.

"If you'd like, I can call back the other Eyes," the little, lavendar light said. "They can build a wall of leaves around you that will protect you from all nastiness and keep the Black Place away from you."

"Will such a wall be strong enough?" Jewell asked. "I mean, if it's only made of leaves, then how can it keep anything away from us?"

"Because each of the Eyes of the Forest will sprinkle the wall with the same substance that makes us sparkle," the lavendar light said. "It's a very strong, magical substance and can transform itself in any way we need it to."

Daffonia looked at Jewell and smiled. "I told you this was a magic place," she said. Then she turned toward the little Eye. "Please do that for us. I'm sure we'd be able to sleep better knowing we are well protected."

"Besides," Jewell said, "it would be a shame to have to wake Sprig up. He seems so comfortable."

"Oh, Sprig loves to sleep," the little lavendar man said. "But he's always there when you need him."

"And he always will be," the peach-colored Eye said, flying into view. "As long as you don't take advantage of him."

"Is he your leader?" Jewell asked.

The two Eyes looked at each other, then turned back toward Jewell. "Something like that," the lavendar Eye said. "Now, since Sprig is asleep let me introduce all of us to you in case you need anything tonight."

The other two Eyes flew up in streaks of dark crimson and deep yellow to stand with the two Eyes who were already conversing with Jewell and Daffonia.

"This is Poppy," the lavendar Eye told Jewell, pointing to the peach-colored light by his side.

"My pleasure," Poppy said as she curtsied in mid-air.

"And this is Verbena," he said, indicating the deep yellow Eye who stood behind Poppy.

"Charmed," Verbena said as she too came forward and curtsied for Jewell.

"I'm Glory," the crimson Eye said. She flew in a circle around the other three Eyes, then came to a halt beside Verbena and Poppy.

"Glory is a bit of a show-off," the lavendar Eye whispered in Jewell's ear.

"I heard that!" Glory said, pouting.

"And I am Twain," the lavendar Eye said as he bowed, ignoring Glory's remark. "If you ever need us, just yell."

"But never take advantage," Glory added, her crimson wings fluttering.

"No one likes to be taken advantage of," Verbena chimed in.

"Now, close your ears," Twain said. "I'm going to call the others and get that wall built for you."

"How can I close my ears?" Jewell asked, baffled.

"We can help you," Poppy said.

Together Poppy and Verbena fluttered over to Jewell. Each took an ear and gently folded them down to cover the opening to Jewell's ear drums. Then they sat on Jewell's ears to keep them in place while Twain whistled for the other Eyes.

In no time at all, the colorful showcase of lights came rushing from every direction.

"We need a wall to protect these good creatures from the Black Place," Twain told them. "Let's start building."

All at once, streaks of colored light moved around Jewell and Daffonia while the Eyes of the Forest gathered leaves, wove them together, and built a wall that completely encompassed the two travelers. It took only minutes for them to finish the project. When it was done, the Eyes of the Forest began to cover the wall with a fine, glittery dust that fell from their wings as they fluttered them back and forth over the leaves.

"Good work!" Twain praised the Eyes who bowed to him in response. Then he turned to Jewell and Daffonia. "We will all keep watch for you tonight."

Daffonia smiled. "Thank you so very much," she said. "I feel much better about sleeping here, now."

"Good," Twain said. He zoomed over to Jewell and checked on Sprig. "I see Sprig will have no trouble sleeping tonight." He sounded sarcastic.

Jewell chuckled. "That's alright," she said. "He led us out of danger. He can sleep in my fur anytime."

Twain flittered back to a spot where both Daffonia and Jewell could see him. "Well then," he said. "Is there anything else we can do for you?"

"No, thank you," Daffonia said. "We'll be fine."

"Good!" Twain said. "Sleep well."

Jewell watched as Twain, Poppy, Verbena and Glory all found places to bed down around them. All the other Eyes of the Forest sat perched along the top of the wall of leaves they had built. Some of them lay on their sides resting while others kept watch. The wall itself shimmered in hues of every color imaginable almost as if it were a beautiful beacon of comfort. It worked. Jewell felt content and safe. She lay down her head in the bed of ivy for the last time that night. "Good night, Daffonia," she said.

"Good night, Jewell."

In seconds, they were all sound asleep.

CHAPTER 6

When Jewell awoke it was a few hours past sunrise. The first thing she noticed was that the wall of leaves was gone and she looked around to see if Daffonia and the Eyes of the Forest were still nearby. Daffonia was beside her, but the Eyes were nowhere to be seen. "Daffonia," she said. "Are you awake?"

"Aaaawwwww," Daffonia stood up and yawned. "I'm awake. Did you sleep well?"

"Very well," Jewell said, rising to her feet to stretch. Most of her pains were gone, but there were still a few that remained around her ribs on both sides of her body. "The wall is gone. So is the entrance to the Black Place."

"That's alright," Daffonia said. "It's morning. It doesn't really matter, now. We'll be moving on today, anyway."

"But the Black Place is gone, too," Jewell said, worried. "How can that be?"

"If you remember, I told you that I'd seen it before," Daffonia said. "But I've never seen it in the same place twice. Actually, I thought there were a few of them scattered throughout the forest, but it seems that maybe there's only one that moves around."

"So we might see it again?" Jewell asked.

"I don't know," Daffonia said. "But I suppose it's possible." She gave Jewell an accusatory glance. "Maybe you'll know enough to steer clear of it next time."

"Will I ever." Jewell bent over to lick her paw and saw a surprise that awaited them lying on the ground. "Look!" she said. "Look at all the berries!"

The pile was almost a foot high and mounded over with berries of various sizes, shapes and colors. Some of them Jewell recognized as the kinds she'd been eating, but the rest she'd never seen before. All of them looked and smelled delicious. "Where did they come from?"

"I would have to guess the Eyes of the Forest left them for us," Daffonia said.

There was a rustling among the ivy where Jewell had slept all night and she turned her head to see what was causing it.

"Hey!" Sprig flew up from beneath the ground cover. "What's the big idea, dumping me off like that?" He straightened himself up, flew over to Jewell, and sat on her nose. "Well, that was a fine 'Good Morning' for someone who saved your hides yesterday." "I'm sorry," Jewell said. "I forgot you were even there."

"Did your friends leave the berries?" Daffonia asked.

"Probably," Sprig said, looking at the pile that was on the ground. "Although I wasn't awake to see them do it, so I couldn't say for sure."

"Well, let's eat," Daffonia said. "Then we can be on our way."

"Where are we going today?" Jewell asked. She felt a sharp pain shoot through her back leg and she couldn't help but wince.

Daffonia hesitated before she answered. "Well, that depends on you," she said.

"Please," Sprig cut in. "No more surprises like yesterday."

"Don't worry," Jewell said, acting a little cocky. "You can bet I won't be running into any dark places ever again."

He nodded once. "Glad to hear it!"

"Can't we go to the garden?" Jewell asked. "I learned to listen when I'm told not to do something."

"Have you?" Daffonia asked. She began to eat the breakfast left for them by the Eyes of the Forest.

"Sure I have," Jewell said. She felt insulted.

"Then there must be something else you have to learn," Daffonia said, "because we're still in the forest."

Sprig shook his head and sighed. "Oh, this is going to be a long journey for you."

Jewell frowned. "I hope not. I had enough after yesterday. I'm ready to move on to lesson number two. There will be no more trouble for me."

"Time will tell," Sprig said, crossing his arms. "Time will tell."

They dug in to the pile of berries and finished them in no time.

"Are you traveling with us today?" Daffonia asked Sprig.

"For a day or two," Sprig said. "It really depends on how much trouble that one decides to get herself into." He pointed his tiny finger at Jewell as he floated through the air alongside them.

"No more trouble," Jewell said. "I'm telling you!"

"Mmmhmmm," Daffonia and Sprig said together.

"We'll see," Sprig added.

They began to walk through the forest together, taking in the scents of pine, morning dew, and moss. Jewell felt much better now that she'd eaten and she was enjoying the show of lights once again as the Eyes of the Forest kept their watch on them. She even caught a few glimpses of Tempo flittering between patches of sun and it gave her a warm, familiar feeling.

They walked for a time, without seeing anything new or unusual, but after a few hours the wounds in Jewell's body began to hurt again from the dust and fungi that settled in her fur. Even Daffonia managed to re-open a cut on her shoulder that had begun to heal when they walked through the branches of a very old larch tree that hung all the way to the ground. They had spoken very little. Jewell was lost in memories of her family and never noticed the silence between them until nearly noon when the sun reached it's zenith indicating that mid-day was at hand.

"It's been quite an uneventful morning," Sprig said, breaking the quiet.

"Thank the stars for that," Daffonia said. She stopped walking and looked around.

"Still," Sprig said, hovering in mid-air. "We don't seem to be making much progress."

Jewell didn't like the sound of that. "How do you know?"

"Well," Daffonia started to say, but before she could finish her thought, Jewell interrupted her and jumped in the air. "Look!" she said, then began to run.

"Ohhhh, noooo!" Sprig took off after her in a streak of spring green light.

Daffonia leapt across the forest floor and caught up with them in only a few strides. "What is it?"

"Flowers!" Jewell said. "Flowers! These are the first flowers I've seen since I entered this forest."

"Wonderful news!" Sprig said. His wings fluttered in a brilliant flash of green sparks as he hovered a few inches above Jewell's head. "Just wonderful!"

"Oh Jewell," Daffonia said in a stern, but relieved tone of voice. "You scared the living stars out of me. I thought you were on another collision course with yourself, but this is actually terrific."

"Why?" Jewell asked, panting. "What does it mean?"

"It means that we're making progress after all," Daffonia said. "It means you have actually learned something."

Jewell buried her nose in the pink cyclamen and breathed deeply. "They don't have much of a smell," she said. "But they're pretty."

"That they are," Daffonia said, looking around as if she were planning something. "I think we should rest here for a bit. I smell food." She trotted off after her twitching nose to find the source of the smells.

Jewell smiled and looked at Sprig. "So I'm making progress," she said.

"That you are," Sprig said. "But you could be doing much better. If only I had a way to know what it is you are here to learn. I might be able to do something to help you."

"Why can't you?" Jewell asked.

"Ah, I don't know." Sprig sighed and settled on a nearby tree branch. "Probably because it would be too easy and painless for all of us. You really don't learn much that way." He crossed his legs Indian style and leaned forward. "It's always the lessons that are hardest to learn that we seem to remember the best."

"And the most painful," she said. She began to lick the wounded areas near her ribs.

"No! Leave it alone!" Sprig shook the tiny branch he was sitting on as he jumped up, then flew down to Jewell's side. "Let me look at that. You probably made it worse. You have to leave these things alone to heal, you know."

"I didn't know," Jewell said, feeling defensive. "It hurts. I couldn't help it."

"Well, you're going to have to be strong and ignore it for a day or two." Sprig dipped in and out of the dog's long hair in search of yesterday's wounds, talking to himself as he did so. "Let's see." He moved to a different area. "That one's alright" She felt him switch to her belly. "That one's healing nicely." He went to her back leg. "Mmmmhmmm."

"How does it look?" Jewell asked. "Am I healing?"

"Well, you didn't do too much damage," Sprig said, "thanks to all this hair. What kind of dog are you anyway? I've never seen so many different shades of black and brown hair on one dog in my life. And it's all so long!"

"I'm not sure," Jewell said.

Sprig held up a few strands of Jewell's hair and studied it. "Well, what kind of dogs were your parents?"

"My mother was a Belgian Shepherd," Jewell said. "I heard my family say that. But my father." She thought a minute. "I'm not sure. I think he was a different kind of shepherd, much larger than my mother, and more of a light brown."

"Well, that explains all the colors in you." Sprig dropped the strand of Jewell's hair that he'd been holding and fluttered back to his tree branch. "It also explains why your hair is so long. Belgian Shepherds have nice, long hair just like yours."

"I loved my mother's hair," Jewell said, looking away. "I miss her."

"Where is she now?" Sprig asked.

"I don't know," Jewell said. "I haven't seen her since I went home with my new family."

Sprig yawned a long-winded yawn, stretching his arms as he did so. "I'm ready for a nap," he said, dropping the subject. He lay on his side on the tree branch and used his folded arms as a pillow.

"You sure do sleep a lot," Jewell said, but Sprig didn't seem to hear her. He was already dozing off, leaving her to herself while Daffonia was gone in search of something for them to eat.

Jewell lay down on the ground beneath the tree where Sprig had fallen asleep. She didn't know what else to do with herself and she was afraid to get in any more trouble if she went nosing around on her own, but she was already growing bored.

She got up and began to walk around the immediate area, keeping a watchful eye on how close she was to the tree where Sprig lay sleeping. She could just see the sparks his wings made as they rubbed together with each breath he took.

I'll be fine as long as I can keep him in sight, she thought to herself.

She wandered a little and found another patch of cyclamen. These were white, but also had very little scent to them. Still, they were pretty to look at. She began to realize some of the other things that she hadn't seen in the forest that she might have expected to see. There were no bugs of any kind. No birds, no little scurrying animals like those she was used to chasing in the woods back home.

She checked on her distance from Sprig, but couldn't see his sparks anymore. She turned and headed back the way she came looking around for his tree, but she was distracted by an unfamiliar sound. She heard a soft weeping to her right. "Who's there?" she quietly asked. She listened, but there was no response. She waited a few moments and the weeping began again. Jewell looked around in every direction, but could not see anyone. Still, the weeping continued. "Who's there?"

Again, there was no response.

"Why are you crying?" she asked, then listened carefully for the little voice that would match the soft weeping. This time she heard it. Between sniffles, the quiet response was barely audible, but Jewell had her ears primed for even the slightest sound.

"I hurt myself," came the teary reply.

"Where are you?" Jewell asked. "I can't help you if I can't find you."

"I'm down here. In front of you."

Jewell looked at the ground, but still saw nothing. Further along in front of her, however, she caught a fleeting flash of deep crimson, as it sparkled beneath a group of cyclamen leaves. She recognized it as the light from one of the Eyes of the Forest.

"Come out in the open where I can see you," Jewell said.

"I can't. I hurt myself."

Jewell didn't know what to do. The Eyes had protected them the night before and now one of them needed her help. She was so much bigger than the tiny creature, it seemed impossible for her to try to do anything. She could easily crush the little Eye with just her nose alone if she tried to lift her. "Stay there," Jewell said. "I'll go get Sprig to help you."

"No," the little Eye said. "I'm frightened. Don't leave me alone."

"But I can't help you," Jewell said. "I'm too big. I'll only hurt you worse if I try to get you out of there. Can't you drag yourself out in the open somehow?"

"No." The weeping began again in earnest.

Jewell was frantic to help. "What am I going to do?"

"Just keep me company," the little voice said between sobs. "I won't live much longer anyway. I just don't want to be alone."

Running through Jewell's head were the words of both Daffonia and Sprig telling her not to get in any more trouble, and to listen when someone tells her to do something. But she hadn't listened to Daffonia who had distinctly told her to stay put. Now here was someone who needed Jewell more than Jewell needed to listen to Daffonia. *They're going to be so angry with me*, she thought to herself.

"Please stay." The little voice broke Jewell's heart with its melancholy tone.

The heck with Daffonia's orders, Jewell thought. Let her be angry with me.

Jewell lay on the ground near the crimson sparks that jumped out from under the cyclamen leaf. "I'll stay with you," she said. "What's your name?"

"My name is Glory."

"What?" Jewell jumped straight up. "I just met you last night. How did you get hurt? Why are you going to die?"

Glory sniffled a few times, then began to tell Jewell what had happened to her. "I left you this morning after Poppy, Verbena and I had gathered as many berries as we could find," Glory said. "Some of the others who had kept watch on the wall helped us."

Jewell sat on the bare ground to listen to Glory's story.

"When Twain and the others dismantled the wall, the entrance to the Black Place was still there," Glory said. "When we made our last run for berries and returned to you, however, it was gone. We looked everywhere, but couldn't find it. Eventually, we left to go about our own business."

"Then, what happened?" Jewell was anxious to get to the bottom of it.

Glory breathed heavily for a few moments before answering. "Well, whatever was in there was angry with us because it followed us." She took a deep breath. "One minute we were flittering around the trees, and the next thing I knew the black space was right beside us. I didn't see it. But something reached out and smacked me into a tree. My wings broke." She started to cry again.

"There must be a way to fix them," Jewell said. She was not going to give up. "I broke my leg once. My family took me to a man who wrapped it up and it healed."

"You're lucky to have someone to take care of you," Glory said. "Poppy and Verbena didn't even know I was hurt. I was knocked unconscious and fell to the ground. When I woke up, I was all alone with two broken wings. There's no one to fix them for me."

"There must be someone who can do it," Jewell said, refusing to give up. "You can't die just because your wings are broken."

"My wings are my life," Glory said. "They're what gives us the sparkle of living. Without them I cannot fulfill my purpose."

"I can't let you die because of that," Jewell said. She had to find help. "You helped us last night, now I'm going to help you." Jewell started to walk away to look for Sprig's tree or signs of Daffonia, but she only went a few steps before Glory's call stopped her.

"No! Don't go," Glory cried. "I don't want to die alone under this leaf, on the ground when I've spent most of my life in the air. Don't go, Jewell. Please don't go."

Suddenly, Jewell had an idea. "I won't have to," she said to Glory. "I can stay with you and call for help."

"Don't bother, Jewell. It's no use."

"Oh, yes, it is!" Jewell said. She began to howl as loud as she could. She howled and howled like a wolf using every different sound she could make. Soon, Glory stopped crying and started to listen to the sound of Jewell's voice.

"Oh, that's so pretty!" she said to Jewell. "It's like music."

Jewell stopped howling and looked in her direction. "Really?" she said. "I think you hit your head harder than you remember."

"Oh, no!" Glory said. "Your voice is so strong and comforting. Sing for me some more, Jewell."

Jewell started to howl once more, this time making her sounds as pleasing as she could. It didn't take long before Daffonia came bounding through the foliage with Sprig right behind her in a streak of green sparks.

"What's the matter?" she called to Jewell.

"Be careful!" Jewell warned. "Don't come any closer."

Sprig came to a halt right above Daffonia's head. "What have you done now?"

"I haven't done anything!" Jewell said. He was starting to make her angry. "It's Glory. She's hurt!"

"Glory?" Sprig asked. "Where is she?"

"Down there," Jewell said, pointing with her nose to the place where she saw the crimson sparks.

"Let me see." Sprig zoomed in the direction Jewell had indicated. As fast as he flew into the cyclamen patch, he flew out equally as fast only seconds later.

"She wasn't kidding," he told Daffonia. "Glory has two broken wings. She's going to die if we don't get her to the garden fast."

"Can you take her?" Daffonia asked.

"I'll call the Eyes and we'll all take her." Sprig looked at Jewell. "Close your ears," he warned.

Jewell frowned. "Just whistle," she said. "Glory's life is at stake."

Sprig nodded to Jewell, then released his call to the Eyes of the Forest. In seconds, they were gathered around Glory. They lifted her out from under the cyclamen leaves, and quickly carried her away on a tiny bed of moss.

"Where are they taking her?" Jewell asked Sprig.

"They're taking her to the garden where she will be healed," he said. "I'm going with them. Glory is my sister."

"Oh my," Jewell said. "I'll miss you Sprig. But I understand."

"Thank you for finding her," Sprig said. "She would have died if you hadn't been here."

"Go take care of your sister," Daffonia said. "Come back to us when you can. We'll be fine in the meantime."

Sprig nodded and in seconds, he was gone.

"Now what?" Jewell asked.

"Now we continue on our way," Daffonia said. "We'll find something to eat as we go."

"That's fine with me." Jewell stared after the procession that was already out of sight. "I'm not that hungry just now anyway."

CHAPTER 7

They continued through the forest in silence for some time, but Jewell knew she was going to have to tell Daffonia the truth of how she wandered off. She secretly hoped the subject wouldn't come up. She liked Daffonia. In fact, she respected her. She didn't want her to be disappointed.

"What happened to Glory?" Daffonia asked.

Jewell was startled. She'd been so deep in her own thoughts that the sound of Daffonia's voice seemed out of place. "That thing in the Black Place did it," she said. "The Monster Shadow. Glory told me that the entrance to the Black Place was still there when the Eyes of the Forest broke down the wall of leaves this morning. But when they were bringing back the last few berries for us, it was gone. Later, when they were flying around in the woods the entrance suddenly appeared beside them. The Monster Shadow reached out through the entrance and smashed Glory into a tree. It knocked her unconscious and she fell to the ground where I found her."

"How could that have happened?" Daffonia asked. "Was she alone?"

"No," Jewell said. "Poppy and Verbena were with her, but they never saw it. Glory told me they never knew what had happened to her."

Daffonia sighed and shook her head. "I had no idea that place was so dangerous."

"I don't understand why Amethyst was able to come to my rescue when the Monster Shadow was trying to reach out and get me, but she couldn't help someone as wonderful as Glory when she was in the same kind of trouble." Jewell exhaled deeply. "It doesn't make sense."

"It probably happened so fast, there wasn't enough time for Amethyst to get there," Daffonia suggested. "Maybe there wasn't enough time for her to even know what was going on." Daffonia looked around a bit, sniffing the air as she did so. "If you remember, Jewell, you were in the Dark Place for quite awhile. Amethyst might have been right there waiting for the chance to help you."

Jewell shrugged her shoulders as she looked at the small spots of sunshine that seemed to be appearing everywhere. "There must be a way to destroy it," she said.

Daffonia cast her a look of disbelief. "I can't imagine how," she said. "We don't even know what it is."

"There has to be someone who does," Jewell said. "Someone must have encountered it before."

"Maybe," Daffonia said, then stopped.

"What?" Jewell asked. "You were going to say something. What were you thinking?"

Daffonia looked thoughtful, hesitating before she spoke. "I was thinking that someone in the garden might know what it is," she said. "But we can't ask anyone until we get there."

Jewell nodded. "And we can't get there until I'm done with whatever it is I'm doing out here in the forest."

"The best we can hope for is that we'll be able to avoid the Black Place until we get to the garden," Daffonia said.

Jewell stopped walking and turned to face her. "But if it moves around, then it could sneak up on us while we sleep."

"You're right." Daffonia had a nervous look on her face. "We're going to have be very careful from now on until our journey is through."

"How do you know it won't go in the garden?" Jewell asked.

"Because nothing bad can get that far through the forest," Daffonia said. "It's the way Abba made the forest."

"If someone named Abba made it, then why is it called Noah's Garden and Noah's Forest?" Jewell asked in a haughty tone.

Daffonia smiled. "Because Noah is the caretaker of it all," she said. "Abba created everything, but Noah was put in charge of watching over this forest and the garden at its center."

"I thought you said Abba takes care of it all." Jewell was getting confused.

"He does," Daffonia said, "but on a different level. Abba is everywhere at once. Noah is only where he is at any given time."

Jewell shook her head, baffled. "I don't understand."

"You will," Daffonia said. "You're not the first creature who doesn't understand it and you certainly won't be the last. Nor will you be the first one who learns to understand it." Then, speaking as if to herself, Daffonia added, "Let's hope you won't be the last."

Jewell heard what Daffonia said, but she was so confused she chose to let the subject drop and started forward through the trees. They walked in silence for a few minutes until Daffonia brought up what Jewell had hoped to avoid.

"How is it that you found Glory?" Daffonia asked.

Jewell hesitated, afraid to admit that she'd disobeyed Daffonia's direction to stay put. But she realized it was quite obvious what had happened and so decided to tell her the truth. "I tried to stay with Sprig," Jewell said, "but he went to sleep in the tree and I got bored waiting for you to come back. I explored a little, and I did my best not to go so far that I lost sight of him. When I turned around to head back I heard her crying. She begged me to stay with her. I didn't know what to do so I started to howl so you'd hear me and come running just like you did."

"It wasn't wrong for you to explore," Daffonia said. "Some of the most important discoveries have been made by explorers. At least you didn't go running off without thinking at all. But imagine what might have happened if you hadn't been so careful about staying close."

Jewell thought about it for a few moments. "So there's more than one reason not to run around?"

"Sure there is," Daffonia said. "Just think of the things you miss when you don't take your time. You would never have been there to find Glory."

"So what I did wasn't wrong?" Jewell asked. She couldn't believe it.

"No it wasn't."

"But I don't understand," she said. "You told me to stay put, but I didn't. Why wasn't I wrong this time?"

"Because you were careful," Daffonia said. "You didn't go very far. You used your head."

"I lost sight of Sprig's tree, though." Jewell lowered her head. She was ashamed to admit she wasn't as careful as Daffonia thought she was. "I was actually looking for it when I heard Glory in the leaves."

"Even better," Daffonia said. "You recognized your mistake and you took steps to fix it. I think you're learning how important it is to be conscientious."

Jewell looked at her and cocked her head to one side. "What does that mean?"

"What did you really want to do when you realized you couldn't see Sprig's tree?" Daffonia asked her. "What was your first instinct?"

Jewell tried to remember what went through her head at that moment. "I guess I really wanted to explore a little more."

"Why didn't you?"

"Because I didn't know what I might run into after last night," Jewell said. "I didn't want to run into the Black Place again, and after finding Glory in the condition she was in, I was afraid to lose sight of you and Sprig in case something awful happened to you, too. It just didn't seem right to take that chance."

Daffonia nodded her head and smiled. "That's what being conscientious is. Conscientious means you did something because you knew it was the right thing to do. Regardless of what you might have wanted to do, you did what you felt was right."

"Jewell! Daffonia!"

They were startled, their conversation interrupted. Together they turned toward the sound of their names and saw streaks of deep yellow and peach racing at them from among the trees.

"We heard Sprig's whistle," Poppy said as she and Verbena

soared up to Jewell and Daffonia. They halted in mid-air, sparks popping out of their fluttering wings.

"Where did he go?" Verbena asked.

"You're a little late," Jewell said, a mixture of anger and sadness in her voice.

"What happened?" Poppy asked, both arms stretched out from her sides, palms up.

Daffonia stepped forward. "Jewell found Glory hurt not too far from here," she said. "Sprig was with us. He called the Eyes to help take Glory to the garden."

"She was with us earlier," Poppy said. "But then she just . . . disappeared."

"That's because that Monster Shadow in the Black Place slammed her into a tree," Jewell said. "Both her wings are broken."

"Her wings?!" Poppy said, sounding shocked.

"Both of them?!" Verbena asked. "That's awful! She'll die without her wings."

"How long ago did Sprig leave with the other Eyes?" Poppy asked, her eyes beginning to fill with peach-colored tears.

"Quite awhile, actually," Daffonia said. "Jewell and I have been walking for some time. They probably made it to the garden by now."

Jewell jumped up, excited. "Is it that close?" she asked. "If the garden is so close then we should be able to go there right now. Why don't we just go?"

Daffonia and the two Eyes looked at her quickly then acted as if she hadn't said a word.

"We'd better fly like the wind," Verbena said. "They may need our help in the healing."

"You're right," Poppy said. She turned to Daffonia. "Did they take her right to Astilbe?"

"Who's Astilbe?" Jewell asked. All these new names and new acquaintences were beginning to make her head spin.

"I would imagine so," Daffonia said. "Glory was in quite a state by the time Sprig and I reached her."

"Then we'll go right to Astilbe, too," Poppy said. She followed close behind Verbena who had already zipped away in a streak of deep yellow.

By this time Jewell was completely frustrated with being ignored. "I want some answers!" she yelled.

Daffonia turned slowly toward her and stared at her for a few moments. Finally, she walked up to Jewell until their noses were almost touching. "What is the matter with you?" she asked.

Jewell cringed a little from the serious look on Daffonia's face. It was a side of her she hadn't seen, yet and she was unnerved by it. "I want some answers," Jewell repeated in a softer tone of voice.

"The polite way to say that is, 'I would like some answers, please.'" Daffonia continued to stare into Jewell's eyes, still standing nose to nose.

"Alright," Jewell said, feeling sheepish. "I would like some answers, please."

Daffonia pulled back her head, then took a step away from Jewell, turning as she headed further through the woods. "Much better," she said. "Now, what are the questions that need answers?"

Jewell watched Daffonia take four steps away before she started to follow her. "First of all," she said, feeling self-assured once more, "I'd like to know why the Eyes of the Forest can get to the Garden so fast, but we can't."

"I can," Daffonia corrected. "You can't."

"Fine," Jewell said. "I can't. Now, why can't I?"

"Well, to put it as simply as I can," Daffonia said, "you can't go directly to the garden because you cause too much trouble. You're too unsettling, too wild. You have so much to learn, so much growing up to do."

"I do not!" Jewell said. "I'm five years old already. I'm plenty old enough to take care of myself."

"Whether or not you can take of yourself is not the issue," Daffonia said.

"Then what is?"

Daffonia looked sideways at Jewell and shook her head. "You really don't understand, do you?"

Jewell did not respond. She continued to wait for the answer to her first question.

"Alright," Daffonia said. "The issue is not whether you can take of yourself or not. The real issue here is whether or not you can take care of someone else . . anyone else . . Everyone else."

"What?" Jewell was dumbfounded.

"Jewell," Daffonia said, "we're not here to run around, play, and have fun all the time. We're not here to cause trouble and get each other in trouble. And we're certainly not here because one creature wanted someone else to take care of."

"Alright, already," Jewell said, annoyed. "What are we here for, then?"

Daffonia stopped walking. They approached a patch of sunshine on a small, rocky area where blueberries grew everywhere the sun's rays touched. She looked lovingly at Jewell as she sat down in the outer edge of the sunny circle. "We're here for each other," Daffonia said. "That's all. We're here for each other."

Jewell was speechless. What a crazy idea! "You're kidding!" she said.

Daffonia looked serious. "No, I'm not kidding," she said. "We're here to take care of each other, to teach each other, and to help each other."

Jewell stuck her nose in the air and turned away. "I take care of myself."

"You told me your family takes care of you," Daffonia reminded her.

Jewell looked at her from the corners of her eyes. "Yeah, well, they feed me and stuff," she said.

"Why don't you take care of them in return?" Daffonia asked.

Jewell thought about it for a minute. "I don't know," she said, looking away. "They don't really need anything from me."

Daffonia stood up. "Of course they do!" she said. "They didn't get a dog so they'd have another mouth to feed, Jewell. They got a dog for companionship. They got a dog for the love a dog has to give. They got a dog for protection from intruders." She walked to the edge of the shade they were in and looked at the berry bushes. "Do they have any children?"

"Yes," Jewell said.

"Then they probably got a dog to keep an eye on their children, too," Daffonia said. "That's your purpose Jewell. To take care of the family that takes care of you by giving them your love and companionship, your protection and your concern."

Jewell took in everything Daffonia said and mulled it over in her mind, but she needed to figure it out. She'd never considered any of those things before.

"Do you remember when we were first getting to know each other and you told me about all the things you do with your time?" Daffonia asked.

Jewell nodded, then laid on the ground with her head between her front paws.

"You told me about all the trouble you and your friends cause in your neighborhood," Daffonia said. "You told me that you did those things out of boredom. But do you remember that I told you how you were only bored because you didn't know your purpose?"

Jewell lifted her head, surprised. It was beginning to make sense to her. "Yes, I do."

"Well," Daffonia said, "now you know your purpose."

Jewell stood up and smiled. "Do you mean to tell me that my family needs me?" she asked. "Really?"

"They sure do."

Jewell stuck out her chest and pranced. "I'm important to them," she said.

Daffonia shook her head and frowned. "Don't get so carried away," she said. "You're not important to them the way you are today."

Deflated, Jewell stopped prancing and sat back down. "Why not?" she asked.

"Because you don't know how to take care of them yet," Daffonia said. "You have to learn."

"Oh." Jewell was disappointed. She lay her head on the ground between her paws once more.

"Don't be discouraged," Daffonia said. "You did a great job getting help for Glory. That was a big step in the right direction."

"I only howled because I thought I was going to be in trouble," Jewell said, looking at the ground.

"Don't start being modest, now." Daffonia sounded sarcastic. "C'mon, let's eat a little before we move on." She stepped into the sunlight and headed for the berries.

"I'm not hungry," Jewell said, sulking.

Daffonia turned to her. "Jeeweelll," she said in a stern tone.

"Oh, all right!" Jewell stood up and followed her into the sunny patch where she began to nibble on the big, juicy blueberries growing there. "Who's Astilbe?" she asked after devouring a few mouthfuls of berries.

Daffonia hesitated a moment while she finished chewing. She swallowed, then looked at Jewell. "Astilbe is something like a mother figure for all the Eyes of the Forest," she said. "She's the oldest and wisest of the Eyes. She takes care of them so they can keep watch on everyone else in the world."

"She takes care of all the Eyes in the whole world?" Jewell asked. "That's impossible!"

At that moment a soft, yellow patch of wings flew right past Jewell's nose and landed on Daffonia's back. "Nothing is impossible where love is concerned," Tempo said in a soft, feminine voice. "Astilbe has an incredible amount of love to share."

"Tempo," Jewell whispered. "I've seen you up in the trees. You're so pretty."

"Thank you," Tempo said, gently fluttering her wings twice. "I'm most comfortable in the sun. My wings absorb the heat like a blanket. I just love the sunshine." She turned her small body a bit in order to face Jewell better. "I will rest here with you and eat, if that's alright with you and Daffonia. Then I will be back up in the sky, high above your heads."

"Why are you watching us?" Jewell asked. "In case we get in trouble?"

Tempo let out a soft chuckle. "No," she said. "There is no trouble for Daffonia to get into. But you, Jewell. You have so much to learn. I am watching simply to keep track of all that you do, and to keep a record of your journey. That's all. Nothing more."

"But why?"

"So many questions, Jewell." Tempo fluttered her wings twice more. "But the time for answers only comes when you've earned the right to know those answers. You aren't ready yet." She flew a few inches into the air, then hovered around Daffonia's head until she landed at the tip of her ear. "But you wil be ready soon, Jewell. I have confidence in you."

Jewell stuck her chest out and pranced past the butterfly. "Thank you." She bent over and pulled a mouthful of blueberries from the bushes nearby.

"You're welcome. Now I suggest you two get some food in your stomachs. You still have quite a journey ahead of you."

Jewell sat down in front of Daffonia and Tempo. "May I ask one more question?"

"Of course you may ask," Tempo said, flying over to a white flower that grew on the end of a thorny vine.

"How old is Astilbe?"

"Seven thousand years old," Daffonia said.

Jewell's mouth fell open, dropping all its contents of blueberries to the ground in a most un-ladylike movement. "No way," Jewell half-sighed in disbelief.

"It's true," Daffonia said.

"How can it be?"

"She came to the forest with Noah," Tempo said, "along with quite a few others."

"Where did they come from?" Jewell asked, attempting to clean up her mess.

"It's a long story," Daffonia said. "It has something to do with a great flood that happened a long time ago. Noah had two of every kind of creature on a boat with him and his family. When the flood was over, they settled somewhere else first. But when the world started to corrupt itself they moved here, where the world outside could only get in by a special calling to individual creatures in need of something that's missing in them, in their heart. Do you understand what I mean?"

"I think so," Jewell said. "It sounds so fantastic, though."

Daffonia chuckled. "Oh, Jewell," she said. "There are so many things in this world that no one knows of. Some can be seen, others cannot. But these things exist none-the-less."

"How do you know?" Jewell asked.

"Because I've been fortunate enough to see them for myself," Daffonia answered.

"I want to know what else is out there," Jewell said.

"In time you'll know all that you need to know," Tempo said. "But for now, I think you should eat so you can make some progress on your journey before calling it a day."

"What about the Black Place?" Jewell asked.

Daffonia looked worried for a moment, then turned away to pick another mouthful of berries. "We'll think of something," she said.

Jewell, however, was not so sure they would.

CHAPTER 8

Jewell thought about all Daffonia had told her for a few hours while they walked in peaceful quiet, but she was deeply bothered. She was learning quite a few new things that made perfect sense, but there were many others she simply could not accept. Finally, she had to say something. She looked sideways at Daffonia, then turned to face straight ahead. "You know," she said, "I'm finding it hard to believe your story about the flood. And Astilbe being seven thousand years old. That's just impossible."

Daffonia said nothing at first. It was almost as if she hadn't heard her. Then, just when Jewell thought she was being ignored, Daffonia let out a loud sigh. "It doesn't matter whether you believe it or not, Jewell. The truth is the truth no matter what."

Jewell looked at her, then shook her head. "I don't understand what you mean."

Again, Daffonia was quiet for a long time before she spoke. "What color is the grass?" she asked.

"Green, of course."

Daffonia nodded and kept walking. "If I couldn't see and I asked you that same question, what would you tell me?"

"I'd still tell you the same thing," Jewell said. "The grass is green."

"Why would you still tell me the same thing?"

"Because that's what color it is." Jewell was getting frustrated.

Daffonia stood still and turned to face her. "What if I told you that in my mind the grass is red?"

Jewell frowned. "I'd tell you you're wrong."

Daffonia leaned back and stared at Jewell for a second. "But I've built it up in my mind that the grass is red."

"Then you'd better change your thinking because the grass is green."

"But I still choose to believe it's red because I've never seen it for myself," she said, "and I've always envisioned it as being red."

Jewell was now so angry with the conversation her fur stood up along her back. It seemed to her that Daffonia was making an issue out of nothing. "You can believe whatever you want to believe," she said. "Someday you might see if for yourself and know you were believing a lie the whole time."

"How could it be a lie if I'd never seen it?" Daffonia asked. "I wouldn't even know better."

"Because it would." Jewell had enough. She wanted to jump at Daffonia and wrestle her to the ground, but she wasn't like one of her friends back home. "The grass is green. You can't change that just because you say so."

"But what if I don't know better?"

Jewell stared at her, using all her willpower to control her temper. "Why are you trying to aggravate me?" she asked.

Daffonia smiled. "Just keep up with me," she said. "Now, what if I didn't know better?"

"You would if you'd listen to what I'm telling you."

"Why should I listen to you?"

"Because I'm telling you the truth." Jewell was now poised and ready to pounce. She had reached the end of her self control.

"EXACTLY!" Daffonia stood on her hind legs and waved her fronts in the air as if she were cheering. Her smile lit up her entire face. "That's exactly my point."

"Which is?" Jewell still did not understand.

"The truth is the truth no matter what else you may say or think," Daffonia said. "The truth never changes. But a lie, on the other hand, a lie can change by the minute."

And finally, it made perfect sense to Jewell. "So you're saying that if I don't want to believe the things you tell me, then it's my loss because I'm missing out on the truth."

"Bingo!" Daffonia jumped in the air, then pranced once around Jewell.

"Alright, then," Jewell said, trying to calm her down. "I believe you."

Daffonia stood still and looked at her. "Don't pacify me, Jewell," she said. "I want you to, at least, open your mind and try to believe me. The real faith in these things will come in time. You have to change your thinking a little in order to accomodate new realities, but the first step is to simply open your mind to them."

"Alright," Jewell said. "I'll keep my mind open."

"Good enough." Daffonia nodded. "Now, what do you think we should do tonight?"

"What do you mean?" Jewell asked.

"About the Black Place," Daffonia explained. "Should we sleep in shifts so that one of us can keep a watch for it while the other sleeps?"

Jewell did not answer. She had stopped for a moment to sniff the ground near a very large patch of unusual, white, bell-shaped flowers trailing down a single stem. She hadn't seen these flowers before. "What are these?" she asked.

Daffonia walked over to her side. "The Eyes of the Forest call those Valley Lilies."

"But we're in the forest," Jewell said.

"I know." Daffonia smiled. "The Eyes brought them here from the Outside Place. They grow very well in the forest."

"They have a smell, too." Jewell breathed in the aroma from the small, but fragrant flowers. "I like these."

"You'll find quite a few flowers that you'll like," Daffonia said. "Each time you see a new flower, you'll know you've learned something you needed to know. Each new flower brings you a little closer to the garden."

"Really?" Jewell was excited. "What did I learn?"

Daffonia looked at her, tossed her head back, and laughed.

"What's so funny?" Jewell was insulted.

"Oh, Jewell," Daffonia said. "What do you think you learned?"

Jewell shrugged. "I don't know. To keep an open mind, I guess."

"Well, alright then," Daffonia said. "Now, what about tonight? What do you think we should do?"

"Hmmm," Jewell said, thinking it over. "This may sound silly to you, Daffonia, but I think we should walk through the night rather than stop to sleep. It would throw off the pattern we've been keeping for the past two days. If one of us gets really tired then we can stop, and maybe use your idea to sleep in shifts."

Daffonia frowned, then began to nod as she seemed to think about the idea for a minute. "You know," she said. "That actually sounds like a pretty good plan. Then tomorrow we can find a sunny place and rest in the sun for awhile. Maybe we'll even run into one of the Eyes who has some word on how Glory is."

At the mention of Glory's name Jewell became sad. "You know," she said to Daffonia. "I don't really know Glory, and she did seem to be quite a show-off, but I liked her. I like all of the Eyes of the Forest. They seem to really care about us."

"They do," Daffonia said. "They care about everything and everyone. That's their purpose."

"You're like that, too," Jewell said, walking close beside her.

"What do you mean?"

"You seem to care about everything and everyone," Jewell said.

"I do," Daffonia said. "We're all supposed to care that way. If the people cared more about the world in general, they wouldn't build those big pollution makers that destroy everything from the air we breath to the soil that grows our food. If they cared about each other they'd be trying to help each other, teach each other, guide each other instead of competing with each other and even killing each other."

"Not where I come from," Jewell said. "I don't see all that."

"House pets seldom do," Daffonia said.

"What do you mean by 'house pets?'" Jewell asked.

"People keep different creatures as pets," Daffonia said. "Like you and other dogs, not to mention cats and birds and horses and all kinds of animals."

"They don't keep me in the house," Jewell said.

"No," Daffonia said. "I didn't mean that. What I meant is they keep creatures they take care of. They don't let them run around outside long enough to go wild. They feed them and make sure they're always healthy."

"Like they do for me," Jewell said.

Daffonia nodded. "Exactly. But the people who care for the different creatures know all about the problems in the Outside Place. They know all about the pollution and the violence out there."

"But we live in the country," Jewell said. "Everyone seems to get along very well. I never saw anyone kill someone else. And the air seems to be quite clean." Jewell looked around the forest and took a deep breath. "Although, it isn't as clean as the air here is."

"Even the country has been polluted by the air that drifts in from the cities where the big pollution makers are," Daffonia said. "Many people who live in the country used to live in the city and know all about the bad things that happen there. That's why they left."

"Do you think my family ever saw a person kill another person?" Jewell asked. "Or that they knew someone who killed another person?"

"It's possible," Daffonia said, sounding sad. "It's very possible."

"How awful," Jewell shook her head and sighed. She tried to picture such a thing in her mind, but had to shake off the terrible image.

"Yes, it is," Daffonia said.

They walked in silence for nearly an hour more. Jewell could not get the Outside Place, as she had come to think of it, off her mind. She was beginning to see it in an entirely different light. It had always been her home and playground. She was happy when she could run free and do as she pleased, and miserable when she was tied up, confined. But she was starting to see her confinement as less of a punishment and more as a way for her family to protect her. Probably from herself more than anything. That thought did not sit well with her. So when Daffonia finally spoke Jewell was thankful for the interruption.

"The sun is beginning to set," Daffonia said. "Are you sure you want to walk through the night?"

Jewell looked at the sky and nodded. "I'm sure. I think it will be safer for now, at least until we know what that thing is. Maybe if we knew what it was, we could figure out how to get rid of it."

"I agree with you," Daffonia said. "And I'm also ready to walk through the night with you if you think we can."

"I run around all night back home," Jewell said. "It's easy."

"Maybe where you come from," Daffonia said, sounding nervous. "But I've heard stories from other travelers who've come through the forest at night."

"What kind of stories?"

"Scarey stories," Daffonia said. "They say the forest is totally different at night. They say there are totally different creatures that come out at night that are very dangerous, but that if you sleep through it, it doesn't bother you."

"What doesn't bother you?" Jewell asked, thinking those stories would be silly.

"The forest, I guess," Daffonia said. "I don't know really. Maybe the different animals. I know racoons, bats, owls, and such are out at night, but I never thought of them as being quite so frightening. I guess I don't know."

"Haven't you ever travelled through the forest at night?" Jewell asked.

"Honestly," Daffonia said. "No, I haven't. Not this forest, anyway. I've been all over the garden at night and when I was in the Outside Place I traveled through those wooded areas at night, but I've never traveled through Noah's Forest at night." Daffonia looked around curiously and appeared to be thinking. "No, I never had reason to travel through here at night."

"Why not?" Jewell asked. "Didn't it make sense to get where you were going faster by travelling longer?"

"I never thought about it," Daffonia said. "But I am now."

"You're not afraid are you?"

"A little," Daffonia said. "You're used to being out at night. I'm not."

"Don't be afraid," Jewell said. "There's nothing to it. It's just like running around during the day except that you can see a little better when the sun is out."

"Well, if you're not afraid, then I'm not afraid," Daffonia said, lifting her chin gallantly in the air.

Jewell laughed. "Good!" she said. "Then night travel it will be!"

"I hope you know what you're doing," Daffonia said.

Jewell smiled. "Trust me, Daffonia. I know what I'm doing."

CHAPTER 9

The sun had been set for a little over an hour as Jewell and Daffonia continued on their journey. The sounds of crickets and owls, rustling leaves and toads could be clearly heard echoing through the trees.

"It's mighty dark out here," Daffonia said with a nervous quiver in her voice.

"It's not much different than where I'm from," Jewell offered. "The only lights I see in my neighborhood are lights from the houses, but most of them are so deep in the woods that you have to be fairly close to them before their lights help you see where you're going."

"Are sure you're not afraid?" Daffonia asked, her voice shaky.

"I'm sure," Jewell said. "Besides in this forest you have the Eyes twinkling all night long. Look at how much prettier their colors are without the sunlight."

Daffonia looked around the forest for a few seconds. "You know, you're right, Jewell. It is very pretty in the forest at night."

"It's much prettier than the woods that I'm used to," Jewell said. "Even at night I've never seen the Eyes of the Forest back home. But I'll tell you," she added. "I like knowing they're there."

Daffonia stopped walking and began to look around, sniffing the air with a feeling of concern emanating from her.

"What is it?" Jewell asked.

"Ssshhh!" Daffonia said. "I heard something."

"You'll hear alot of things in the forest at night," Jewell said. "Don't be afraid just because you can't see it."

"No," Daffonia said. "It's not a sound like I've heard in the daytime."

"That's because there are things that sleep all day that only walk at night," a little, masculine voice said, startling the travelers.

Daffonia and Jewell both jumped at the unfamiliar sound.

"Who's there?" Jewell asked. "Show yourself."

"I'm not hiding," the voice said, sounding angry. "I'm just much smaller than you."

Jewell felt an insistent tugging at the hair on her legs and she pulled her foot away. A mere second after she did so something hit her on her other leg.

"Down here, you dope!" the voice said. "Look down here and stop being so ignorant!"

Jewell looked down at her feet. Standing on her left paw she saw a little round man wearing a red, pointed hat and green shorts with suspenders over a white, short-sleeved shirt. On his feet were flat, brown shoes with white knee socks. He had a brown beard with red and white strands of hair running through it. When he took off his hat to bow to her, she saw that his hair was the same color as his beard. He wore it long, all the way down to his shoulders, but it was tied back somehow so that it made a very small tail near the back of his neck.

"What is it?" Daffonia said.

"Who is it?" the little man said, slapping Jewell across the leg at the same time. "Let's get this straight right now," he yelled as loud as his little voice could yell. "My name is Tolebit! I'm one of the many sprites that live in this world. Just because we haven't met doesn't mean that I don't deserve respect!"

"I apologize," Daffonia said sincerely. "I didn't mean to be so rude. It's just that I've never traveled through the forest at night and I'm not very comfortable doing so now."

"No excuses!" Tolebit admonished as he started scaling Jewell's leg using her hairs as handles to pull himself up.

"That hurts!" Jewell yelped, twitching in response to the pain.

"Be still!" Tolebit orderd. "How do you expect me to climb up onto your neck if you keep moving around like that?"

"Why don't you ask one of us to lift you up?" Jewell asked

impatiently. Under her breath she added, "You nasty, little slug."

"I heard that!" Tolebit yelled. "My ears are very keen. Don't think you're going to get any help from me if you keep up that disrespectful banter."

"I don't think I need any help from you," Jewell retorted.

"Careful," Daffonia whispered to Jewell. "You never know. We might need his help for something."

"Like what?" Jewell whispered back to the deer.

"Like updating you on Glory's condition, for starters," Tolebit said as he struggled past Jewell's shoulders, then hoisted himself onto her neck.

Daffonia and Jewell looked at each other, surprised.

"How do you know Glory?" Daffonia asked him.

"I know everyone," Tolebit answered. "I heard through the grapevine what happened to her," he continued. "And I heard the same way how she's doing."

"So, she's alive?" Jewell asked, excited.

"Now why should I tell you anything?" Tolebit asked. "You don't need me for anything. Remember?"

"You're the most annoying creature I've ever met," Jewell said. "I'll be in the garden soon enough and I'll find out for myself."

"Maybe," Tolebit said. "But you could know now and put your mind at ease."

"I don't need to," Jewell said. "You just gave me the answers anyway. She's doing fine, obviously."

"Not obviously!" Tolebit said, tweeking Jewells right ear.

"Ouch!" Jewell yelped. "I'll throw you to the ground if you do that again!"

"Try it," Tolebit dared. "I'll hang on to your long, mangy hairs and you'll only cause yourself more pain."

"Stop it!!" Daffonia finally cut in. "Both of you!"

"It's her fault," Tolebit started.

"Be quiet!" Daffonia said. "I want to know exactly how Glory is doing. Will you tell me? Please?"

Tolebit was quiet for a moment while Jewell comtemplated throwing him to the ground, anyway.

"I'll tell you," he began, "even though Miss Attitude here will also get the news."

Clearing his throat, Tolebit started to tell what he had heard.

"The Eyes of the Forest got her to Astilbe in time," he began. "Both of her wings were broken very badly. Astilbe reset the breaks and put twig supports on them to hold them in place while the breaks heal."

"That's great news!" Jewell said, her tail wagging in rapid sweeps.

"I wasn't speaking to you," Tolebit said.

"That's great news," Daffonia repeated.

"Not such great news," Tolebit said.

"Why not?" Jewell asked. She felt him slap her in the head and she winced then bent forward a bit knocking him a little off balance. She felt him tip from side to side before he spoke.

"I wasn't speaking to you."

"Ooooo, you little. . . . ," Jewell mumbled under her breath.

"I heard that," Tolebit said arrogantly.

"Why isn't that great news?" Daffonia cut in.

"Because Glory fell unconscious while the Eyes were transporting her," Tolebit answered. "She hasn't awaken yet."

"Wha. . . . ," Jewell began, but Daffonia gave her a look that told her it was better to hold her peace while Daffonia did the talking.

"What does that mean?" Daffonia asked.

"No one is quite sure," Tolebit replied. "But Astilbe believes it has something to do with the Monster Shadow."

Jewell's ears perked up. From the corner of her eye she saw Tolebit with his hand raised and ready to slap her again, so she held her tongue while Daffonia asked all the questions.

"Do you know anything about the Monster Shadow?" Daffonia asked.

"No more than you," Tolebit answered. "Why? What do you want to know?"

"Jewell and I were talking," Daffonia began.

"You mean this mut?" Tolebit cut in as he banged his little fists on Jewell's head a few times.

"Why are you so abusive?" Daffonia asked, sounding exasperated and angry.

"She rubbed me the wrong way," Tolebit answered.

"Then why are you sitting on her neck and not mine?" Daffonia asked.

"So I can be close enough to pound on her whenever I feel the need," Tolebit answered.

"That's not very nice," Daffonia lectured. "Jewell is a wonderful friend. She's here to learn just like everyone else that's here. It's obvious that you never made it to the garden yourself."

"I never had the desire to go to the garden," Tolebit said defensively.

"That doesn't mean that Jewell shouldn't earn her entrance into it," Daffonia said. "Now I suggest you leave her alone or I'll help her throw you to the ground. We'll leave you there and go on our way."

Tolebit seemed thoughtful for a little while as he sat on Jewell's neck without making a move. Daffonia stared him down while she waited for his decision.

"Alright," he finally said. "I'll do my best to behave. But it isn't easy for me."

"Your best will be good enough for starters," Daffonia said.

"May I speak now?" Jewell asked as she caught Tolebit ready to strike her again.

"Toollebit!" Daffonia warned.

Tolebit lowered his arm slowly.

"I told you it isn't easy for me," he said. He leaned forward over Jewell's head. "Yes, you may speak, now."

"Well," Jewell began, "as Daffonia was saying, we were talking. It seems that there must be someone who knows about the Monster Shadow and how it is that the Black Place can move around throughout the forest."

"What if there is?" Tolebit asked, holding his left arm down with his right.

"If there is then maybe we can learn about it and figure out a way to get rid of it?" Jewell said.

Tolebit kept still for a few seconds longer while he seemed to wrestle with himself.

"What's the matter?" Daffonia asked.

"Nothing," Tolebit answered. "I was just thinking that I might know someone who has all the answers for you about that place. To visit him, though, will take you out of the way of your journey to the garden."

Jewell let out a slight whimper at the thought of being delayed in getting to the garden.

"That decision is entirely up to Jewell," Daffonia said. "This is her journey. I can't make those choices for her."

Tolebit looked at the top of Jewell's head and said, "Well, Mongrel, what do you say? How important is it to you?"

"Oohh," Jewell whined. "I don't know. I really want to get through this place so I can go back home to my family."

"It's up to you," Daffonia said as Jewell looked to her for help.

"Why should I go?" Jewell asked, feeling a twinge of guilt the moment she'd spoken the words.

Tolebit climbed up to Jewell's right ear and whispered in it. "What if Glory's life depended on it?"

"Does it?" Jewell asked excitedly as she flipped her head around, knocking Tolebit off balance and leaving him holding on to her by a single hair.

"You idiot!" he yelled. "That's the last time I tell you anything."

Daffonia nudged Tolebit with her nose, lifting him back onto Jewell's neck.

"I'm sorry," Jewell said to the sprite. "I got excited."

"You sure did," Tolebit said. "But I don't know if Glory's life depends on you making this side trip or not. I'll tell you this, though," he continued. "There are a lot of other lives that do. That might even include your own. And Daffonia's."

Jewell looked at Daffonia again, this time with conviction.

"Maybe I have a larger purpose than you thought," she said to Daffonia.

"Maybe you do," Daffonia agreed.

"What do you think?"

"It's your decision where we go," Daffonia said.

"Then we're going to see Tolebit's friend," Jewell said decisively.

"He's not my friend," Tolebit said. "I never said that. I only said that I know of someone who might have all the answers you're looking for about that monster thing."

"Good enough," Jewell said. "Take us to him."

"If you insist," Tolebit said. "How good is your night vision?"

"Good enough," Jewell answered.

"What about yours?" Tolebit asked Daffonia.

"I'm a deer," Daffonia replied. "I have excellent night vision."

"Alright, then," Tolebit said. "Turn around and head back the way you came. When you get to a place where five white birch trees clump together, you'll find a path to the left. Take that path and follow it as long as you possibly can."

"Then what?" Daffonia asked.

"Yeah, then what?" Jewell echoed.

Tolebit leaned back and tied himself in place with Jewell's hair. "Then you can wake me up and I'll take you the rest of the way."

"What is it about all the male creatures in this place?" Jewell asked Daffonia. "They're always sleeping."

"Not all of them," Daffonia said. "Only the two you've met so far."

"Oh," Jewell said, rolling her eyes. "That gives me so much confidence in this little guy's friend who knows everything."

"The decision is still yours." Daffonia let out a deep breath as if she were trying to stay calm. "We can forget this whole thing and continue on our way."

Jewell thought about it. "No," she said. "If it's going to help Glory, or anyone for that matter, then we should probably take the chance and go."

Daffonia nodded. "I'm with you," she said, smiling. "Lead the way."

CHAPTER 10

They had been traveling for nearly an hour and Jewell was growing hungry, but there didn't seem to be anything to eat on the way to see Tolebit's friend. She was beginning to wonder if she should have decided to take this chance. Maybe it wasn't such a good idea.

"I think I see the five birch trees up ahead," Daffonia said.

Jewell saw where she was looking and turned to see if Daffonia was right. "I see them too," she said. "Now we just have to find the path on the left that this annoying little man told us to look for."

"He's not that bad," Daffonia said. "He's just a defensive creature. He's a little insecure. That's all."

"That's enough," Jewell said. "It figures that he would choose me to ride on."

Daffonia studied Tolebit for a few seconds. "He looks cute sleeping all wrapped up in your hair."

"I'm glad I can't see him," Jewell said. "I'd probably bury him somewhere."

"Oh, Jewell," Daffonia said. "You have to have a little compassion for creatures like Tolebit. He's not so bad once you understand him."

"Oh, I understand him, alright," Jewell said. "He lives just to aggravate others like me."

Daffonia laughed, but Jewell didn't see the humor in what she had said. "What I don't understand is why he never made it to the garden."

Daffonia looked at him again and nodded. "I wonder how long he's been in the forest."

Jewell shrugged. "We'll have to remember to ask him when he

wakes up. Here," she said, changing the subject. "We're at the five birch trees. Now where's the path?"

Daffonia hopped past Jewell and stood at the beginning of a small path that seemed to lead into another part of the forest. "Right here," she said.

Jewell tried to look down the path, but it was difficult to see much in the dark, especially through the overgrown state of the trees. And the smell was different. It smelled like mildew and mushrooms. "He'd better not be leading us on a wild goose chase," Jewell said. "I don't like the looks of that one."

"I don't think he is," Daffonia said. "I don't know why, but I believe him."

"Well, if he is," Jewell said, stepping on to the beginning of the path, "we'll find the Black Place and throw him in it." She stood beside Daffonia, looking down as far as she could see. She didn't want to do this, but if there was any chance it would help Glory, then she had to. "Well, here goes nothing."

Together they started down the path near the clump of five white birch trees as Tolebit had directed them.

"How far do we go?" Jewell asked.

Daffonia shook her head. "I'm not sure," she said. "Tolebit said to follow the path as long as we possibly can.

"What is that supposed to mean?" Jewell was annoyed.

"If we take it literally," Daffonia answered, "it could mean that we should follow it until we're exhausted and can't go any further."

"Or it could mean to follow it until we're bored with it." Daffonia turned to look at her. "Or it could mean to follow it until it ends."

"Great!" Jewell said. "Now what?"

"I suppose we just keep walking," Daffonia said. "As long as there's a path let's just follow it."

Jewell grumbled. "Oh, this just keeps getting better," she said, her voice dripping with sarcasm.

"Hush," Daffonia said. "Let's just do as Tolebit told us. Someone has to find out about that awful Black Place."

"Hey," Jewell said, "I just had a thought."

"What's that?"

"It occurred to me that maybe you have a larger purpose than you thought, too," Jewell answered. "Maybe there's a greater mission we're on than either one of us knows."

"Interesting," Daffonia said. "I'm not sure I like the idea, but it's still an interesting one."

"I think it's an exciting one."

"You would."

"You know something else?" Jewell asked.

"What's that?"

Jewell quickly scanned the immediate area. "I don't see any Eyes around here at all. Do you think they're all asleep?"

"They couldn't ALL be asleep," Daffonia said. "They don't need much rest to begin with. Usually the Eyes of the Forest only sleep when they know they're completely safe. Their purpose is to be ever watchful. That means all the time. It's unusual that there would be no Eyes around anywhere."

"Oh, no," Jewell said, suddenly very worried. "You don't think something awful happened to Glory?"

"I hope not."

"Even worse."

"What's even worse?" Daffonia asked.

"I had a thought that's really bad," Jewell said.

"What's that?"

"What if Tolebit led us right into the Black Place?" Jewell asked. "What if we're in it right now.?"

"It doesn't look like it did when we were in it before," Daffonia said as she looked around. "It looks like the forest, but without the colorful Eyes blinking all over the place."

"So, what do you think?"

"I think we're in a different part of the forest," Daffonia said. "I think it's a place that the Eyes are either not welcome in or are afraid to enter."

"I thought the Eyes were everywhere."

"So did I," Daffonia said. "But I may have just been proven wrong."

"Well, I for one think it's time to wake up the tiny monster and torture him until he tells us where we are and what's going on," Jewell said.

"Who? Tolebit?"

"That's exactly who I'm talking about."

"He said to follow the path as long as we possibly can."

"I'm not sure I even WANT to follow it anymore until I know exactly what he's up to," Jewell said. "I don't trust him."

"Oh, come on," Daffonia said. "He hasn't done anything to give us reason not to trust him. Just because he's annoying doesn't mean he's misleading us."

"Yeah? Then why hasn't he ever been to the garden?"

"Because I chose to stay out here and help ingrates like yourselves get there first," Tolebit said from on top of Jewell's neck.

"Good to see you awake," Jewell said, deliberately letting her sarcasm show.

"Don't bother being nice to me," Tolebit said. "I've been awake longer than you think."

"Good," Jewell said. "Then you already know that I'm not too happy going down this path."

"So I hear," Tolebit said as he stretched and yawned.

"I think Jewell has a valid concern," Daffonia said. "Why aren't the Eyes of the Forest around here?"

"Oh, ye of little faith," Tolebit said, shaking his head.

"Well, why aren't the Eyes around here?" Jewell asked.

"Because they're not needed in this part of the forest," Tolebit said.

Jewell felt the air by her left ear whoosh by and she knew Tolebit had swung at her again. She was surprised that he had missed.

"Why not?" Daffonia asked.

"Because this whole area is greatly protected by Oscar. The Eyes would be wasting their time here when they're so badly needed in other places," Tolebit said. "Oscar is a very strong psychic."

"What does that mean?" Jewell asked.

"It means that Oscar can see things with his mind," Daffonia said.

"Yes," Tolebit said, "but only to an extent. Oscar keeps this part of the forest protected in all ways. The Eyes are welcome to come here to rest and they do quite often, but their watchfulness is not needed here."

"Well, I don't see any Eyes sleeping, either," Jewell noted.

"I would imagine that all the Eyes who can be are at Glory's side right now," Tolebit said. "Any ninny could figure that out for themselves."

Jewell tensed. "Don't start with me Tolebit."

"Come on you two," Daffonia cut in. "You've both been doing so good until now."

"How much farther do we have to walk, anyway?" Jewell asked, trying to forget Tolebit's belittling remark.

"Well, it's obvious that you've gone as far as you possibly can," Tolebit said.

"What does that mean anyway?" Daffonia asked.

"I don't know," Tolebit said. "That's the way the directions were given to me so that's the way I pass them on. I think it's different for everyone. It's all relative, you know."

"What is?" Jewell asked.

"Everything."

"Daffonia," Jewell said with a growl underlining her words. "He's getting on my nerves."

"I think what Tolebit means is that every creature has different limits," Daffonia said. "Some can go longer without eating, others can go longer without sleeping, while still others can go longer without getting bored."

"I see who the smart one in the group is," Tolebit grumbled.

Jewell growled at him in response, but Tolebit did not seem to be shaken by it.

"What next?" Daffonia asked.

"Look for a huge boulder," Tolebit answered. "Once we find it we have to sit and wait for Oscar to come out. He'll know we're there, don't you worry."

Jewell let out a short, low growl as she began to look around for the boulder.

"How long have you been in the forest, anyway?" Daffonia asked Tolebit.

"A long time," Tolebit said. "I couldn't really tell you anymore. I lost track."

"But you never made it to the garden?" she asked him. "Don't you want to see it?"

"I suppose so," Tolebit said. "But I gave up trying so long ago that I don't think about it much, now."

"How close did you get to it?" Daffonia asked.

"To the lilies."

"The Valley Lilies?" Daffonia asked.

"No, the Day Lilies," Tolebit answered. "I got that far before I got, . . sort of . . . stuck, I guess."

"What else did you have to learn?"

"How to be nice," Jewell answered for him.

Whap! Tolebit slapped Jewell across the top of her head. "I am nice!"

"Tolebit," Daffonia said in a reprimanding tone. "What you just did wasn't very nice."

"I don't have any patience with nincompoops," he said.

Jewell turned to Daffonia and let out a frustrated breath. "Don't waste your time with him," she said. "I see the boulder over there. Let's just wait for this Oscar creature so we can find out about the Monster Shadow."

"I think I want to ride on Daffonia's neck after this," Tolebit said as they closed the fifty feet between them and the boulder. "This ride is becoming a hostile one."

"That's fine with me," Daffonia said. "It might be better for everyone. But I warn you, Tolebit. Slap me once and I'll dump you on your rear end and leave you there."

"I'll behave," Tolebit promised.

"You'd better."

"I'll be glad to be rid of you, anyway," Jewell said.

"And good riddance to you!" Tolebit said.

They approached the boulder and stood a moment. "What does Oscar look like?" Jewell asked.

"Have you ever seen an owl?" Tolebit asked her.

"I have, many times," Daffonia said. "They're in the garden."

"I've seen them back home," Jewell said.

"Well, that's what Oscar is," Tolebit said. "He's an owl. A very old, wise owl."

Jewell flipped her head to the side. "Great. A bird."

"Not just a bird," Tolebit warned. "Oscar is special. He knows things like Astilbe knows things."

"That reminds me," Jewell said. "Aren't you changing seats?"

"Right now, as a matter of fact," Tolebit said. "Daffonia, can you stand neck to neck with this mut so I can climb onto you. The stench in this seat is making me nauseous."

Daffonia stood next to Jewell while Tolebit made his way through Jewell's fur, then transferred himself on to Daffonia's neck.

"Much better," Tolebit said as he positioned himself comfortably on Daffonia. "Shorter hair, but I'll make do."

Jewell shook herself off now that Tolebit was no longer buried in her hair. "How do you know so much about the garden if you've never been there?"

"I talk to other creatures," he said. "And I listen to them talk to each other. I even tried to steal my way into the garden on a few occasions, but the Eyes caught me every time."

"Good for them," Jewell cheered.

"You know you shouldn't have done that," Daffonia said. "You have to earn your way into the garden. You can't just hitch a ride with someone else."

"I know," Tolebit said.

"What happened to your companion?" Daffonia asked. "Didn't someone meet you when you entered the forest?"

"Not exactly," Tolebit said. "I sort of stumbled into it by accident."

"No one stumbles into the forest by accident," Daffonia said. "You must be allowed to enter."

"Well, I don't know about that," Tolebit said. "All I know is that I was on the outside and then I was inside, but once I was here, I couldn't get out."

"What were you doing when you entered the forest?" Daffonia asked. "Were you looking in? Did something catch your eye?"

"Oh, alright! I'll tell you," Tolebit said, waving his arms in the air. "I saw one of the Eyes of the Forest fly in."

"From the outside?" Jewell asked.

"Yes, brainiac," Tolebit said. "From the outside. That was before the big pollution makers were built, back in the days when the Eyes were easier to see in the Outside Place. Oh, she was beautiful. I just had to see her, again."

"So what happened?" Daffonia asked.

"I saw her fly in and I wanted to follow her," Tolebit answered. "But every time I tried, this squirrel kept stopping me. It chased me and followed me. It even grabbed me around the arm a few times and carried me away from the border."

"So what did you do?" Daffonia asked.

"I kept trying different ways until I finally got in."

"No," Jewell said. "It couldn't have been that easy."

"Why not?" Tolebit asked. "Didn't you just run right in without stopping? No one tried to make you go away."

"How do you know?" Jewell asked.

"I told you," Tolebit said. "I know everybody. They tell me things."

"Tolebit," Daffonia said. "You would never have been able to see the forest if you weren't meant to come in. Only those who need the forest are allowed in. Don't you see? Noah knows you're wandering around out here because you were allowed to come in. He's probably been waiting for you to figure it all out so you could gain admittance into the garden."

"Figure all what out?" Tolebit asked.

"Figure out what it is you need to learn," Jewell cut in. "Like manners, for starters."

"Why you," Tolebit said taking a swipe in the air at Jewell. "You're lucky I'm not riding on your neck, anymore."

"No," Jewell said. "I'm thankful."

Jewell bowed to Daffonia. "I thank you for taking that nasty, little burden off my neck."

"Oh, please," Daffonia said. "Stop it, will you?"

Jewell sat down by the boulder and leaned her body into the huge rock. "How long do we have to wait?"

"I don't know," Tolebit said. "I've never been here."

"Then how do you know there's even such a creature as Oscar?"

"Because I listen," Tolebit said. "And I believe the first time I'm told something."

"Enough," Daffonia said. "Tolebit, I swear. One more snide word out of you and I'll stuff your mouth with moss."

Tolebit grumbled something inaudible, but kept silent after that.

"Well, I'm bored," Jewell said. "Now what?"

"Now you exercise some patience for a change," Daffonia answered. "This may just be important enough for you to finally do that."

"You're right," Jewell agreed. "I'll give it my best try this time."

"Good girl."

"I'm going back to sleep," Tolebit said.

Jewell took a deep breath. "That's the best idea I've heard in quite a while," she said. "You go right to sleep, Tolebit. We'll wake you if anything happens."

"Too late," Daffonia said to her. "He didn't hear you. He's snoring."

Jewell shook her head in frustration. "I don't know how you can stand him."

"Because I **under**stand him," Daffonia said. "A little compassion goes a long way, Jewell."

"I suppose. But I'm not even sure what compassion is."

"When it's time for you to learn, you will," Daffonia said. "For now let's just wait for Oscar. It's still very early in the night hours. We may have a long wait ahead of us."

Jewell grumbled as she lay on the ground near the boulder and placed her head complacently between her paws to wait for the mysterious owl named Oscar to appear. "I hate this stuff."

CHAPTER 11

"This is ridiculous," Jewell complained. "We've been sitting here for hours. I don't think this Oscar character even exists. I think Tolebit made it all up."

"Well, if he did," Daffonia said, "I'll be mighty disappointed in him. But think about it, Jewell, how else are we going to find out about that Black Place unless we follow up on all the possibilities. If this turns out to be a dead end, then so be it."

Jewell looked curiously at Daffonia, then shook her head. "You amaze me," she said to her. "I'm growing angrier with that little nuisance on your neck with every minute that passes. You, on the other hand, just shrug your shoulders and say, 'Oh, well.'"

"Why are you angry?" Daffonia asked.

"Because I think we've been lied to," Jewell said angrily. "I think we've been played for fools."

"For what reason?"

"I don't know," Jewell said as she sat up. "Maybe Tolebit just wanted company. Maybe he wanted a ride here. Who knows?"

"That's right," Daffonia said. "Who knows, indeed?"

"What are you saying?"

"I'm saying that you shouldn't be judging those you hardly know without proof to back up your judgement," Daffonia said. "Tolebit's only negative trait is that he's extremely annoying."

"Is he ever!"

"But he hasn't done anything to hurt us," Daffonia said. "He hasn't lied to us, he hasn't led us into any place that will harm us. I can't find any reason not to trust him."

"Oh, give him time," Jewell said sarcastically.

"You're not being fair to him," Daffonia said. "How can a person prove to be trustworthy unless we give that person the chance?"

"And how do we do that?" Jewell asked. "By letting him lead us into a trap?"

Daffonia shook her head. "No, Jewell," she said. "By trusting him."

Jewell started to comment, but was suddenly silent instead. She looked at Daffonia, then at Tolebit who was sound asleep on Daffonia's neck, then nodded her head as the point Daffonia was trying to make suddenly became crystal clear. "You know," Jewell said. "You're right. I never thought about it that way, but you're right."

"I'm glad you understand," Daffonia said. "Because I think you might want to consider how many chances your family has given you to prove your trustworthiness to them."

"What do you mean?" Jewell asked, concerned. "I'm trustworthy."

"Are you?" Daffonia asked.

"Sure I am."

"Well, if you consider the fact that they can trust you to run around the neighborhood like a nut, then you're right," Daffonia said. "Or we might consider the fact that you can be trusted to tear up the garbage in the neighborhood whenever you're let loose, then you're right again."

"But I always go home," Jewell said defensively.

"And I'll bet they're thrilled to have you home," Daffonia said. "Especially smelling like you must smell from the swamp you run through and the garbage you've played with, not to mention all the complaints they must be getting about you from the other neighbors in the area."

"Then why don't they make me go away?" Jewell asked.

"Maybe they've been trying to," Daffonia suggested. "Maybe they keep letting you run loose because they're hoping you don't come back."

The very thought that her family might not really want her made Jewell very sad all of a sudden. She hung her head as a tear began to roll down the side of her furry face.

"Or maybe they keep letting you come home because they love you so much," Daffonia said. "Even though you're so much trouble."

Jewell looked up at Daffonia with her sad, tear-filled face. "Do you think so?" she asked. "Do you think they really love me that much?"

Daffonia gave her a comforting smile. "I think so," she said.

"Oh, I miss them so much," Jewell said. "I wish I could go home now."

"You can't go back until you're ready to."

"I'm ready now," Jewell said eagerly.

"Just because you want to, doesn't mean you're ready to," Daffonia said. "The process of growing up and maturing is what makes us ready to do all the things we must do. In order to be successful at anything, you need to be prepared for it."

Daffonia looked lovingly, yet empathetically at Jewell. "No, Jewell," she said. "You're not ready to go home, yet."

Jewell was quiet as she lay back down on the ground next to the boulder and let her head rest across her front legs. She was sad.

Suddenly, from the darkness of the forest came a rustling, sweeping sound.

Daffonia jumped in place, then looked around, quickly. "What's that?"

"What's what?" Jewell asked.

"That sound!" Daffonia said, still looking around.

"I don't hear anything."

"Well, stand up and stop feeling sorry for yourself!" Daffonia demanded. "Listen with me."

Jewell did as she was told. The very moment she was on her feet she heard the sounds Daffonia was talking about.

"What is it?" Daffonia asked, again.

"It sounds like the wind blowing through the trees," Jewell said.

"It's an awfully loud wind," Daffonia said.

"Mighty strong, too," Jewell said. "Look at that!"

Daffonia looked in the direction Jewell indicated and her face took on a startled, frightened expression. "Jewell!" she yelled as the sounds grew too loud for a dog to comfortably hear. "We've got to get out of here! I think we've been tricked."

"Here!" Jewell yelled, running behind the boulder for safety. "Come here with me and crouch down low. Let the boulder hide us from whatever is coming."

Daffonia did as Jewell suggested and joined her companion on the other side of the over-sized rock to hide from the unknown intruder.

"My ears are hurting!" Jewell yelled as the windlike rustling grew ever louder.

"Mine too!" Daffonia said. "Is Tolebit alright?"

Jewell checked on Daffonia's rider. "He's sleeping right through it!" she reported.

Suddenly, a huge shadow covered the entire area making the darkness of the forest as black as pitch.

"I think it's the Monster Shadow," Daffonia said in a shaky voice as the shadow seemed to swoop down to the ground, then rise back up into the air.

"I don't know," Jewell said, watching the shadow descend on them. "It seems different some how."

"What do you mean?" Daffonia asked. "It's a huge shadow and it's looking for us. It knows we're here."

"Stay here." Jewell began to inch her way around the boulder.

"What are you doing?" Daffonia asked, panic invading her voice.

"I'm trying to see what it is."

"Don't be a fool!" Daffonia warned.

"I don't think it's the Monster Shadow," Jewell said. "It doesn't 'feel' as scary as the Monster Shadow."

At that moment the huge shadow that had been circling around above their heads began to grow smaller and smaller until all that was left was the sound of flapping wings.

"What happened?" Daffonia asked in almost a whisper now

that the din was gone.

"I'm not sure," Jewell replied. "But I'm going to find out."

"Wait," Daffonia said. "I'm coming with you."

Together, they walked out from behind the huge wall of stone and looked around cautiously.

"Do you see anything?" Jewell asked.

"Not yet," Daffonia said. "What about you?"

"Me neither," Jewell said. "I thought it might be Oscar, though. I mean, we don't have any idea what he really looks like except that he's an owl."

"Did someone call my name?" a voice behind them said in an old, but worldly tone.

Daffonia and Jewell turned around in unison. Together, their eyes scaled the height of the boulder until they came to rest on the stately, beige figure that stood perched at the very top of the mammoth stone. He appeared soft, his head moved a fraction of an inch to one side, then to the next, always moving as if he were constantly on the alert.

"Oscar?" the travelers asked together.

"That is my name," the tall owl replied. "Who is asking?"

"I am Daffonia," the deer replied humbly, "and this is Jewell."

"Ah, yes," the owl replied. "The newcomer and her companion."

"How did you know?" Jewell asked.

"Jewell," Daffonia whispered in a reprimanding tone. "He's psychic."

"That I am," Oscar replied. "What brings you to see me?"

"I thought you were psychic," Jewell said brazenly. "You should know."

"That I do," the owl replied. "That I do."

Spreading his wings to a span of nearly six feet, the owl leaned forward and swooped down upon his visitors. Daffonia and Jewell dropped defensively to the ground as the large owl descended on them.

"Get up!" Oscar demanded as he came to rest on an outcrop in the boulder. "I'm not going to hurt you. I only thought it best to converse eye to eye with you."

Together the travelers stood up, realizing as they did so, that they were, indeed, eye to eye with the great wise owl.

"I do know why you are here," he said to them. "But I must advise you against trying to find or destroy the Monster Shadow. It is a very dangerous entity."

"We just want to know what it is," Daffonia explained. "We haven't really decided to try to destroy it. We met Tolebit in the woods and he said you would know."

"There is really no other reason to know what it is unless you are planning to destroy it, now is there?" Oscar said. "Most creatures avoid evil and negativity. There are only two reasons I know of why one would want to know more about this particular entity." His head moved from side to side, ever so slightly, while he seemed to study them one by one. "Either you want to join the evil, which I already know is not the case with either of you."

"Maybe it is with Tolebit," Jewell said.

"No," Oscar said, looking at the sprite. "That is not the case with him, either."

"Well, I'm glad you understand we aren't interested in joining anything evil," Daffonia said.

"Ah, that's true," Oscar said. "But the only other reason you'd want to know about the Monster Shadow would be to try to find a way to destroy it."

"Unless we planned to tell someone else who could destroy it." Daffonia looked at him, then put her head down. "But, then, again, you're psychic."

The owl seemed to think deeply for a few moments before he spoke.

"And what about you, Jewell?" he asked. "Shouldn't you be concentrating on getting to the Garden instead of chasing the Monster Shadow?"

"I'm not chasing the Monster Shadow," Jewell explained. "It seems to be following us, though, along with whoever tries to help us."

"What about the Garden?" Oscar asked.

"I am on my way to the Garden," Jewell replied. "But we have to know what that thing is. It tried to kill me and it has seriously harmed Glory. She is one of the Eyes of the Forest. Now Daffonia and I are afraid to go to sleep in case it sneaks up on us."

"I know all about Glory, Sprig's sister," Oscar said. "In fact, I am just returning from visiting her."

"How is she?" Jewell asked.

"Still asleep," the owl replied sadly. "Her recovery is most uncertain."

"Jewell is the one who found her and summoned Sprig to her rescue," Daffonia bragged.

"I heard," Oscar said, slowly moving his head from side to side in short, jerky motions. "Alright," he said. "I'll tell you about the Monster Shadow."

"Tolebit told us you would," Daffonia said.

"That little imp?" Oscar said. "Oh yes, there he is asleep in your fur. Well, let him sleep. He does that best."

"Forget about Tolebit," Jewell said. "Tell us about the Monster Shadow."

"Very well," Oscar replied. "The Monster Shadow is the result of the Black Place itself."

"Well then, what is the Black Place?" Jewell asked, feeling restless.

"Sit patiently and listen," Oscar advised in his slow, dramatic manner. "The Black Place developed because of all the newcomers who enter the forest in search of something. As you know, Jewell, the newcomers are here to learn and to become better individuals as they drop their bad habits along the way. However, what makes each of us the kinds of beings we are is nothing more than energy. Everything we feel, think, say, and do is made of one form of energy or another. Energy cannot be destroyed. It can be changed and modified, but it cannot be destroyed. It is one of the few constants in the entire universe."

"What's a universe?" Jewell asked, feeling bewildered. So many new words, new ideas.

"The universe is all of the worlds that exist," Daffonia explained. "And there are many of them, believe me."

"That's right," Oscar said. "As you walk through your journey in the forest, you are shedding some bad habits, those nasty traits. And as you do, the way you think and the things you think about change. But what happens to the energy that made up those negative, nasty, evil thoughts and characteristics?"

"They change to good thoughts and stuff," Jewell answered.

"Some of it does," Oscar said. "That's very true. At the same time, however, those traits in you that were already good further develop, as well. Much of the bad that was in you is pushed right out." He looked straight ahead at them. "Shedded, if you will."

"Where does it go?" Jewell asked.

"That's a very good question," Oscar replied. "In the very beginning, the bad energy left behind by the visitors who came to the forest merely floated around in the atmosphere. There was so little of it that it was of no consequence to anyone. But as time went on, there was more and more bad energy being left here. Eventually a little bit of bad energy from one place would bump into bad energy from another place as they floated around. As is true to nature, like attracts like."

"So they stuck together when they met?" Jewell asked.

"To put it quite simply, yes," Oscar replied. "As more time went by the little bits of bad energy that had been distributed throughout the forest began to grow as they all joined together. Eventually, the masses of bad energy all joined entirely into one, huge mass. That is what we know as the Black Place."

"What about the Monster Shadow?" Daffonia asked. "How did that thing form?"

"It was an inevitable result of all that bad energy finally joining forces," Oscar said. "It developed a consciousness. It was predictable. It was bound to happen. The Black Place was no more than a mother's womb in which to develop a child. Unfortunately, the child that this mother developed needed direction just like all children do until they grow up and mature enough to think rationally for themselves. The only direction the Monster Shadow has ever had came from the bad energy into which, and from which, it was born."

"Wait a minute!" Daffonia said. "What if the Monster Shadow is still just a baby? What if it hasn't even been born yet? You said the Black Place is a sort of mother's womb, only a really bad one. Well, what if the Monster Shadow is trying to be born?"

"That's right!" Jewell said. "It reached right out from the Black Place to swipe at Glory and smash her into a tree. What if Daffonia is right?"

"Then I pray for Abba to help the forest if the Monster Shadow is released into it," Oscar replied, looking away.

"Can we prevent it from being born?" Jewell asked.

"Unfortunately, that would go against the laws of nature," Oscar said.

"And the laws of the Garden," Daffonia added.

"But we're not in the Garden," Jewell argued. "We're in the forest. By destroying the Black Place and the Monster Shadow we might be protecting the Garden and keeping the forest safe for more visitors who need its help."

"The Monster Shadow cannot go too near the Garden," Oscar said. "The intense beauty and goodness that emanate from the Garden pushes the Black Place away. It wants nothing to do with it."

"Why not?" Jewell asked.

"Ah, now there's a very good question," Oscar stated. "Even I don't know the answer to that one. I only know that it's true."

"How do you know that?" Jewell asked.

"Because I've seen it with my own two eyes," the owl replied. "Not once, but on many occasions in recent times."

"Maybe too much goodness will destroy it," Daffonia suggested.

"No," Oscar said. "It is made up of energy. It cannot be destroyed. It can only be changed."

"Then how do we change energy?" Jewell asked anxiously.

"Oh, another good question?" Oscar said.

"That means he doesn't know the answer," Jewell said to Daffonia.

"Jewell!" Daffonia reprimanded her.

"Actually," Oscar began, "I know what must be done. Unfortunately, I do not know how to do it."

"Then tell us what has to be done," Jewell said.

"The energy must be redirected," Oscar stated.

"What does that mean?" Jewell and Daffonia asked in unison.

"Somehow, you have to change the direction that the energy is going," Oscar said. "If it's moving clockwise, then you must change its direction to move counter-clockwise. If it's heading north, then you must change it to move south. In this case, the energy is moving toward intense badness. It must be changed to move toward goodness."

"But how?" Jewell asked.

"If I knew how, don't you think I would have done it myself?" Oscar asked. "I don't know how. I only know that's what must be done."

Suddenly, Jewell felt deflated.

"Don't despair," Oscar told them. "Keep your faith in Abba and keep your sights on Noah's Garden. That's all you need to do. When the time is right, I'm sure the Good One will take care of these matters for us."

"Who's the Good One?" Jewell asked.

"Abba," Daffonia answered.

"For now," Oscar said, "you will find refuge and rest for as long as you like right here with me. The Black Place has never come here."

"Why not?" Daffonia asked.

"I'm not sure," Oscar said, "but I suspect my psychic abilities are the main reason. I believe the Monster Shadow fears I will know and understand it completely, thus knowing exactly where its weakness lies. I don't think it can afford to take that chance. Also, there's nothing for it here. Evil feeds from evil, but there is none of that here."

Daffonia stood up and walked a few steps before turning back toward Oscar. "If you came close enough to the Black Place, would you understand it completely?"

"I believe so," Oscar said. "I already know it better than anyone else in the forest. I'm not sure I want to know the depths of its evilness, though. I'm quite comfortable that it has chosen to stay away from me."

"May I ask you one more question?" Daffonia asked.

"Of course," Oscar replied. "What is it?"

"You seemed to know quite a bit about Tolebit, earlier," she said. "Do you?"

"Know him?" Oscar asked as he chuckled for a few seconds. "I know all about him."

"He said he was never here before," Jewell broke in. "How do you know him?"

"When he first entered the forest he was quite lost," Oscar said. "He's been floundering for many, many years. I sent one of the Eyes to give him directions to come here so that I might help him, but he has never had the courage to walk the path to me alone. Every time he has been here, he has slept through it and so, he has never seen me."

"Why don't you just go to him?" Jewell asked.

"That would be the easy way out, now wouldn't it?" Oscar asked.

Jewell was silent.

"I think you may have already learned that the easy way is not the best," Oscar added.

"I have," Jewell replied.

"We can talk more about Tolebit another time," Oscar said. "Get some rest. You still have a long journey ahead of you. You'll need your strength."

"Thank you for all the information," Jewell said. "If you see Glory, would you let her know that I asked about her?"

"That I will," Oscar said.

"And thank you for your hospitality," Daffonia added.

"You are most welcome," Oscar said. "It's too bad Tolebit had to sleep through another opportunity to speak with me."

With those words, Oscar bowed to his guests, spread his wings and was gone, pushing the air around them with his wide, sweeping flaps in a huge whoosh of turbulence.

"Wow!" Jewell said when the owl was gone.

"Wow, is right!" Daffonia seconded. "I'm not sure I'll be able to sleep, now."

"Me, neither," Jewell said. "But we have to try. Oscar is right. We're going to need all of our strength. Especially if we run into the Black Place."

"I agree," Daffonia said, laying down next to the boulder. "Alright, then. Good-night, Jewell."

"Good-night, Daffonia," Jewell replied as she lay on her side in the pitch dark forest and felt herself immediately begin to drift off to sleep.

CHAPTER 12

"Where are we?" Tolebit asked in a sleepy voice.

"Who's that?" Jewell was just waking up. She saw Tolebit's movements as he stretched his limbs, but her vision had not fully focused.

"It's me you idiot!" he snapped. "Where are we?"

"Where you sent us," Jewell said. "To see Oscar."

"Is he here?"

Jewell sat up. "Nope. You managed to miss him, again."

"Drat!" Tolebit said angrily, stamping his foot on Daffonia's neck.

Annoyed, she jumped up throwing Tolebit onto the ground beside her. "Tolebit, you arrogant little snipe!" she snapped at him.

"Oh, let me bury him," Jewell said as she stood up and stretched fully along the ground. "Let me bury him so deep that no one will ever find him."

"I was just disappointed," Tolebit tried to explain from his place under a mushroom where he'd gone to hide. "I didn't mean to disturb you."

"You need to think before you do things, Tolebit," Daffonia said in her motherly tone of voice. "You don't mean to do a lot of things, but somehow you manage to do them, anyway."

"I'm sorry," Tolebit said.

"What were you disappointed about?" Daffonia asked.

"He wanted to see Oscar," Jewell chimed in. "I told him he managed to miss him, again."

"Well, Tolebit," Daffonia said. "If you hadn't slept through it, you would have met him, finally."

"Well, anyway," Tolebit said, emerging from under the mushroom. "What did he say? Did he say anything about the Monster Shadow?"

"You were right on that part," Daffonia said, lying back down. "He explained everything to us about the Monster Shadow except how to get rid of it."

"But that's the most important part!" Tolebit said. "Why didn't he explain that to you too?" He sat on the ground and leaned against Daffonia's stomach.

"Because he didn't know," Jewell said, walking over to the other two.

"Now what do we do?" Tolebit asked.

"Go back the way we came," Daffonia said. "We'll just have to continue our journey to the Garden and see what happens."

"I want to go with you," Tolebit said.

"Well, I for one don't want you tagging along," Jewell said. "You're a pain in the backside, and I'm not putting up with your nasty mouth, anymore."

"Who does she think she is?" Tolebit asked, pointing his thumb at Jewell.

"Actually," Daffonia began, "I have to agree with Jewell. You've been nothing but nasty since we met you. Unless you start exercising some manners and common courtesy, I don't want you traveling with us, either."

Tolebit hung his head sadly for a few moments, then perked up and stood with his hands on his hips. "Fine! I'll go to the Garden on my own." He turned and began to walk away toward the path they'd traveled during the night.

"You mean like you've been doing for,. . . . how long now?" Jewell asked.

Tolebit stopped walking and stood still.

"Come on, Tolebit," Daffonia said, sidling up to him. She nudged him from behind, causing him to fall forward.

"Hey!" Tolebit said. "That was uncalled for!"

"So are you," Jewell said. "But you're here, anyway." She turned to Daffonia. "Come on. Let's get going. We've wasted enough time as it is."

"Who made you the boss?" Tolebit remarked.

"Tolebit!" Daffonia warned.

"Well, she is being mighty bossy," Tolebit mumbled.

"Not another word!" Daffonia said. "Do you hear me Tolebit? Not another word no matter what."

"I heard you," he replied.

"Alright then," she said. "Climb on and let's get going. You'll never get there alone."

Tolebit scaled Daffonia's front leg, but when he got to her shoulders, her hair wasn't long enough for him to hold on in order to hoist himself up onto her neck. "I can't go any further," he complained.

Jewell came around to Daffonia's side and lifted him the rest of the way onto Daffonia's back.

"That was nice of you," Daffonia said to her.

"No, it wasn't," Jewell responded. "It was the only choice I had. If he couldn't get on your back, then that makes me the next closest ride for him."

"Oh, Jewell." Daffonia smiled.

"Let's go," Jewell said as she started back down the path.

"I don't know why she has such a bad attitude toward me," Tolebit said.

"Quiet!" Daffonia warned him.

They walked until they passed the five white birch trees and continued back the way they came. Tolebit managed to stay silent most of the way, but Jewell knew it wouldn't last too long. When he finally spoke, all she could do was grumble internally.

"So what else did Oscar have to say?" he asked.

"I knew it was too good to be true," Jewell mumbled under her breath.

"What?" Tolebit asked innocently. "I only asked a question."

"He explained about the Monster Shadow like we told you," Daffonia said.

"But what did he say, exactly?" Tolebit asked.

Daffonia explained to him all that had transpired while she and Jewell visited with Oscar. She did her best to relay Oscar's information about the Black Place and the Monster Shadow.

"Well, I'll be!" Tolebit said, sounding truly amazed.

"He also told us that Glory is still unconscious," she added.

"Poor Glory," Tolebit said, shaking his head. "It doesn't sound too good for her."

"No, it doesn't," Daffonia agreed.

"Hey, Tolebit!" Jewell broke in. "Is that concern I hear in your voice? It almost sounded like you had feelings for someone besides yourself."

"I have lots of feelings," Tolebit answered defensively. "I keep them to myself, that's all."

"Maybe you should share them a little more," Daffonia suggested. "You might become a bit more likeable."

"I am what I am," Tolebit said.

"Well, you don't have to be," Jewell said.

"I like myself the way I am," Tolebit told her.

"Yeah, but no one else does."

"That's not true!" Tolebit replied.

"No?"

"Are you two done now?" Daffonia asked, but neither of them answered.

When they were close to the place where they had met Tolebit, they stopped for a brief rest.

"Which way?" Jewell asked.

"Whatever you think," Daffonia said. "It's your journey, remember?"

"Might I make a suggestion?" Tolebit asked in somewhat of a sheepish manner.

"No!" Jewell said.

"Why not?" he asked. "I made it to the Day Lilies. That's farther than you got."

"But you got stuck there," Jewell said.

"Wait a minute, Jewell," Daffonia said. "It might not be a bad idea. Remember what we talked about on our way to see Oscar? It can't hurt to hear him out and give his idea a try."

Jewell looked from Daffonia to Tolebit a few times, finally settling her vision on Daffonia. "OK," she said. "What's your suggestion?"

"Well," Tolebit began, pulling himself up as if he were suddenly put in command of an army. "There's a clearing up ahead a few hundred yards from here. It's not a large clearing, but it is a clearing none-the-less. The sun shines very brightly in that spot so there are all kinds of berries there. We haven't eaten in a day so we might as well eat while we can. I'll take you as far as I can toward the Day Lilies. After that it will all be new to me."

"We might see Tempo, again," Jewell said.

"Who's Tempo?" Tolebit asked.

"She's a beautiful, yellow butterfly who's been watching our journey," Jewell said.

Tolebit frowned. "I don't have one of those," he said. "That's not fair."

"I'm sure there's a reason," Daffonia said. "When we have the chance, we'll ask someone."

"And they had better have a good answer," Tolebit said, crossing his arms in front of him.

"In the meantime, we might as well follow his directions," Daffonia said to Jewell. "I think you're still going to have to learn something in order to pass through each phase that we come to. Let's just hope that enough has happened to teach you along the way so that we might be able to make progress a little quicker with Tolebit's help."

"And glad to help, I am," Tolebit chimed in.

"Oh brother," Jewell said, shaking her head. She took a deep breath and sighed. "Alright," she said. "It sounds like a decent enough idea. Which way to the clearing?"

"Straight ahead to a field of Valley Lilies just past where you found me," he said. "A left turn through the center of the field will take us to the clearing where the berries are."

Together, they walked a little while longer until they were right back where they had started from the night before.

"Alright! We're back at the place where we met you," Jewell said as she looked further ahead. "So the field of Valley Lilies should be straight ahead."

"That's right!" Tolebit said as they continued to walk through the forest. "In fact, you should be able to see it from here. It's very close, actually."

"I see it," Daffonia said. "Come on."

Together they walked the two hundred feet to the carpet of little, white bells.

"Now what?" Jewell asked.

"There's a tiny pathway that cuts right through the center of the lilies," Tolebit said. "We have to follow it to the end."

"Is this it?" Jewell asked, sniffing the ground for signs that others had passed the same way.

"Right on the mark!" Tolebit said.

"You're not kidding, it's a tiny path," Jewell said. "We're going to trample quite a few of these flowers by crossing through here."

"Just be careful," Daffonia advised. "We don't want to harm more than we have to."

"Oh, don't worry about these flowers," Tolebit told them. "They're quite resilient."

"If you say so." Jewell started through the field of flowers as carefully as she could with Daffonia following directly behind her. When they had walked so far into the field that lilies could be seen all around them with no apparent end, she stopped. "How big is this area?"

"Oh, it goes on for quite a way," he said.

"How far is 'quite a way,' Tolebit?" she asked.

"Well, it takes some time to get to the end of the field," Tolebit answered. "But it's worth the walk."

"I suppose it would be," Jewell began, "if the scent from these flowers wasn't so strong. They're tickling my nose." She began to sneeze.

"Bless you," Daffonia said after Jewell had sneezed four times in a row.

Jewell nodded her thanks, but began a new sneezing frenzy almost immediately.

Daffonia shook her head, then turned toward Tolebit. "Maybe we should run through the field."

"It is beginning to seem like a good idea," Tolebit agreed.

"Come on, Jewell," Daffonia said between sneezes. "We're going to run the rest of the way. Follow me!"

Daffonia began to move quickly, making great leaps through the flowers while Tolebit held on to her ear with all his might. Jewell did her best to keep up with the deer even as her sneezing continued. The longer she ran, however, the less pungent the aroma of the lilies seemed to be. Eventually, her sneezes came farther apart allowing her a chance to catch her breath a little. It wasn't long before the end was finally in sight.

"I see green up ahead!" Daffonia hollered back to Jewell who was now close behind her.

"Is that the end?" Jewell called back. "Are you sure?"

"It's the end alright!" Tolebit yelled.

"Daffonia?" Jewell asked. "What do you think?"

"It seems to be!" Daffonia replied.

Jewell did her best to see around Daffonia and was able to see for herself that there was, indeed, a clearing of sorts. The sunshine was very bright on the area ahead and Jewell hoped Tempo might be there to greet them. Jewell was even beginning to catch the sweet smell of berries that she had learned to identify as food.

As they finally broke out of the field of Valley Lilies into the clearing where the sunlight shone so brightly, Jewell started to smell all sorts of sweet smells that she did not recognize at all.

"This place. . . . smells. . . . wonderful!" she said between panting breaths as she looked for glimpses of yellow wings.

"Oh! Does it ever!!" Daffonia seconded. "There's all sorts of delicious food here."

"Sure there is!" Tolebit chimed in. "Why there are apples there on that tree and there are pears on that tree and there. . . . "

"Whoa! Wait a minute?" Jewell broke in. "Daffonia. What is he talking about?"

"New kinds of food for us," Daffonia answered as she pranced her way to Jewell with Tolebit on board. "And look around, Jewell. Tell me what else you see."

Jewell did as she was told. Her eyes grew huge when she noticed all the different colored flowers that grew among the trees surrounding the clearing. "What are they?" she asked the other two. "Just look at them all!"

"There are primroses there," Tolebit began, pointing to their left. "And those are bluebells," he continued, pointing straight ahead. "And. . . . "

"Oh, it doesn't matter," Jewell said. "It's a good sign, isn't it, Daffonia?"

"It sure is." Daffonia agreed.

"What did I learn this time?" Jewell asked, baffled. "I don't remember anything important happening."

"I'm not sure," Daffonia said.

"You're able to go this far simply because you were willing to take a chance and go see Oscar." The voice came from the flowers to their right.

"Tempo!" Jewell said, her tail wagging wildly from side to side.

Tempo's wings fluttered a few times, before settling back in the open position to enjoy the sun. "And Tolebit is learning to control his nasty remarks more and more," she said. "Otherwise, I would not have been able to find you here."

"But all I did was take a chance," Jewell said. "That wasn't so important. It only took us a few hours out of our way."

"That's true," Tempo said. "But still, you were willing to give that time up to try to help the others in the forest. And you gave Tolebit a fair chance simply by weighing his advice."

"We didn't get anywhere, though," Jewell said. "All we did

was gather information on the Monster Shadow. It's still out there somewhere."

"The effort is the main thing," Daffonia said, stepping up to stand beside Jewell. "You were willing to go just to find out if there was something that could be done about it. The information may turn out to be very valuable to someone else. Now you have it, but you wouldn't know so much if you hadn't made the decision to go out of your way to get it."

"So that's important too?" Jewell asked. "Going out of my way to try to help even though I wasn't able to help."

"Sure it was," Daffonia said. "Sometimes, it's the mere thought that counts."

"For real?" Tolebit chimed in. "How is that so?"

"Because it softens your heart," Tempo said, flying around a bit before settling on to a different flower. "It's the first step toward tearing down the walls that separate you from the others around you. And many times, it makes you wish you could have done more. Then the next time you find yourself in a similar situation, you will do more."

"What if I don't want to do any more?" Tolebit asked.

"Oh, give it up!" Jewell said in a disgusted voice as she walked away from them.

"Tolebit," Daffonia began, "my only advise to you is to do whatever you want to do. You're too pig-headed for learning anything new."

"That's not true!" Tolebit argued. "I want to learn."

"Then why don't you just take someone else's advise for a change," Jewell yelled back having heard their conversation. "Instead, you're always arguing with us. I'll bet you've argued with everyone you've ever met. It's no wonder you couldn't get past the Day Lilies. You're too pig-headed."

"Let's not start again," Daffonia cut in sternly. "Let's enjoy our good fortune at having met Tolebit so he could lead us into such a beautiful place."

"Haven't you been here before?" Tempo asked Daffonia.

"Not to this particular area of the forest," Daffonia answered. "I've seen the primroses and bluebells and such before, but just not in this exact spot. It's very pretty."

"Thank you," Tolebit said as he stood on Daffonia's neck and bowed to them proudly as if he'd created it all.

"Why, you're welcome, Tolebit," Daffonia said.

"Now, let's eat!" Tolebit jumped from Daffonia to Jewell, then shimmied down Jewell's leg.

"Is it all edible?" Jewell asked.

"It certainly is," Daffonia said. "There are even some grasses by those prickly bushes that I think you'll find most enjoyable."

"What are they?" Jewell asked.

"Which? The grasses or the prickly bushes?"

"Both," Jewell replied.

"The grasses are very nutritious," Daffonia began. "People call them herbs. We just call them grasses. The prickly bushes are another kind of berry. You might want to be careful with them after your experience in the Black Place," she advised. "Only the Eyes of the Forest are small enough to pick them without getting hurt. Maybe Tolebit could as well."

"Yeah! He is a small man, isn't he," Jewell joked.

"Oh, be nice, Jewell," Tempo gently admonished her. "He's done quite well for you."

"I suppose so," Jewell said, looking around the area of the clearing. "I guess I'll try the larger fruit first, since I'm starving."

"Good choice." Daffonia smiled.

"I'll be on the blossoms if anyone needs me," Tempo said, her wings gently fluttering before she moved to a higher branch.

"We'll talk more when our stomachs are all filled," Daffonia said. "For now, let's enjoy."

"I agree," Jewell said, walking toward the pear tree first.

CHAPTER 13

They took their time as they ate and explored the new area for nearly an hour, then laid down to rest in the shade of an apple tree, fully sated. Jewell marveled at the new flavors she experienced, the new flowers she smelled, and the wonderful way her belly felt now that it was full, once again.

"Hey!" Jewell suddenly said. "Where's Tolebit?"

"Don't tell me," Daffonia teased her. "Are you actually worried about him?"

Jewell looked embarassed as she hesitated a moment. "Not really," she said. "I just don't want him taking off on us before he gets us as close to the garden as he can." She looked around, briefly. "I notice Tempo isn't here, anymore. I don't know why, but I feel so attached to her."

"I'm sure she had somewhere else to be," Daffonia said. "Don't worry, she'll be back. She's got a job to do for us while you're here, but right now we're safe so she may have something else to take care of." She smiled at Jewell. "Is that what made you worry about Tolebit?"

"I told you, I wasn't worried about him."

"Oh. I see," Daffonia said, a knowing smile appearing on her face.

"I'm right here," Tolebit's lazy reply sounded from the other side of the tree. "This is a wonderful place, don't you think?"

"I certainly haven't eaten this much since I arrived here," Jewell said. "I have to hand it to you, Tolebit. You did alright this time."

Tolebit didn't even jump at the bait as Jewell expected him to, but crawled toward them from the other side of the tree and lay curled up in her full tail. "So, tell me what else Oscar told you two," he said, changing the subject. he rolled onto his back and stuck his full belly in the air.

"Why are you so interested in what Oscar had to say?" Jewell asked him. "You should have stayed awake and heard it all for yourself."

"Well, I just couldn't," Tolebit said. "I was much too tired."

"Were you?" Daffonia asked him. "Or were you afraid?"

Tolebit sat up as far as his full stomach would allow him to. "Afraid?" he asked. He settled back down, closed his eyes, and pushed his hat over them. "I'm not afraid of anything," he said in a pompous tone.

"If that's so," Jewell began, "then why is it that you've never managed to stay awake whenever you've had the chance to meet Oscar?"

She waited for his response while he continued to lay under the apple tree in silence.

"Well?" she pried.

"I told you," Tolebit began without moving an inch. "I've never been there before."

"Then how is it that you know the way there?" Daffonia asked. "I've lived in this forest for more years than I could ever count, but I never knew about Oscar."

"I suspect there's a lot of the goings on in the forest that you don't know about," Tolebit replied, still laying with his hat over his eyes.

"That may be true," Daffonia said, "but that doesn't answer the question about how you knew the way."

"One of the Eyes told me a long time ago," Tolebit said.

"Why is that?" Daffonia asked.

Tolebit hesitated a moment before answering. "I haven't a clue," he said. "Maybe she liked me."

Jewell could no more resist an opening like that than she could have resisted a nice, juicy steak a week ago. "No one likes you, Tolebit," she said, reaching out to nibble on more of the grasses that Daffonia had introduced her to.

Tolebit lifted his hat off his eyes and turned to look at her. "Just because you don't like me doesn't mean that everyone doesn't like me." He turned his head back to the center and placed his hat over his eyes once more.

"All bickering aside," Daffonia said. "Think about it, Tolebit. What made the Eye of the Forest tell you about Oscar?"

"Yeah," Jewell jumped in. "Did she just fly up to you and say, 'Hey! I'll bet you didn't know about the owl named Oscar?'"

"Not exactly," Tolebit said.

"What then?" Daffonia asked. "Why did she tell you?"

"Who said the Eye that told me was a she?" Tolebit asked defensively.

"Wasn't it?" Jewell asked with a slight chuckle.

Tolebit didn't answer, but lay back with his eyes closed and his hat over them, once again.

"Is he sleeping?" Jewell whispered to Daffonia.

Daffonia inspected Tolebit, nudging his little legs with her nose. "I don't think so," she whispered to Jewell.

They looked at Tolebit, then at each other. Finally, Jewell lay her head between her paws and sighed. Daffonia quickly inspected him one last time then curled her legs beneath her body and closed her eyes.

Together, the three weary but sated travelers rested under the apple tree with the early afternoon sun shining all around them. Jewell felt herself doze off, then begin to dream. She dreamt of her antics with her friends from the neighborhood where she lived, but she no longer felt the same excitement in her dream as she had when she used to run with them. She dreamt of her family and felt her heart fill with joy at the sight of them. Through her dreams Jewell even relived parts of the experiences she'd had in Noah's Forest already.

As she dreamed, she began to feel uneasy. Her unease eventually brought her out of her dreams and into the early stages of waking. Her waking process continued, but Jewell's consciousness remained partly in the post-dream state as the rest of her thoughts centered on trying to pinpoint the cause of her unease. The more awake she became, the more alert she was to the fact that the cause of her unease was the result of something in the forest, something nearby. Slowly she forced her eyes to open so she could look around, but it was too dark to see anything and she decided that she had not really opened her eyes at all. Once again, Jewell tried harder to focus and lifted her head to look around. She felt her head move and she was sure that her eyes were open, but still it was too dark to see anything.

Jewell looked around allowing her eyes to adjust to the darkness. As she did so, she noticed something else that added a larger disturbance to her feelings. There were no Eyes of the Forest anywhere to be seen. Where could they have gone?

Once Jewell's eyes were adjusted to the surroundings, she began to see that Daffonia was as close to her as she'd been before and Tolebit was still sleeping on his back.

Suddenly, the ground beneath them began to shake. It shook consistently as if something huge were walking across it, making the earth move with every step.

"Oh no!!" Jewell said, quickly rising to her feet. "Daffonia! Tolebit! Wake up!"

Shaking, pounding, big footsteps coming closer.

"Daffonia!" Jewell said as she pushed her nose roughly into her friends cheek. "Wake up, Daffonia! Wake up now!!"

Daffonia awoke with a start. "Is it night time already?" she asked alarmed.

"No!" Jewell said. "We're in the Black Place again and that thing is coming for us. We've got to get Tolebit and get out of here."

"How?" Daffonia asked. "We have no Eyes to guide us."

"Tolebit will know," Jewell said as she made it to Tolebit's side in one step and began to wake him up. "Tolebit!" Jewell yelled into his face. "Wake up, Tolebit!"

Tolebit didn't budge.

"Hurry, Jewell," Daffonia warned. "We've got to do something."

Jewell looked from Tolebit to Daffonia, then back to Tolebit. "Tolebit!" Jewell yelled, then rolled the little sprite over with her nose.

"Who's making all the racket?" Tolebit yelled, annoyed. He got to his feet and dusted off his hat before placing it back on his head.

"We're in the Black Place!" Jewell yelled at him. "We've got to get out of here. Climb on my back! We've got to run."

Without thinking about it or saying a word, Tolebit ran to Jewell's front legs and, with a little help from Daffonia, was on the dog's neck before any of them could blink an eye.

"Which way to the Day Lilies from here?" Jewell yelled to Tolebit as the noise from the approaching Monster Shadow grew.

"Straight ahead through those trees," Tolebit said, pointing so that Daffonia could see and lead them.

Together they were off like a shot following Tolebit's directions precisely.

"Between those two maple trees, straight ahead and look for the path on the right," he instructed them. "Over that small hill, that's it, keep going."

The faster they ran, the more the Monster Shadow's rumblings diminished. They ran over the hill and continued on, still inside the Black Place.

"How big is this thing?" Daffonia asked between panting breaths.

"Yeah!" Tolebit said. "And how do we get out?"

"I'm thinking," Jewell began, breathing hard. "I think the closer we get to the garden,. . . .huff, huff,. . . . the closer we are,. . . . huff, huff,. . . . to getting out of here."

"Oh yeah!" Tolebit said. "That's right. Didn't Oscar tell you that it was turned away by the goodness in the garden?"

"That's right!" Daffonia agreed. "Great idea, Jewell!"

"Thanks!" Jewell replied between heaving breaths. "How much farther, Tolebit?"

"Not much," he said. "We'll be coming to a huge tree standing all by itself. Its trunk is wider than if you and Daffonia stood head to head and measured length from tail to tail. You can't miss it. It's the only one in the forest that I've ever seen like it. It's truly one-of-a-kind."

"What then?" Jewell asked.

"Run around its right side," Tolebit said. "Only the right side."

"Why not the left?" Jewell asked.

"Because there are poisonous plants on the left side that will give you an awful, itchy rash," he said.

"I'm running out of steam," Daffonia said. "I haven't had to run this much in. . . .I don't even know how long."

"Keep going," Tolebit said. "The great tree is just ahead."

"I see it!" Daffonia yelled. "This way."

"No!!" Tolebit yelled. "To the right! To the right!"

At the last minute, just before reaching the tree, Daffonia steered herself to the right with Jewell close behind. Immediately upon passing the great tree, they found themselves back in the sunlight with darkness left behind them. Daffonia bounced to a sudden halt while Jewell ran right into the deer nearly knocking her to the ground.

"I'm sorry," Jewell huffed and panted. "I couldn't stop myself."

"That's alright," Daffonia replied, panting and gasping herself. "I'm glad I was here. . . .to stop you. . . .from tripping and rolling."

"And possibly hurting me," Tolebit finished for her, back to himself now that they were all safe.

"Look at it," Daffonia said, fighting to catch her breath.

"It's growing fast," Jewell said. "We've got to do something."

"Not now," Tolebit said. "Let's try to get as close to the garden as we can first."

"Tolebit's right," Daffonia said. "That way if we run into trouble trying to destroy it we'll be closer to the help we need."

"What do you mean?" Tolebit asked alarmed. "Who's going to try to destroy that thing? Certainly not us!"

"Someone has to do something," Jewell said. "It's growing too fast." She looked from Daffonia to Tolebit. "Why is it growing so fast?"

The three of them looked at each other in wonder. Suddenly, from the corner of Jewell's right eye she saw the shadow of something big move over her as it cast itself on the ground blocking the sun from her back. She felt the warmth disappear as a chilling, angry cold passed over her from above and she knew exactly what it was.

It was the Monster Shadow reaching out to take what it had come for. . . . her and Tolebit.

She sprung into the air, twisting herself around toward the huge shadow and opened her mouth just as she witnessed a massive lump of an arm lift Tolebit in the air. It began to draw him into the empty, dark expanse of nothingness. Jewell growled an infuriated growl of warning just as she wrapped her jaws around the puffy lump of an arm that was the Monster Shadow. To Jewell's surprise she felt nothing, but continued to move right through the thing she had tried to bite. Still, she had some measure of success as the angry shadow released Tolebit and let out a low-pitched and painfully angry yell. Jewell's tail moved at the right time, and Tolebit was able to catch the hairs from it as it brushed right through his arms while they flailed frantically in an attempt to get hold of anything that would stop him from falling to certain death.

When Jewell landed on solid ground, she spun around, immediately searching for Tolebit. "Where is he?" she asked Daffonia who stood by witnessing the awful event with mouth agape and eyes as big as saucers.

"I don't know," Daffonia answered in robot-like fashion. "It all happened so fast."

Frantically, Jewell searched the ground as Daffonia watched the Black Place retreat quickly. "Tolebit!!" Jewell yelled.

"PPffftt! Ppffftt!!"

Jewell and Daffonia both heard and stopped to listen closer.

"I'm back here!" Tolebit said.

"Tolebit?" Jewell asked, turning around to find him.

"Where is he?" Daffonia asked.

"Back here," Tolebit yelled. "On the dog's tail!"

Jewell looked behind herself and saw Tolebit's little feet dangling from beneath her long hairs while he tried desparately to hold on to her tail while it continued to swish back and forth from excitement.

"Now," Tolebit began, sounding aggravated. "Do you think you can stand still long enough for me to climb aboard?"

Jewell was suddenly so relieved to see that Tolebit was alive that she had to force herself to stand still. "I'll do one better than that." With that she lifted her tail right over her back, allowing Tolebit to simply drop down onto her. "How's that?" she asked.

"Just wonderful," Tolebit said, out of breath.

"Jewell!" Daffonia said, suddenly. "That was incredible! You were wonderful! I couldn't be more proud of you right now if you had saved Noah himself!"

Jewell looked at Daffonia as if her friend had lost her marbles. "Are you sure Daffy doesn't suit you better?"

"Now don't get smart," Daffonia warned. "I'm merely giving you a well deserved compliment."

"For what?" Jewell asked. "That thing is a menace."

"And so were you not too long ago," Daffonia reminded her.

Jewell stood in silence taking in the implications of Daffonia's words. Suddenly, she felt Tolebit drop onto the back of her head. "What are you doing?" she asked him.

"Why, he's hugging you," Daffonia said. "I don't believe it. Someone pinch me. I'm dreaming. I must be."

"Stop that, Tolebit," Jewell said sternly.

"Why?" Tolebit asked. "You saved my life. You, of all creatures. You saved my worthless, little life."

"No one's life is worthless," Daffonia said. "Everyone has their purpose. Don't you ever say that again."

"I'm just so grateful," Tolebit said. "And after the way I've treated you. I don't deserve this. Now I'll be indebted to you forever." Then as an afterthought, Tolebit sat up and slapped himself in the forehead with the palm of his hand. "Oh no!" he said sounding terribly upset. "I'm indebted to her."

"Oh, shut up, Tolebit!" Jewell verbally jumped at him. "You don't owe me a thing."

"Yes, I do!" he said. "You saved my life. I have to repay you somehow."

"No, you don't," Jewell said sternly. "I'm releasing you of all indebtedness."

Tolebit gave her a suspicious look, then crossed his arms and nodded. "Oh," he said. "Is that how it is? I see. Well, fine. I don't owe you a thing."

"Right," Jewell said. "You are both making a big deal out of nothing. I was threatened. It's a natural instinct for a dog to react the way I did when being threatened. It's no big deal."

Jewell looked up once more at the area near the great tree where the incident had occurred. In truth, she was deeply shaken. But it was a relief to see that the Black Place had retreated completely.

"It's gone," she said to Daffonia.

"For now," Daffonia replied.

"Now what?" Tolebit asked.

"Now we find out where we are," Daffonia said. "And try to decide how much farther we can all go before we need rest again."

"I'm with you," Jewell said, and they began to survey this new area of the forest.

CHAPTER 14

"Look at that!" Tolebit was pointing to an area that was full of color just to their right.

"What are they?" Jewell asked, amazed at all the new colors she was seeing already.

"Buttercups and Lupines," Daffonia said, smiling.

"I haven't seen those since before I entered this forest," Tolebit said. "What a sight for sore eyes they are."

"They're so pretty," Jewell remarked as she and Daffonia looked at each other knowingly.

"Tolebit?" Daffonia said his name like a question. "Do you know what that means?"

Tolebit looked at her curiously. Then suddenly, his face lit up with a huge smile that quickly spread across it. "No," he breathed in awe. "Me? Did I really learn something finally? It can't be."

"I think the flowers speak for themselves," Daffonia said.

"I don't believe it," Tolebit breathed. "What happened?"

Jewell looked at Daffonia and said, "I think I know."

"Shouldn't Tolebit figure it out for himself?" Daffonia asked her.

"Probably," Jewell agreed, "but I doubt that he can."

"Now wait just one minute!" Tolebit spoke up. "I learned to say, 'Thank you.' I think that's why I'm able to see these."

"Exactly," Daffonia said.

"For the first time in your tiny life, I imagine," Jewell mumbled under her breath.

Daffonia stepped up to Jewell. "You're making such progress," she said to her. "Don't let your first impressions of Tolebit cause you to fall short of your goal. You don't want to end up in the forest like he did for all these years," she warned.

"You're right," Jewell agreed. "I really have to work on that. It's just that he made me defensive right from the beginning."

"I know he did," Daffonia said, "but he's been trying hard to control himself."

"I really have," Tolebit chimed in. "Now I learned something new. Finally!"

"How does it feel?" Daffonia asked him.

"Mighty darned good!" he replied, sticking his chest out.

"Good," Daffonia said.

"Didn't I have to learn something too in order to be at this level?" Jewell asked.

"Of course," Daffonia responded. "But it's possible that your courageous efforts a little bit ago are what did it for you. It's also possible that you may be ahead of yourself in allowing Tolebit to travel with us. The truth is, I've never traveled with two newcomers at once so I'm not sure just what to expect or how this will work, now."

"I think," Tolebit said, "that Jewell and I will hold each other back at different times, depending on which one of us still has not learned something important in order to move further toward the garden."

"You're probably right," Daffonia said. "But, I don't know for certain."

"Great," Jewell remarked sarcastically. "I'm at the mercy of a half pint. This just keeps getting better."

Tolebit hung his head sadly as both Jewell and Daffonia watched him. Daffonia gave Jewell a look of admonishment, the meaning of which was not lost on her.

"Ah, Tolebit," Jewell said, feeling very bad all of a sudden. "I didn't mean anything by that. You have to understand that I've been missing my home a lot. I'm anxious to get to the garden so I can go back and be part of my family the way I was supposed to be all along."

Tolebit raised his head and looked at Jewell, a small smile beginning to show. "Really?" he asked.

"Yeah, really," Jewell said. "You're not so bad most of the time."

"That's wonderful!" Daffonia said.

"Come on," Jewell said to Daffonia. "Let's see where this little guy takes us."

"As far as I can," Tolebit offered happily. "In fact, there should be a grouping of large rocks up ahead through those trees," he said pointing to a thicket of evergreens. "There are about five of them all together, if I remember correctly. It might be hard to see them at first because they're covered almost entirely with ivy."

"Wait a minute," Jewell said. "I thought he never made it to this level before. How could he know what else lies ahead?"

"I never saw the buttercups and lupines before," Tolebit said. "But the paths and markers don't really change."

"That's very true," Daffonia said. "I've done this many times, and the only thing I've ever seen happen is that I've ended up going in circles in ways I never could have seen coming. That's why the guides, like myself, leave so many of the decisions up to the students, like you, Jewell."

Jewell shook her head. "It's so confusing."

"Sometimes, it is," Daffonia said. "But so is all of life. That's why it's so important to always learn new things."

Jewell nodded.

"Come on, Jewell," Tolebit said in a gentle voice that was so unlike him. "We've got more traveling to do and those rocks are covered with ivy. They might be fully hidden by now."

"We'll find them," Jewell said, smiling.

They walked for a time in silence. All the different kinds of flowers they'd seen so far were scattered through the forest everywhere they looked and it occurred to Jewell that something wasn't quite right about that.

"Daffonia?" Jewell asked.

"Yes?"

"I remember seeing some of these flowers back home where I lived before coming here," Jewell said. "But it seems to me that some of them shouldn't be growing at the same time as some of the others."

"Which ones do you mean?" Daffonia asked.

"Like the buttercups," Jewell said. "I think I saw those before, but they weren't growing at the same time as those first flowers we saw."

"You know," Tolebit chimed in, "that bothered me too when I first came here. But you know what I learned?"

"What?" Jewell asked.

"One of the Eyes told me that in Noah's Forest, and especially in Noah's Garden, it's common to find Spring and Summer flowers growing together because there are no season changes here. There's only one season in this forest."

"That's true," Daffonia confirmed. "Especially in the Garden where every kind of plant that you've ever seen, and many that you've never heard of, all grow at the same time. It's the most beautiful place you'll ever see."

"I can't wait to get there," Tolebit said.

"Me, neither," Jewell said. "By the way, Tolebit," she added. "That wouldn't be the same Eye of the Forest who told you about Oscar, would it?"

Tolebit was silent.

"You know who I mean," Jewell continued in a teasing manner for a change. "I mean the Eye who told you about the flowers growing at the same time because there are no seasons here? Is that the same Eye who told you about Oscar?"

"Yeah," Tolebit said, blushing.

"Well, what's the big secret?" Jewell asked.

"Ohhhhh," Tolebit whined.

"What's the matter?" Daffonia asked, slightly alarmed at the worried tone in Tolebit's voice.

"Oh, I might as well tell you," Tolebit said. "Remember how I tried to chase one of the Eyes into the forest from the Outside Place?"

"Yes," Daffonia said. "I remember."

"Well," Tolebit began hesitantly, "I used to watch her outside of the forest all the time. I thought she was the most beautiful creature I'd ever seen in my life. I wanted to follow her and be close to her. I wanted to go everywhere she went. I wanted to know everything there was to know about her."

"You fell in love with her," Daffonia said softly.

Tolebit gave her an awkward, sideways glance. "I guess I did."

"There's nothing wrong with loving another," Daffonia said warmly.

"There is when she's one of the Eyes of the Forest and I'm just a sprite from the outside," Tolebit said sadly. "I don't have wings or anything magical like the Eyes do. I didn't know I couldn't go in the forest. I kept trying and trying."

"Why didn't you just wait for her to come back out?" Jewell asked.

"At first, that's exactly what I did," Tolebit said. "But I never knew where she would come out. Sometimes I'd be sleeping outside the forest perimeter and she'd sneak up on me from behind."

"Did she know how you felt about her?" Daffonia asked.

"Sure she did," Tolebit said. "The Eyes know just about everything."

"So tell me," Jewell said. "Why couldn't you wait for her this time? Why did you have to get into the forest?"

"Well, I started waiting," he said. "But time was going by. First a few days went by, then I lost count when I started to imagine never seeing her again. Such a magnificently soft shade of pale orange. Like the color of a peach with those subtle variations of yellow and sometimes red. Oh, she's so beautiful," Tolebit finished, lying back with his arms beneath his head as he seemed to see her standing before him.

"So she's the one who told you about some of the secrets of the forest?" Jewell asked.

Tolebit was silent as his daydreaming continued uninterrupted.

"Tolebit?" When she received no response, Jewell glanced at Daffonia who simply smiled in return. "Tolebit!" Jewell said as she jumped over a little tree in order to purposely shake Tolebit up and bring him out of his reverie.

"What?" he asked, sounding annoyed.

"Is that the Eye who told you about the forest?" Jewell asked, again.

"That's the one," Tolebit sighed as he lay back once again.

"What's her name?" Daffonia asked him.

Tolebit was silent.

"Tolebit?" Daffonia asked softly.

"What's the big secret, Tolebit?" Jewell asked.

"Poppy! Are you happy now? The Eye that told me is Poppy," he blurted out angrily.

"We met her," Jewell said, astonished at the coincidence.

"Did you?" Tolebit asked suddenly sounding happier. "When did you meet her?"

"After our first encouter with the Black Place," Daffonia said. "She was one of our protectors that night."

Together, Jewell and Daffonia described what had happened when they first ran into the Black Place and how the Eyes of the Forest built them a magical wall to keep them safe.

Tolebit listened intently. His full attention directed solely on their story. "It's a small world," he sighed when they were done.

"One more thing," Jewell added. "It was shortly after that when I found Glory in the cyclamen. She had been with Poppy and Verbena when the Monster Shadow attacked her. Later, after Sprig and the others took her to the garden, I ran into those two again and told them about Glory. They flew off to the garden right away."

"Then that explains why I haven't seen her in a couple of days," Tolebit said sadly. "I thought that was the case. The Eyes of the Forest are like that. Their first priority is always each other. I could never fit into Poppy's world."

"Wait a minute," Jewell said, a thought having occurred to her. "What made Poppy tell you so much?"

"What do you mean?" Tolebit asked.

"I mean," Jewell began, "wasn't she betraying some secret code of silence in revealing so much to you?"

Daffonia stepped forward. "Jewell," she said, "do you remember what Oscar told us?"

"About what?" Jewell asked.

"About Tolebit knowing how to find him," Daffonia reminded her.

"What are you talking about?" Tolebit questioned.

"Well," Daffonia started, glancing briefly at Jewell before she continued. "Oscar told us that he sent an Eye to tell you how to get to him so he could help you reach the garden. But you never went to him alone. Instead, you went with other travelers and slept through the entire visit."

"That's right," Jewell said. "And you told us you were never there when in fact you had been. You had just never met Oscar."

"Actually," Tolebit said, "the most I ever saw was what I saw with you two when I woke up and you were still at the boulder. You're right," he admitted. "I never met him, but I honestly don't remember ever being where we were, either."

"That's alright," Daffonia reassured him. "Did you know Oscar told Poppy to give you directions to find him?"

"She never told me," Tolebit said sadly. "Why do you think that is?"

"I'm not sure," Daffonia said. "I'm sure she meant well, though."

"I've got an idea," Jewell said. "I'll bet she didn't tell Tolebit because she didn't want him to know she'd been to see Oscar. Now why do you suppose that is?"

"What are you trying to say?" Tolebit asked.

"What I'm saying is that there's a reason why Poppy went to see Oscar in the first place," Jewell replied.

"I'm getting confused," Tolebit said. "She never told me she'd been to see him. She only told me she knew of him."

"Oh, I see," Daffonia cut in. "You know, I think you're right, Jewell." Daffonia turned to face Tolebit, and smiled. "Poppy told you how to find Oscar because Oscar told her to."

"Well, now I know that much," Tolebit replied. "It did seem

rather strange at the time when she told me about it, but I was so happy to have her near me that I never thought of it, again."

"So, it follows that there's also a reason she went to see Oscar in the first place," Daffonia said.

"Maybe I'm assuming too much in thinking this," Jewell said. "But it just came into my head."

"First instincts are usually correct instincts," Daffonia assured her.

"The only way I'll ever know is when I can ask her myself," Tolebit said. "And with Glory still unconscious, who knows when that will be?"

Jewell suddenly felt bad for Tolebit and wanted to do something to cheer him up, but she didn't know what. "Well," she said. "At least some things are beginning to make more sense than they did before."

"I guess," Tolebit replied half-heartedly. "I guess."

"Hey!" Daffonia called suddenly. "I think we've reached the five large rocks Tolebit said to look for."

"Where are they?" Tolebit asked, lifting his head to look around.

"Right over there," Daffonia indicated with her nose. "They're all covered with ivy, just like you said they'd be."

"Yup," Tolebit confirmed. "That's them alright."

"Now what?" Jewell asked.

"Now we only have a short stretch to go and we'll be at the Day Lilies," Tolebit answered a bit more cheerfully.

"OK," Daffonia said as they approached the rocks. "Lead on, Tolebit. The sun will start to set very shortly and we should try to cover as much ground as we can before then."

"Follow the path that you'll find to the left of the rocks," Tolebit said. "It will lead you right into the field of Day Lilies."

"Are they beautiful?" Jewell asked eagerly.

"That they are," Tolebit said. "There you'll see beautiful, tall lilies of every color you can imagine. White, red, orange, yellow, pink, striped, spotted and different combinations of colors. It's a magnificent display."

"Then I can't wait to get there," Jewell said as they located the path to the left of the five rocks and started down it.

"Assuming you can go there at all," Daffonia reminded her. "You may not have learned enough to experience something new, just yet. We can only follow Tolebit's instructions and wait to see."

"That's right," Jewell said. "But if we don't reach it, we'll know it's because of me and not because of Tolebit."

"That's very true," Daffonia said. "That's very true."

CHAPTER 15

They traveled for the rest of that day without reaching the Day Lilies and decided to spend the night where they were. The next morning they started out again, but when the sun showed them the middle of the day had arrived with no progress, Jewell knew in her heart that she was the reason they weren't reaching their destination. She looked at Tolebit and sighed. "Did it take this long for you to reach the Day Lilies?"

Tolebit hesitated. "Well, not really, I'm afraid."

"Then I must've done something wrong," Jewell surmised. "But what?"

"I don't know," Tolebit replied softly, shaking his head.

"Daffonia?" Jewell asked, lamenting. "What did I do wrong?"

"Maybe nothing," Daffonia answered. "It may be something you simply haven't done yet."

"Well, how do we figure it out so we can go on?" Jewell asked.

"It's the situations we run into that teach us along the way," Daffonia said.

"Forget about that," Tolebit commented. "This path is quite boring as far as events along the way are concerned. I've been down this way many a time in my years in the forest and I've never encountered anything even remotely unusual."

"Well, there's a first time for everything," Daffonia said as she stared off into the forest. "Look over there. We have company again."

Jewell and Tolebit looked into the forest as Daffonia had indicated.

"In broad daylight," Tolebit said. "It seems to be growing stronger with each day. Why is that happening, now?"

"My guess," Daffonia said, "is that you and Jewell are like a magnet for its evilness."

"But we're not evil," Jewell complained. "How can it be so drawn to us?"

"Because you both still have those small, dark areas within you that must be overcome in order to reach the garden," Daffonia explained. "It's those dark parts of you that it feeds from."

"That's right!" Jewell said. "Oscar told us that as we overcome our weaknesses, the Black Place devours the bad energy we leave behind."

"So are you telling me that it's waiting for us to learn enough to reach the next step?" Tolebit asked. "Or are you saying it's trying to suck the bad energy that is left in us right out of us."

"Honestly," Daffonia said. "I think the Black Place would like to shorten the entire process by consuming both of you the way it tried to do a few days ago."

"But it had surrounded you, too," Jewell said.

"That's right," Daffonia said. "But we all managed to escape unharmed."

"Something just occurred to me," Tolebit said to Jewell. "Both times that you were inside the Black Place you managed to escape. But both of those times there was also a creature of greater goodness in there with you. First, Daffonia and Sprig together. Then, Daffonia by herself. The second time was harder to escape and I think it's because I was in there with you."

"What are you getting at?" Jewell asked.

"Is it just me, or does it seem that when the Black Place is in contact with a greater goodness, it is weakened somewhat?" Tolebit suggested.

"Yes!" Daffonia said. "And when it is in contact with more, shall we say, imperfection, that it is strengthened."

"That's my point!" Tolebit said excitedly.

"You know," Jewell said, "you may have something there."

"Well, now what do we do?" Tolebit said. "That thing approaches quickly as we speak."

"Let's walk while we think of how this new idea might be of use to us," Daffonia suggested.

"I'm in full agreement," Tolebit said. "It's blackness makes me very uncomfortable."

"I wish Sprig were here," Jewell said. "He seems to know how to keep that thing away from us."

"Well, he's not," Daffonia said. "And understandably so."

"That's right," Tolebit said. "We have to figure this out for ourselves."

"I'm sure neither of you will like this idea," Jewell said. "But I have to say it."

"Go ahead," Daffonia encouraged her.

"Well," Jewell hesitated. "Daffonia,. . . . you can go directly to the garden if you left our company. Is that true?"

"Yes, it is," Daffonia replied. "But I'm bound by my assignment to accompany you to the garden. I cannot just desert you and go on ahead."

"You could if there was an emergency," Jewell said. "A tragedy, of sorts."

"But there is no tragedy," Daffonia said.

"Not yet." Jewell said. "But if Tolebit or I run directly into the Black Place, there's a good chance we cannot get out unless someone like you or one of the Eyes of the Forest were to come in after us."

"That may be true," Daffonia said. "But I wouldn't advise you to do such a thing."

"I know I have no intention of running into that place," Tolebit said.

"Besides," Daffonia said, looking back behind them. "Why would you want to give that awful thing more strength than it has gained already?"

"I don't," Jewell said. "But if one or two creatures of great goodness can weaken it enough to let it's guard down and release one who is imperfect, then how much damage would the entire population of Eyes of the Forest do if they all entered the Black Place at the same time?"

At the very moment Jewell finished explaining her theory, a great, grey shadow fell over the threesome.

"Ruuuuuuuunnn!" Tolebit yelled, causing Jewell and Daffonia to bolt before he had even finished his warning.

As they ran out of the shadow, Jewell turned to Daffonia. "That. . . .was close," she said between gasping breaths.

Daffonia looked at Jewell to respond, but came to such an immediate halt that she nearly tripped over her own legs. "Where's Tolebit?"

"Isn't he still on my back?" Jewell asked, startled.

"No, he's not." Daffonia turned to look behind them. "And the Black Place is nearly gone."

Jewell looked behind them and saw that Daffonia was right. The Black Place continued to retreat even as they stood in one spot. "Maybe he just fell off me." Jewell started back the way they'd come to look for him.

"Tooollllebiiit!" they called together, searching the ground around them, but there was no response to their calls.

"Maybe he's unconscious," Daffonia suggested.

"Even if he were," Jewell said, "I'd still be able to locate him by his smell."

"And?" Daffonia asked.

"And there's no smell of him anywhere," she said.

"We're right back where we started from," Daffonia said. "I think the Monster Shadow reached out and grabbed him again."

"I should have sensed it coming," Jewell said. "My canine instincts should have sensed danger. What good am I as a canine if I can't even sense danger? How can I ever protect my family if I don't know when they're in trouble?"

"I'm sure the Monster Shadow is more perfect in its evilness than any of us are in our attempt to reach a greater goodness," Daffonia said. "If anyone should have sensed its approach, it should have been me."

"Then it's strong enough to hide its own presence?" Jewell asked.

"It seems so," Daffonia said sadly looking further down the path. "Which may be why Amethyst was only there to save you that one time. She is ultimate good, much better than me or most creatures I know. If the Monster Shadow is able to hide from her, then we really do have a very serious problem."

"It's gone," Jewell said.

"I know."

"Now what?" Jewell asked. "It's got Tolebit. We can't just leave Tolebit like this. We can't leave him in that terrible place."

"We have to reach the garden first," Daffonia said.

"I'm sorry, Daffonia," Jewell argued, "but not this time. Another being is in trouble. We can't possibly turn and walk away from this situation. He needs our help. We have to get him out of there."

"No," Daffonia said. "It was meant to be this way."

"WHAT?" Jewell yelled. "Are you telling me it was meant to be that the Black Place should grow stronger by wholly devouring us? Are you telling me it's a good thing, to accept it, and just walk away?"

"Maybe Tolebit wasn't meant to ever reach the garden," Daffonia suggested.

"How do you know?" Jewell asked. "Unless you know without a doubt that there's a good reason for this to have happened, I'm not going to accept it."

Daffonia stood silent, staring at Jewell uncertainly.

"That's all the answer I need." Jewell turned to head back down the path. "I'm going after to him."

"You can't!" Daffonia argued. "You have to come with me to the garden."

"Go yourself," Jewell called back to her. "And while you're there round up some help. If Tolebit and I die in there, I imagine it spells doom for all of Noah's Forest."

"Jewell! Don't!" Daffonia yelled after her, but Jewell kept running as fast as she could to find the Black Place.

Within minutes, Daffonia was by her side, running along with her.

"I told you to go to the garden for help," Jewell said. "Or you can just chalk the whole thing up to fate and forget about us both." She stopped briefly to look around for signs of the Black Place.

"But Jewell," Daffonia said, stopping with her to look around. "This wasn't the plan."

"What was the plan?" Jewell asked angrily. "I may not know everything, but there's one thing I learned since I've been here and that's the difference between what's right and what's wrong. I know that it can't be right to abandon Tolebit without knowing for sure if he's alive or dead. I wouldn't want to be in his position, wishing someone would help me and eventually losing all hope when no one shows up for me. How would you feel in there?"

Daffonia looked at Jewell, then at the ground.

"You'd be frightened to death!" Jewell told her. "So would I."

"You're right," Daffonia agreed. "But I still can't let you go after him. I'm responsible for your safety until you reach the garden."

"Then go to the garden and get help," Jewell ordered, "because I'm going after Tolebit no matter what you say."

"Then I'll go with you," Daffonia said.

"For what?" Jewell argued. "Use your head, Daffonia. We barely made it out the last time when you came in to help me. If Tolebit hadn't known the exact way to go through the forest, we'd probably still be running around aimlessly in the shadow of that thing. Your goodness isn't enough to weaken it. You have to go for help."

"I can't," Daffonia said. "I'm charged with staying by your side. Besides, you learned not to go running around aimlessly. I thought that was one of your first lessons."

"It was," Jewell agreed. "But this time, I'm not running around aimlessly. I have a definite purpose for running this time and I don't expect to see you running next to me again. You'll do no good by coming along and you know it."

"Noah will be so angry," Daffonia worried.

"Not if he's as good as you say he is," Jewell said, looking deeper into the forest.

"There it is!" she cried, just able to make out the Black Place deep within the trees.

"It's teasing you," Daffonia warned. "It knows you're looking for it. Don't you understand? It wants you, too. It was a great ploy for it to grab Tolebit knowing you'd come looking for him. Don't play into it's hands, Jewell. You're doing exactly what it wants you to do."

"And if you follow me, you'll be doing exactly what that thing expects you to do," Jewell advised Daffonia. "Now surprise it and go to the garden for help. Wait until I'm inside its perimeters. Then turn tail and run as fast as you can to the garden."

"Why should I wait that long?" Daffonia asked.

"Because if it sees you go before that it may realize things are not going to go according to its plan," Jewell warned. "It may retreat before I can reach it."

Daffonia shook her head in understanding.

"Now, I'm going before it really is too late for that aggravating little guy," Jewell said, smiling mischievously. "See you soon, Daffy."

With those words, Jewell took off into the fastest run of her life, heading straight toward the Black Place which hovered in the forest as if waiting just for her. Seconds before she entered its bounds, Jewell looked back in time to see Daffonia still standing where she had left her. Even from her considerable distance away, Jewell could see the anguish in Daffonia's stance and she knew she was causing her friend a great amount of grief and concern.

As Jewell crossed the perimeter of the Black Place, Daffonia's image was lost behind a clouded veil of grey that quickly turned black as pitch. Immediately, she picked up Tolebit's scent, but knew it would take some time for her eyes to adjust to the intense darkness so she stopped. The last thing she needed was to get caught up in those dead thorn bushes, again. Jewell stood still in one place until her eyes were able to focus in the dark. It was maddening for her because she had caught Tolebit's scent and knew he wasn't too far away, but she could not do a thing about it, yet. Jewell was determined to keep her head. She was angry at this place for having stolen Tolebit from right off of her back. She was angry at the constant fear this place had caused in all three of them during their travels. She was even angrier that, in some small way, her own short comings were part of what was making this awful place grow stronger. She wanted vengeance for her anger.

As Jewell waited for her eyes to adjust to the incredible darkness, she heard a noise that she hadn't heard before. She listened and was able to make out an intermittent wailing sound, as if there was a creature crying in the distance. Maybe it was just a trick. Maybe the Black Place was trying to get her to start searching before she was ready, thereby leading her straight into a trap. But the wailing went on, coupled infrequently with what sounding like short screams.

Jewell knew in her heart it wasn't a trick. The sounds she heard were coming from Tolebit who was nearly frightened to death already. Jewell knew this because even through the intense dry heat in this awful place she could smell Tolebit's terror and it made her maddeningly anxious to reach him before it was too late.

CHAPTER 16

It seemed to take longer than Jewell expected for her eyes to adjust to the intense darkness of the Black Place. She was riddled with anxiety and fear over Tolebit's potential demise as she waited for her surroundings to come into focus. The air was stifflingly hot and dry. It took mere moments before she desparately needed water, but there was no doubt she would find none here. Finally, when she could see well enough to identify objects in her path, she proceeded forward, deeper into the abyss. She heard Tolebit's fearful whimpering and proceded toward it, passing the dead thorn bushes she had been trapped in the first time she'd entered this horrible place. She could still see the roots of the bush Daffonia pulled out of the ground in order to free her. How much Jewell had changed since then, such a short time ago.

Just past the thorn bushes, Jewell saw dead pine trees that still stood, lifeless and barren as if they had been burned to a crisp, yet remained standing in place. The ground beneath her feet crunched and crackled from the dried, dead branches and leaves over which she walked. Their brittle sounds mingled with Tolebit's soft, frightened cries. She had to find him. She determined to let nothing stop her. Jewell wanted to call out to him, but she was afraid to draw the attention of the Monster Shadow.

Suddenly, she caught the scent of something other than dry heat or Tolebit's aroma. It was a putrid smell. It was the smell of decay. She hadn't smelled it the first time she'd been in the Black Place, trapped in the dead thorn bushes. But the farther she walked, the stronger the odor became. She didn't like it one bit, but her instincts told her that if she followed the awful smell, she just might find Tolebit close by.

The whimpering grew louder, more frightened. What was she going to do? How could she find him without alerting the Monster Shadow?

Then it dawned on her. The Monster Shadow already knew where she was. She was certain it had watched her run toward this place. But if it knew she was here, then why hadn't it shown itself yet? Something told her Tolebit was nothing more than bait meant to bring her right to the heart of this place for whatever nefarious reason the Monster Shadow had. Oh, the heck with it!

"Tooollleeeebit!!" she yelled. "I'm coming Tooolleebit!"

There was no response. The whimpering had grown to a fever pitch and Jewell began to run faster toward the sound, her paws hurting from the snapping things beneath her feet.

"Ouch!" she said aloud as she stumbled over something that caught her front leg. She felt a sharp pain in her paw as it was punctured. Briefly, she inspected the wound, licking it until she located the object that was stuck in it. Once found, she worked on it with her teeth until she had a firm hold on it and could pull it out. "Yiippe!" she let out as she freed the piece of dead wood from the pad on the bottom of her front paw. Immediately, Jewell tasted her own blood, but she knew the wound was not severe enough to keep her from reaching Tolebit. She was determined that nothing would keep her from saving him.

She got back to her feet, and began to run. The pain in her paw lessened with each step as the numbness began to set in. "Tooollleeebit!!" she called to him again. To her joyful surprise, she received a response.

"Help me!" the tiny, weakened voice called out.

There was no mistaking it.

That was definitely Tolebit!

"Toollebit!" Jewell called. "I'm coming. Hold on. I'm coming for you."

This time, there was no response, only the whimpering that had begun, again.

As Jewell raced toward him, Tolebit's scent grew stronger along with the smell of fear he emitted. She was getting closer. Excitedly, Jewell looked around to see if she might be able to see him. She was amazed and saddened at the death that surrounded her. Everything in this place was dead. There were carcasses of birds and small animals lying everywhere she looked. Nowhere did she see a single sign of life. There wasn't so much as a green leaf or pine needle anywhere. This place had drained every living thing of its last ounce of life energy.

Jewell surveyed the vast, dark wasteland and suddenly realized the whimpering had stopped. She could no longer hear Tolebit. Even his scent had all but disappeared. "Ooh!" she cried. Why was she distracted? Why wasn't she paying attention to what she was looking for? To compensate for her mistake, Jewell ran faster. She was afraid for him even worse than before she lost track of his scent. Especially now that she'd seen all the death that surrounded her. What if Tolebit was dead? What if the Monster Shadow killed him because she was trying to save him? The very thought brought Jewell to an immediate halt and left her standing in the middle of nowhere, surrounded by desolation, engulfed by a suffocating, dry heat that left her panting and gasping for air. Jewell was suddenly lost, not only geographically, but emotionally as well.

It couldn't be. He couldn't be dead. She stood in place, still as a stone, listening and sniffing the arid air, looking around slowly, deep into the darkness as far as she possibly could. "Tolebit," she said softly, a tear forming in her eye.

Nothing.

Suddenly, from the corner of her eye, Jewell saw a flash of light. She turned to her left to see what it was, but nothing was there. She jumped defensively around to her right, but found only blackness and death. Quickly glancing to her left once more, she saw it again. A flash of some kind had appeared in the distance. It was all she had to go on now. She took off running after whatever it was that had caught her attention.

No matter how far or how long Jewell ran, nothing changed. She grew thirstier by the minute. Her front paw was completely numb. But if there was still a chance for her to save Tolebit, she was determined not to let that chance slip away.

As Jewell ran she saw the flash again, but this time she knew exactly what it was.

Fire!

Something burned in the distance. It wasn't a constant kind of fire, but rather it was made up of flashes of fire. Jewell had never seen anything like it. The deep orange of the flames as they grew huge, releasing parts of themselves into the air, then disappearing altogether, seemed to have a life of their own. It was almost as if the flames were moving through some weird kind of dance steps, only showing themselves at peak moments of the dance. Jewell was frightened by it. She'd seen the man in her family light fires in the yard, but the flames were yellow, golden, like the color of Verbena, the yellow Eye of the Forest. But these flames were different, much different. Jewell wanted to turn right around and run from these flames, so intense was her fear of them. But she couldn't. She had to be brave and save Tolebit.

Jewell ran, her fear growing with each step, the frightening flames growing larger as she approached them. She could hear their voices crackling and popping as they spoke their destructive language. But even more frightening was that she had picked up Tolebit's scent once more. But his scent was mixed with all of the other strange smells around her, making it difficult for her to determine what his condition actually was.

When Jewell was as far from the flames as the length of her street back home, she caught the putrid smell of decay again. It quickly grew to a sickening level causing her stomach to turn, but she didn't stop. She pushed herself forward even though her head was growing dizzy from the mixture of smells, her thirst, and the pain in her front paw which had begun to travel up her leg.

"Tooollleeebit!!" she yelled as loud as she could manage.

She could feel the heat of the flames now. Her lungs burned with the dense, dryness that eminated from them.

"Tooolllleebit!!" she called again as she stopped running, now only half the distance away. They seemed to be shooting right from the ground, then straight up into the air. Smaller offshoots danced in the air for seconds before burning themselves out.

"Tooollleebit!!" Jewell called out one more time, not knowing where to go from here.

Then she saw it.

She'd recognize it anywhere.

The Monster Shadow stood alone on the other side of the fire. It stood taller than the tallest flames. It stood wider than the widest tree Jewell had ever seen. And in the thick, bulbous appendage that seemed to be the beast's hand lay Tolebit. He was lying limp and lifeless as far as Jewell could tell from her distance away, but she'd recognize his red, pointed hat anywhere.

What was she to do? She stared at Tolebit's tiny body. Instinctively, she began to bark at the huge, dark shape. It was all she could think to do. "Arf, arf," she barked tentatively at first. Then, in a more demanding, deeper tone, she continued, "Whooowhoof, whooo, whooo, whoof!"

In response, the Monster Shadow raised both of its huge arms and let out a loud, deep, gutteral roar such that Jewell had never heard in her entire life. The incredible noise that came from the Monster Shadow shook the ground and everything in sight. Dead trees that still stood trembled, then fell to the ground in explosive crashes, toppling all other trees that stood in their paths. One after another, Jewell watched as the dead trees seemed to shiver from fear, then fell around her, while the flames that separated her from the Monster Shadow continued to burst and spit out of the ground.

She knew she couldn't fight this thing. It was impossible. And she couldn't help Tolebit if she was dead, either.

Just as these thoughts ran through Jewell's mind, the Monster Shadow took a single step forward right into the bursting flames. Suddenly it was on Jewell's side of the fire. One more step forward would bring it within a few feet of where Jewell stood. Frightened nearly to death and uncertain what else to do, Jewell turned and ran. '*Don't worry, Tolebit,*' she thought to herself as the mountain loomed up, enormous before her. '*I'm coming back to rescue you as soon as I figure out how.*' Behind her, the Monster Shadow let out another one of its awful noises that sent more dead trees falling to the ground in front of and behind her no matter where she ran. The lethal branches of one dead tree grazed Jewell's hind quarters as she raced to get out of its way before it landed on top of her. Jewell felt the open wounds the tree branches had ripped through her skin, but she kept running without a clue as to where she was headed.

To her left, beyond the line of lifeless trees, Jewell caught sight of what appeared to be a huge mountain whose immense size dwarfed that of the beast who chased her. She hoped there was somewhere to hide within its bounds and changed direction in order to head straight for the refuge she might find. She ran as fast as her damaged body could carry her, rapidly closing the distance between herself and the mountain. Her lips had begun to crack from the dry heat. Her lungs ached from the dust and ashes she had inhaled as the trees fell around her. Still, she ran, feeling as if she would drop from exhaustion at any time. She fought to keep her footing steady while the ground continued to shake beneath her from the weight of the Monster Shadow that she knew was hot on her tail.

As Jewell took her first step onto the rocky base of the mountain, the Monster Shadow released yet another intimidating roar. The noise it made shook even the huge mountain sending tons of rocks raining down its side. Jewell was struck by quite a few of them, gaining more cuts and bruises from their impact.

"Over here!" she heard a squeaky, little voice call. "Quickly, before it reaches you."

Jewell looked up the mountain side toward the sound of the voice as she continued to make her way over the boulders and crags as fast as she could force herself to climb.

"You're almost here," the voice called to her again. "Hurry! It's coming!"

Still, Jewell could not see who was calling her, but she continued to climb in the direction of the anonymous voice.

"Just a little further," the voice encouraged her. "Hurrry!"

At the very moment Jewell located the source of the voice, she felt a searing heat breeze past her, burning her fur as it just missed catching her in its grasp.

"Step in here," the tiny voice called. "Hurry!"

Jewell saw the cave. Right in its dark opening stood a little chipmunk with two white stripes and one black stripe running down the center of its back. Jewell pushed herself up the last step toward the cave. As her back legs came down on the floor of the cave's mouth, Jewell lost her footing and rolled further into the opening, just missing the second searing touch of the Monster Shadow as it made a grab for her once more.

"Follow me!" the chipmunk ordered as it headed further into the mountain.

Jewell forced herself to her feet out of fear alone and followed the chipmunk for what seemed like miles. The tunnel through which she was being led appeared to go on forever. Jewell was in such immense pain from all the damage she had sustained that her entire body had begun to go numb.

"I. . . . pant, pant,. . . . can't. . . . go on," she said to the chipmunk who kept running deeper into the mountain.

"It's just a little further," the chipmunk said. "You'll be able to rest soon."

Jewell followed, having decided the chipmunk must know what it was doing if it had been able to survive in such a nasty place. But the pains in her body were demanding rest and attention. Jewell stumbled more than once as she followed the spry, little animal.

"Please," she begged as she gasped for air. "I can't."

"We're almost there," the chipmunk encouraged her. "Take a deep breath. Do you smell it?"

Jewell did as she was told. She breathed in deeply and took in the fresh aroma of clean air and water.

Water!

"Yes," she said to the chipmunk. "I smell it."

"Then come on," the chipmunk said. "We're almost there."

Jewell called on all her inner reserves of strength to keep her on her feet long enough to get to the source of the water that her aching body craved.

Finally, she could hear it.

Running water.

And light!

She could smell the light.

It was sunlight. Sweet, pure sunlight.

That was enough to give Jewell the incentive to make those last strides through the dark cave and into the light where she knew the water would also be.

"And heeeerrre we are!" the chipmunk said as they entered a large room within the mountain.

The first thing Jewell did was to locate the water which she saw was straight ahead. She ran for it without slowing down as she reached its edge and dove right in. She drank the water as she came to the surface and began basking in the cooling relief that the water brought to her throbbing, wounded body.

"Feeling better?" the chipmunk called out from the side of the clear pool.

"Much!" Jewell replied, swimming to the pool's edge and lapping up as much water as she could take in.

"Glad to hear it!" the chipmunk said enthusiastically. "What are you doing here, anyway?"

"Trying to rescue my friend." Jewell climbed out of the water and shook herself off.

"Nice rescue," the chipmunk said sarcastically, then jumped out of the way of the shower Jewell had created.

"What is this place?" Jewell asked as she lay down and began to lick the wounds on her hind quarters.

"This is the Great Mountain," the chipmunk replied spreading his arms out as if to show off the surroundings. "And my name is Sam. Welcome to my safe haven for those who have wandered into the clutches of evil."

"What?" Jewell asked as she stopped licking her wounds and looked at Sam curiously.

"You heard me," Sam replied. "This is the Great Mountain and I am . . . "

"I heard that," Jewell said, interrupting him. "But what does it mean?"

"Which part?" Sam asked. "Where you are or who I am?"

"Where we are," Jewell replied. "Is this the forest?"

"This is part of the forest," Sam said.

"Which part?" Jewell asked. "The Black Place or the forest itself?"

"The Black Place is part of the forest," Sam replied.

"But where does this mountain fit in?" Jewell questioned. "How is it that the Monster Shadow can't enter here? Where does this water come from? How does the sun get in here?"

"Whoa, whoa!" Sam stopped her as he ran over to a pile of fruit, grabbed a pear in his mouth, then took it to Jewell and dropped it between her front paws. "One thing at a time. The answer to your first question, first. The Monster Shadow could get in here if it had any clue how to do it. But since it's a basically stupid being, it doesn't so it can't. Second, the water comes from the sky like the sun which is the answer to your third question."

"But how do the sun and rain get down here?" Jewell asked as she bit into the pear.

"There is a very long tunnel that runs straight up to the top of this mountain," Sam began. "The mountain itself is so high that the very top of it extends far past the borders of the Black Place, even though the mountain is inside the Black Place at the moment. The sunlight shines right down through the tunnel into where we are now. The same happens with the rain. When it rains, the water runs down the tunnel and right into this pool."

"Amazing," Jewell breathed in awe. "Do you live here?" she asked Sam.

"Sometimes," Sam replied. "Most of the time I live in Noah's Garden."

"Then what are you doing here?" Jewell asked.

"Trying to save your life."

"How did you know I'd be here?"

"Daffonia told Noah what had happened to a little sprite and a dog she'd been traveling with," Sam answered. "Noah sent me to try to keep an eye on you."

"Tempo was watching us," Jewell said.

Sam giggled. "This place would dry up Tempo's wings in seconds. Besides, she needs the sun. I don't."

"What about Tolebit?" Jewell asked. "How do we rescue him?"

Sam shook his head sadly as he looked at the ground.

"I'm afraid we can't," Sam said. "The Monster Shadow has him now."

"No!!" Jewell said adamantly, rising to her feet in one quick motion. "I'm not going to let that beast have him."

"There's nothing you can do," Sam said.

"Yes there is!" Jewell replied.

"What?" Sam asked.

"I don't know yet," Jewell responded, lying back down. She felt defeated. "But I'm going to figure it out."

"Well, good luck!" Sam said.

Jewell looked at Sam angrily. "Are you the best help Daffonia could find to send for me?"

"At the moment," Sam said. "I'm it!"

"What do you mean?" Jewell asked.

"Just what I said," Sam replied. "My purpose is to keep you safe until more help arrives."

"Tolebit could be dead by then," Jewell complained angrily. "I can't wait for help to arrive. We have to do something now!"

"I'm telling you," Sam tried again, "there's nothing you can do."

"We can defeat the Monster Shadow and steal Tolebit back," Jewell said.

"And just how do you propose to do that?" Sam asked as he ran back to his pile of fruit and brought another piece back for Jewell.

Jewell thought for a moment. "We have to come up with a plan," she said.

"What is this 'we' talk?" Sam asked. "My purpose is to keep you safe, not get myself killed."

"What about Tolebit?" Jewell asked.

Sam looked thoughtful for a moment, then shrugged his shoulders uncertainly.

"I don't know," he said. "The Monster Shadow is dangerously powerful. I don't know what can be done."

"I do," Jewell said. "I saw Amethyst use her horn to make the Monster Shadow go away. And I know this place is evil and doesn't like goodness to get too close. I learned that from Oscar. So let's bring all the Eyes of the Forest in here. Maybe Amethyst would enter, too, if you know how to reach her."

"For what purpose?" Sam asked.

"To overwhelm the evil in here with their goodness," Jewell said. "That much goodness will destroy this place and save Tolebit."

"How do you know that?" Sam asked.

"I don't," Jewell said. "But I suspect it will happen because Sprig, one of the Eyes, . . . "

"I know Sprig," Sam interrupted.

"Well," Jewell continued, "the first time I was trapped in here, he led Daffonia and me out. At the time I thought it was just Sprig who could do that, but when it happened again, Sprig wasn't with us. The second time the Monster Shadow tried to engulf Tolebit and me, it also engulfed Daffonia," Jewell explained. "I believe that because of her great goodness, we were able to find our way out."

"And now?" Sam asked.

"Now there's just Tolebit and me," she answered. "And you."

"So what would you like me to do?" Sam asked uncertainly.

"If you can," Jewell answered, "go to the garden and tell Noah my idea. That's what Daffonia was supposed to do. Even if it turns out that I'm wrong, there still must be someway to rescue Tolebit and destroy this place."

"Alright," Sam said. "You rest here awhile and I'll see what I can do."

"Thank you," Jewell said.

"You're welcome," Sam replied. "Now get some rest. You got mighty beat up out there in such a short time. Let me take your idea to Noah and see what he thinks. I'll only be gone a short time."

Jewell watched as Sam scurried up the tunnel in the roof of the room they were in. When Sam was out of sight, Jewell drank more water, then lay down and quickly fell asleep.

CHAPTER 17

Jewell awoke to the sound of a loud splash. She opened her eyes, quickly remembered where she was, and looked toward the pool for the source of the noise. Something floated toward her, the ripples from its impact in the water were pushing it slowly along. One thing was for certain. Whatever it was, it wasn't moving on its own.

Jewell stood up and walked to the pool's edge, astonished to see the chipmunk who had saved her, floating lifelessly along. "Sam!" she called out, but there was no response. In an instant, Jewell was in the water. She gently grasped Sam's limp form in her mouth, then swam to the edge of the water, jumping out of the pool to quickly deposit Sam on the ground. She began to lick the water from him, concentrating on his chest and back the way her mother had done when Jewell was just a puppy. She remembered how her mother's ministering had made it easier for her to breath and hoped she would be able to do the same for Sam.

"Khuh, khuh," came the sputtering sound from the water-soaked rodent as he finally began to cough the water from his lungs. "Khuh, khuh."

Jewell continued massaging his small body until she was certain he'd be alright on his own.

"That's,..khuh, khuh,. . . . enough!" Sam rolled away from Jewell's rough attention.

"Are you OK?" Jewell asked him. "What happened?"

"Khuh, khuh," Sam coughed a little more. "Forget about going anywhere," he said.

"Why?" Jewell asked. "What's wrong?"

"I'll tell you what's wrong," Sam began, still coughing. "We're surrounded by the Black Place. There used to be a tiny opening on the other side of the hill that I could use to get out of here. It isn't there anymore. I couldn't get out. It was waiting for me. Khuh, khuh, khuh."

"Take it easy, Sam," Jewell advised. "Tell me, slowly."

Sam took a few deep breaths, then he went on.

"It had me, Jewell," he said. "It had me right in its clutches. Look at my tail! It's burnt where it touched that awful beast's body."

"How did you get away?" Jewell asked.

"I was quick, that's how," Sam replied. "But I saw your friend."

"Tolebit? You saw him? Is he alright?"

"He's alive," Sam said. "But alright? I don't know. The Monster Shadow had him in its other hand, if you can call that a hand. I saw him breathing, but he was not awake."

"At least we know he's alive," Jewell said. "That's enough for me right now."

"We're trapped, though," Sam said. "I can't get back to the garden. We're trapped." Sam sat by the edge of the pool of water with a hopeless expression on his face.

"We'll think of something," Jewell said, trying to comfort him.

"Just imagine," Sam said. "I'm supposed to be here keeping you safe, and now we're both trapped."

"You're doing exactly what you're supposed to be doing," Jewell offered. "Don't feel bad, Sam. We *are* both safe."

"I know," Sam said sadly. "But for how long? That thing seems to be growing quickly. It was never this powerful. It was never this huge. It has to be stopped somehow."

"I told you how," Jewell said.

"Even if you're right," Sam said, "it does us no good if Daffonia doesn't tell Noah."

"If she remembers to tell him, would he believe my idea?" Jewell asked.

"We can only hope," Sam said. "We can only hope. In the meantime, we have to figure out what we're going to do."

"What do you mean?" Jewell asked.

"Well, for starters," Sam said, "that pile of fruit and nuts over there is all the food we have. If I can't get out of here to gather more, then what we have will have to last us until we figure out a way to get back to the forest."

"At least we'll have water for a long time, even if we do run out of food," Jewell said.

"That's true, but let's hope it doesn't come to that," Sam said. "I'd hate to have to live on nothing but water indefinitely."

They were both silent as the impact of Sam's words fell heavily on them.

"Well." Sam sat back and sighed. "We might as well make the most of it. Tell me about yourself, Jewell. How have your travels through the forest been? What have you learned?"

Jewell relayed to Sam the whole of her adventure in Noah's Forest so far. She told him about Sprig and Glory. She told him how much she detested Tolebit in the beginning and how he eventually grew on her. She told him about meeting Oscar and about Tolebit's love for Poppy. Throughout her story, Jewell and Sam enjoyed a feast of day old fruit and nuts.

When Jewell was finished, Sam stood up and proudly stuck his chest out with his little fists on his waist. "Now you can add Sam to your tale."

"That's right," Jewell remarked. "Now tell me about yourself," she suggested. "What brought you to the forest? Have you been here forever like Daffonia, or have you been here for a number of years like Tolebit? What's your story?"

"I've only been here a hundred moons," Sam replied. "I entered the forest for no apparent reason, really. I simply ran in one day."

"Didn't anyone try to stop you like the squirrel that kept chasing Tolebit away?" Jewell asked.

"Nope," Sam said. "I just ran in. I'm faster than a squirrel any day. If one of them tried to stop me, I never knew it. Even if one of them had, they would never have caught me. Did you ever watch a chipmunk run through the woods back where you come from?"

"Sure, I did," Jewell answered. "I used to chase them."

"A futile chase at best, I'm sure," Sam replied with an air of importance about him.

"I could never catch one, if that's what you mean," Jewell said.

"That's what I mean," Sam said. "What would you have done with one if you had been able to catch it?"

Jewell considered it for a minute trying to imagine what she might have done if she'd ever caught one. "I don't know," she said. "I never thought about it."

"You just chased it for no reason?" Sam asked.

"Yes, I did," Jewell admitted, feeling embarrassed.

"Hhmm!" was Sam's only response. "Hhmm!"

"Didn't you have to go through the same trials that Tolebit and I have had to go through?" Jewell asked, astonished.

"Nope!" Same replied.

"Why not?"

"Because I hadn't had the kind of interaction with other creatures like you and Tolebit have had," Sam replied. "My lessons here were of a different nature than yours."

"What do you mean?"

Lying on his back, Sam began to explain. "You see," he said. "Some creatures keep to themselves more than others. Like me, for example. I gathered my food, dug my nest, and did little else except during the mating season. I had no interaction with people or animals of any kind. Some chipmunks become close to people, some become prey for other animals, but me? I experienced none of those encounters."

"But how does that make you a better creature than Tolebit or me?" Jewell asked.

"It doesn't," Sam replied. "The truth of the matter is that I needed to learn to interact with others. My life was in peril if I didn't. You see, I had never known the matter of trust because it had never been an issue in my life. I was both too trusting and too suspicious."

"You can't be both of those things at the same time," Jewell argued.

"You sure can," Sam countered. "I never knew how important caution was because I had never been hunted. I never even knew there was such a thing that could happen to me as having another creature consider me to be its next meal. So I scurried here and there without a care in the world."

"That should be a good thing," Jewell said. "Not to have a care in the world."

"It is when you're in Noah's Garden," Sam said. "But the Outside Place is not Noah's Garden. Neither is Noah's Forest, for that matter. Especially not now with the Monster Shadow lurking around, growing stronger day by day."

"So how were you too suspicious?" Jewell asked, trying to get back on the subject of Sam's entry into the forest.

"By being so carefree and used to my own way," Sam began, "I was mentally thrown when I met one of the Eyes of the Forest. I had never seen one before and it frightened the life out of me."

"I thought the Eyes of the Forest are everywhere," Jewell remarked.

"They are, in a way," Sam said. "They can go anywhere they want to go. They had just never come my way before. One of them tried to talk to me, but I scurried away. I had no idea what wonderful creatures they are and I was afraid."

"I see," Jewell said. "What you had trusted without question was what you had grown used to."

"Not exactly," Sam said. "What I trusted was a life without another living creature, short of insects, around me. That makes for quite the reclusive life, when you think about it."

"Weren't there any birds where you lived?" Jewell asked.

"Oh sure," Sam answered, "but there were none that were a threat to me. They took care of their business and I took care of mine. We left each alone."

"That sounds alright to me," Jewell said.

"It does," Sam agreed, "until you consider all the wonderful things you miss out on by living that way. Just imagine being afraid of an Eye of the Forest. Why that's preposterous! But I was. Scared to death, in fact."

"Oh, I get it," Jewell said. "What you're saying is that it may seem safer to stay away from everyone else and keep up your own routine, but you miss out on everything else that life has to offer."

"That's right," Sam said. "Looking back now, I see all the time I wasted living that way. Since I came to Noah's Forest, I've met some of the most wonderful creatures I could ever have hoped to meet."

"Is that why Noah let you in?" Jewell asked. "To learn how to be friends with other creatures?"

"Yes, it is," Sam replied. "With certain, individual creatures. I learned very quickly that when a creature becomes reclusive, such as myself, it loses its usefulness to the rest of the world. Life grows and continues through interaction with others. We learn everything there is to learn from each other. When you think about that alone, you come to realize how important that interaction is."

Jewell did think about it for a minute or two as she tried to break the green, outer casing from a black walnut.

Putting his tiny paws out, Sam snatched the black walnut from between Jewell's paws and said, "Give me that. I'll show you how."

Jewell watched as Sam masterfully released the inner nut from its protective coverings, then handed the nut meat back to her.

"See!" Sam said. "You just learned something from me."

"Thank you." Jewell took the entire nut into her mouth and began to chew.

"The trick is," Sam continued, "to make sure that everything we teach each other is worth learning. For example, learning to cast insults on each other is a worthless thing to learn."

Jewell thought of all the times she had insulted Tolebit.

"For another," Sam continued, "learning to hate is another useless lesson."

Jewell thought of how much she disliked Tolebit at the beginning and she was grateful to have overcome her dislike.

"Learning to be unmerciful and then practicing such a thing is the worst waste of time I can think of," Sam said.

"What does that mean?" Jewell asked.

"Mercy is a sort of favor that we grant to others," Sam said.

"Do you mean like if I were to ask you if you would do me a favor?" Jewell asked.

"Yes," Sam said. "It's like that. Every time you help someone who's in need of help you are granting them mercy. Whenever you forgive someone for having done wrong, you are being merciful."

"Are you saying that learning to turn your back on others is the waste of time?" Jewell asked.

"That I am," Sam said.

"What else?" Jewell asked. "What other things aren't worth teaching?"

"Selfishness," Sam quickly responded. "Keeping everything for yourself including yourself. That's an awful thing to teach someone how to do."

"I don't understand what you mean," Jewell said. "Keeping myself to myself?"

"We need to share ourselves with others," Sam said. "We need to share the things we know that might help someone else. It's selfish to keep knowledge to ourselves."

"Oh," Jewell said, contemplating Sam's words.

"And never teach another creature how to be weak," Sam said. "By teaching that kind of lesson, you destroy the creature you are teaching."

"Then how are we supposed to teach the right things to other creatures?" Jewell asked, her ears held back in humility.

"By our actions," Sam answered. "By the things we do and say. That's how. We need to be good examples to others so that they see a better way to live and be."

"Maybe that's why we couldn't reach the Day Lilies," Jewell thought out loud.

"Is that where you were headed when Tolebit was taken by the Monster Shadow?" Sam asked.

"Yes," Jewell replied, "but we couldn't seem to get there. We kept walking and walking, but we got nowhere."

"Had Tolebit been there?" Sam asked.

Jewell lay her head on her paws and said, "Yes, Tolebit had been there."

"Oh, don't feel bad," Sam said, placing his tiny hand on her paw. "Some lessons in life are so obvious, but others are not. We don't always see our own shortcomings because we've survived as we are for so long that there doesn't seem to be anything wrong with us. But no one is perfect. We can all learn something new or better every day."

"I've learned so much since I came to the forest," Jewell said. "When I look back on what I was like before, I can't believe it was really me. I was awful!"

"Don't ever forget that," Sam said. "But don't dwell on it, either. Use those old memories as reminders of how far you've come and how far you'll always have to go."

"But I did some terrible things," Jewell said. "How can I ever make up for them?"

"Simply by being nicer, kinder, more compassionate, stronger, and everything good from this point on," Sam said. "Just be better!"

"That's what I want to be." Jewell sighed and looked into the pool of water. "Better."

"If you concentrate on doing just that, it will become a natural way for you to be," Sam said. "In no time at all, you won't have to think about being better, anymore. It will simply happen."

"I hope so," Jewell said.

"Let's both get some rest, now," Sam suggested. "We're safe here for as long as we need to be. In the morning we can start brainstorming how to rescue Tolebit."

"I feel like I have to do something now," Jewell said.

"I know you do," Sam said. "But you have some nasty wounds that need a little time to heal. There's nothing you can do for your friend if you're not in tip top shape yourself, you know."

"I'm not so sure there's anything I can do for him, anyway," Jewell said sadly. "The Monster Shadow is huge and nasty. I tried to bite its arm a day or two ago when it had reached out and grabbed Tolebit."

"You did?" Sam asked, amazed. "What happened?"

"I went right through it," Jewell said. "There was nothing there to grab hold of."

"What about Tolebit?" Sam asked.

Jewell thought a moment.

"Wait!" she said, sitting bolt upright. "When I tried to bite it, Tolebit was released. Do you think my bite had anything to do with the Monster Shadow letting go of him?"

"Could be," Sam said. "There's much in this world that we have no idea about. Maybe it felt your teeth, even though you couldn't feel its arm," he suggested. "Or maybe feeling the goodness in you hurt more than your bite ever could have."

Jewell lay back down and shook her head in agreement.

"Maybe," she said. "I hadn't thought about that, but maybe."

Jewell and Sam were silent for a few minutes as they gave it some thought. Finally, Sam yawned and stretched. "Goodnight," he said to Jewell. "We'll talk about it more in the morning."

"Goodnight Sam," she sighed, then closed her eyes and drifted off to sleep.

CHAPTER 18

When Jewell and Sam awoke the next morning, the sun was streaming into the mountain tunnel and sparkling off the pool of water next to where they slept.

"Did you sleep well?" Sam asked Jewell.

"Oh yes," Jewell answered, stretching her limbs as she lay on her side. "I feel much better."

"That's good," Sam said. "Now let's eat something while we try to figure out how to save your friend from the Monster Shadow."

"If he's not already dead, you mean," Jewell replied, feeling sick at the very idea that Tolebit might be gone.

"Don't be so pessimistic," Sam advised her. "The Monster Shadow needs Tolebit in order to draw you to it. If Tolebit dies, what will it have left?"

"A very angry dog who's going to go after it, anyway," Jewell responded glumly.

"And probably get yourself killed as well," Sam added.

"What difference will it make?" Jewell asked as she stood up and walked over to the pile of fruit and nuts. "I will have failed Tolebit anyway."

"You don't know that," Sam said. "Until we come face-to-face with that thing, we won't know anything about Tolebit's condition. Now stop being so depressed and let's get to work."

Sam made a few quick trips over to the pile of food, grabbing a nut or a piece of fruit with each trip and depositing them all by the pool before he finally stopped to sit and talk to Jewell. "Tell me," he began. "What kinds of things have you noticed about the Monster Shadow?"

"Like what?" Jewell asked, not certain what he was looking for.

"For instance," Sam said, "what seems to make it angry? What seems to provoke it to chase you? What characteristics have you noticed about it besides the obvious? What are your thoughts on it as a whole?"

Jewell picked up an apple from the pile of food, then sat thinking as she nibbled on it. It all seemed so overwhelming to her that she didn't know where to begin.

"Let's start with the first question," Sam suggested, biting into a walnut. "What seems to make that thing angry?"

"When I barked at it."

"Is that it?" Sam asked.

Jewell thought a moment more. "Actually," she said, "it seemed to get angry when the Eyes of the Forest kept it away from us that night. Do you remember me telling you how they protected us with a magic wall they built around us?"

"Ah, yes," Sam responded. "That was what provoked it to harm Glory the way it did."

"So we thought," Jewell replied.

"Well, you're probably right," Sam said. "There had to be a reason for it to do such a thing. I've never heard of that happening before."

"Why Glory, though?" Jewell asked. "Why not Sprig? He was the one who flew right into the Black Place to come after us. Why didn't the Monster Shadow try to hurt Sprig?"

"I think it did something worse by hurting his sister," Sam said. "When it wounded Glory, it hurt Sprig in his heart. That's worse than hurting someone physically. Physical wounds will heal, but wounds of the heart seldom do."

"You make the Monster Shadow sound more intelligent than I'd give it credit for," Jewell said. "It seems to be a mindless creature to me."

"Evil is not as mindless as you might think," Sam said. "The difference between the way evil works and the way good works is that evil is conniving, manipulative, and sneaky. Good is simply true, honest, and open. Never underestimate the power of either."

"That's even more frightening than what I went through yesterday when it came after me," Jewell said. "Yesterday I thought it was just some big, dumb thing. Now you're telling me that it's been planning all of this, that it's not just mindless evil, but intelligent evil." Jewell shuddered visibly at the thought. "How can we fight such a thing?"

"Intelligently," Sam said. "Which brings us to the next question. What characteristics have you noticed about it besides the obvious?"

"Do you mean besides its size?" Jewell asked.

"In a way," Sam said. "I'll tell you what. Let's make this easy. Just tell me everything you've noticed about it."

"Ok," Jewell said as she went to the pile and picked up another apple. "These are good, you know."

"I know," Sam said, puffing his chest out. "I wish I'd invented them, but I didn't. Now, tell me about the Monster Shadow."

"Well, I've noticed that I can't get a firm hold on it," Jewell began, "but it seems as if I'm still able to hurt it when I try."

"Good, good," Sam said. "You mentioned that before, but that's a good point. Go on."

"I've noticed how huge it is and how the ground shakes under its weight, even when it walks," Jewell said. "It always seems angry."

"Evil is like that," Sam said.

"Oh, wait!" Jewell said excitedly. "You know what else? I don't think it can get out of here, but we can. What do you think that means?"

"Interesting," Sam said contemplatively. "That's very interesting."

"Well?" Jewell asked impatiently. "What do you think it means?"

"I think that the Monster Shadow is trapped inside its own evil," Sam said. "I think it somehow created this place of desolation and is now stuck here. Tell me," Sam said. "Why do you think it can't get out of here?"

"Because of the time it reached out for me when Sprig led Daffonia and me out of the Black Place," Jewell said. "And because of how it reached out from here to hurt Glory, but couldn't actually get out. And the time it snatched Tolebit and I jumped up to bite through it. There was only a piece of it pushing at the border of the Black Place the times that I saw it with my own eyes."

"Do you mean that it hadn't actually poked through to the forest?" Sam asked sounding intrigued.

"Yes," Jewell said. "It was trying to get out, pushing into the dark, shadowy wall that surrounds the Black Place, but it never actually poked through."

"How far was it able to push the wall?" Sam asked.

"Far enough that I could tell it was some sort of arm," Jewell answered.

Sam sat in silence, obviously thinking deeply before he spoke. "When you bit into it," he began, "do you think it was the Monster Shadow you had bitten into or do you think it might have been the border of the Black Place itself?"

Jewell looked at Sam curiously, turning her head from side to side. "I don't know," she said.

"Hhmmm," Sam replied.

"What difference would it make?"

"I'm not sure," Sam said. "I'm thinking, though, that the Black Place might not have been created by the Monster Shadow, but rather that the Monster Shadow was somehow created by the Black Place."

"That's what Daffonia and I thought at first," Jewell said.

"Except that since the Monster Shadow seems to be trapped inside this place," Sam said, "then maybe the two are actually one."

Jewell was confused. "What do you mean?"

"It's just a thought," Sam said, "but think about this. What if the Black Place and the Monster Shadow are actually one entity? What if they're not two separate things; a place and a creature? What if by sitting inside the Black Place right now, we're actually sitting inside some part of the Monster Shadow itself?"

Jewell thought about it, but couldn't make sense out of what Sam was getting at. "Try saying that again," she suggested.

"Look at it this way," Sam began. "What if the entity, or creature, were the Black Place itself?"

"Do you mean that the Black Place is alive?" Jewell asked.

"Exactly!" Sam said.

"Then what is the Monster Shadow?" Jewell asked.

"Part of the living Black Place."

"Then which came first?" Jewell asked. "Who created who? Did the Monster Shadow create the Black Place or did the Black Place create the Monster Shadow?"

"Who cares?" Sam asked. "What difference does it really make if the two things are actually one."

"Then how do we fight the one?" Jewell asked. "Now we're not only facing the Monster Shadow, but the entire Black Place."

"That is true, but we have an advantage in this mountain," Sam said. "And the mountain is inside the Black Place. That gives us a refuge from which to do battle."

"Now you've lost me," Jewell said.

"Here's what I'm thinking," Sam said. "When you tried to bite into the Monster Shadow, let's assume, for arguments sake, that what you actually bit into was the outer wall that holds all of this together."

"Alright," Jewell said. "Then why didn't it break? Why couldn't I feel anything in my mouth? What would happen if it did break?"

"Slow down," Sam said, laughing. "I think we're getting somewhere, but we have to go through this slowly. What you bit into didn't break because it doesn't have physical substance as you could tell when you didn't feel it in your mouth. If it was something physical that held all this desolation and evil in one place then I think that if you broke it, you would release everything that was held inside to go wherever it could."

"Wow!" Jewell gasped. "I could've done some terrible damage to the forest if that had happened!"

"And how!" Sam said. "But you didn't so let's be glad."

"So then," Jewell continued, "what did I actually do that caused the Monster Shadow to let go of Tolebit that time? If I didn't hurt it physically, then what did I do to it?"

"Call me silly," Sam said, "but I think your noble action for the sake of another was a surge of goodness that inflicted enough pain on it to make it let Tolebit go. The same as Amethyst did when she poked it with her horn."

"Come on!" Jewell said in disbelief. "Is that it? Is that the best you can come up with?"

"That may be all there is," Sam said. "You think of everything in terms of the physical. Can't you see by now that the Black Place is not physical?"

"Except for the Monster Shadow," Jewell said.

"That's true," Sam said. "But I don't believe that the real enemy is the Monster Shadow. I believe that the real enemy is the Black Place itself. I think the Monster Shadow is the child and the Black Place is the child's mother."

Jewell stood up on all fours, suddenly alert and quite a bit shocked. "No!" she said.

"Yes," Sam said.

"Then we're inside that things mother right now," Jewell said.

"In a manner of speaking," Sam said.

"Then what is Tolebit?" Jewell asked. "Food for the baby?"

Sam chuckled. "In a way he is," he said. "This whole place thrives on the bad things, bad feelings, and thoughts that are brought into the forest from the Outside Place. Both you and Tolebit still have some of that left in you. I think that the baby, the Monster Shadow, is growing so quickly that its hunger has increased to a point that cannot be dealt with by the goodness of the forest that surrounds it. The Monster Shadow cannot wait until you and Tolebit discard the last of your angry thoughts and devilish actions. It must be fed *now* and so it has drawn you both into itself in order to drain you physically of all the life that's left in you."

"It will drain the good things out of us too," Jewell argued.

"But it doesn't know that," Sam said. "It's just a baby. Remember?"

"What will happen with the goodness it drains from us?" Jewell asked.

Sam paced quickly back and forth along the pool before he answered her.

"Unfortunately," he said, "not enough to make a difference. You see, if you take alot of red berries and squash them up real good, then mix them with two blue berries, all you end up with is a pile of red berry juice."

"So what's your point?" Jewell asked sarcastically.

"My point is that there aren't enough blueberries in that mixture to turn it blue," Sam answered. "If you consider the red berries as evil and the blueberries as goodness, then you realize that there's so little goodness in that mixture that it becomes completely engulfed by the evil."

"And lost," Jewell added.

"And lost," Sam echoed.

"So what's the solution?" Jewell asked.

"Well, I think your original idea about bombarding this place with goodness from the garden would probably work quite well," Sam said. "Unfortunately, I'm afraid that either Daffonia was unable to convey that message adequately to Noah or those in the garden are concerned with other things. Whatever the case, the bottom line is that we're on our own."

"Great!" Jewell said angrily. "There's not enough goodness in both of us put together to destroy that monster's little toe, assuming it has a toe."

"I agree with you," Sam said. "But don't forget, we are inside the mother the minute we step out of our refuge here in the Great Mountain."

"How does that help us?" Jewell asked. "What can we do to the mother?"

"Fill her with love," Sam said. "As best we can, we'll fill her with love."

"You have got to be kidding," Jewell said.

"Oh, but I'm not," Sam said. "We'll be merciful toward everything we find that still has an ounce of life left in it."

"Nothing out there has an ounce of life left in it," Jewell said.

"Maybe nothing you saw," Sam said. "But those dead trees were alive at one time. Those dead animals you saw lying all over the ground were also alive at one time. There are very few birds that will go into the forest because of this place."

"I didn't see any birds in my travels," Jewell told him.

"Most of them stay in the garden," Sam said. "But there are always new trees being engulfed by this place and new creatures being sucked into it unaware. If we go out and find as many of these as we can, we can bring them back here and do our best to make them healthy, again."

"What good will that do?" Jewell asked. "We don't have a lot of time to play with here. Tolebit's life is at stake."

"Then we'll finish up here and get started immediately," Sam said. "The more goodness we can promote in here, the weaker I believe we can make this whole place including the Monster Shadow."

"You're right!" Jewell said enthusiastically. "If we can weaken it just enough, we might be able to sneak in and rescue Tolebit."

"That's my plan!" Sam said. "Maybe we won't destroy it, but if we can first help your friend, then we can worry about getting rid of the Black Place for good later on. That is, if you want to," he added.

Jewell took a few moments to think about the whole idea. "Let's get Tolebit first," she said. "We'll talk about the rest after that."

"That's good enough for me," Sam said. "We're going to have to go back out of this mountain and into the Black Place to do this, you know."

"I know," Jewell said. "So, let's get going."

"We may not be able to keep the mountain in sight in order to find life somewhere," Sam suggested.

"I know," Jewell said. "Let's get going."

"If you get in trouble, Jewell," Sam said, "I want you to howl. Don't howl for any other reason than if you get into trouble."

"I'll remember that," Jewell said impatiently. "Can we get going, now?"

"If you're sure you want to do this," Sam said.

"What choice do we have?" Jewell asked. "It's the only thing that makes any kind of sense at all, and even this gives us only a remote chance of saving Tolebit."

"That's the way I see it, too," Sam said as he began to walk back down the tunnel that Jewell had followed him into previously.

"Hey Sam," Jewell said. "What if you get into trouble? How will I know? You don't make any sounds loud enough for me to hear?"

"Don't I?" Sam asked. "You'd be surprised at the noises that come out of this tiny body when necessary."

Jewell laughed. "Seriously, Sam," she said. "How will I know?"

"Believe me," Sam replied, "you won't have a doubt in your mind if I end up in trouble. Trust me on that one."

"If you say so," Jewell said.

"I say so," Sam replied. "Now let's get going," he added as he started back through the tunnel. "We've got an awful lot to do and very little time to do it in."

CHAPTER 19

By the time Jewell and Sam reached the cave entrance on the outside of the Great Mountain, they had already begun to feel the dry air from the Black Place as it entered their lungs with each breath.

"This sounded like a good idea when we were deep in the mountain," Sam said. "I forget how awful and desolate it is out here, sometimes."

"We have to do this," Jewell said. "There's no time to waste. We should split up, I suppose," she added doubtfully.

"Right," Sam said sounding equally dubious. "I'll go to the right. You head out to the left. Try to keep the mountain in sight so you can get back to it fast if you have to."

"You do the same," Jewell advised. "I don't want to have to try to rescue you and Tolebit both."

"Point taken," Sam said. "Good luck."

"Same to you," Jewell said as she headed down the mountainside.

Once at the bottom, she turned to look back for Sam, but he was already out of sight. Suddenly, Jewell felt very alone.

"Here goes nothing," she said to herself as she started off into the blackness. It was difficult to see, but it didn't take long for her eyes to adjust to the dark while she and Sam walked through the tunnel. Now she faced the added challenge of trying to search for signs of life in a place where she was lucky to be able to see anything at all. Jewell used her canine talents to sniff for life in the air. The putrid smell she encountered when she started her search for Tolebit was gone, but the smells of dry air and ashes were strong. Maybe she'd be able to find some life if she smelled something different. She walked slowly along, her front paw still a bit sore from the dried tree branch that had punctured it, but she did her best to ignore the enduring pain. She searched the Black Place, always keeping the mountain behind her. Every so often she stopped just to check to see if the Monster Shadow might be lurking nearby, but a large amount of time had already elapsed and she'd seen nothing. She thought she'd at least know it was close when the ground started to shake, but she couldn't forget how it was able to sneak up and snatch Tolebit away without any warning.

After another hour of searching, Jewell began to lose hope, thinking it was all a waste of time. What was she doing looking for life where there obviously was none? Then, she smelled it. It was faint, but it was there.

Jewelled followed the scent for nearly a hundred paces. It grew stronger with each step she took, but she still could not tell exactly what it was. She wasn't even sure it was something living. All she knew was that it was different from the smells she had grown to associate with the Black Place.

She followed the scent until she could no longer tell which way to go. When she looked down, there it was. An injured bird breathing its last gasping breath. Jewell began to lick its wounds and clean the ashes and debris from its feathers. She knew it was alive, but it was also unconscious. Gently lifting it into her mouth, Jewell realized that she and Sam had not determined quite how they were going to go about gathering up whatever living things or creatures they found. Now what was she to do? With no other answer obvious to her, she began to run back to the Great Mountain with the bird in her mouth. It took less than half the time for her to span the same distance back that it had taken her to carefully search, but she reached the Great Mountain and climbed back up to the cave. Inside the cave entrance, she deposited the bird on the ground and began to lick it once again.

"Wake up, little bird," she said soothingly to it, but there was no response. "Don't give up, little bird," she said. "I can't stay with you very long, but I'll take you where it's cooler and easier for you to breath."

Lifting the bird back into her mouth, Jewell ran part of the way through the tunnel until she reached the cooler, moister air. Finding an open area to one side of the tunnel, she said, "I'll leave you here for now, but I'll be back to take you the rest of the way."

With that, Jewell licked the wounded bird once more and headed back through the tunnel, down the mountainside and into the Black Place as quickly as she could. Now that she had found a living creature among the desolation, she had also found new hope that she and Sam might be able to accomplish this far-fetched mission after all.

"Come on, Jewell," she said to herself as she searched the ground for more survivors. "One bird is not going to do the trick. Where are the rest? There's got to be more."

Jewell ran all the way back to the area where she'd found the wounded bird, hoping to find at least one or two more. She did, indeed, find quite a few of them, but it was too late for the rest. She inspected each and every body she could find and eventually did come across one more bird who was still alive. She followed the same procedure as she'd done with the first, running it all the way back to the mountain and part of the way down the tunnel until it was in fresher, cooler air. She placed in on the ground next to the first, then ran back to the cave entrance.

After only a few steps down the mountainside, Jewell heard the most horrendous, high-pitched squealing she had ever heard in her life. It wasn't the deep, guttural roar of the Monster Shadow. It was the complete opposite and it took Jewell mere seconds to realize that what she heard was Sam. From the horrible sounds he made, she knew he was in trouble.

Jewell wasted no time climbing down the side of the mountain Sam had taken. She felt the race against time, and ran toward the screams as fast as she could. "I'm coming, Sam," she said between gasps, hoping Sam might hear her and be reassured.

The sounds coming from Sam were frightening. Jewell could smell him and she feared for his life.

When Jewell came upon him, she could see the white stripes

down his back. He was cornered by something half the size of Jewell herself. It almost appeared to be a dog, but there was something about it that told her it was not. It had a wild scent that was familiar to her. It was also badly wounded. Jewell could smell the blood that oozed from its open sores.

"Get back," Jewell growled at the animal that had cornered Sam. "Get away from him," she warned.

"Sssssss, go away," the wild animal hissed. "I'll kill you, too."

"You don't have to kill anyone," Jewell reasoned with it. "We can help you."

"I need food," the animal hissed. "This little rodent is the only food here. He's mine!"

"We have a whole stash of food in the mountain," Jewell said. "You don't have to harm anyone."

"What mountain?" the animal hissed angrily. "I don't see any mountains."

"Behind me," Jewell said. "Look behind me. I just came from there. Inside is a cool place with water and sunlight and a pile of food that the little rodent you have cornered gathered all by himself."

Sam cast an offended look at Jewell. "Little rodent," he muttered under his breath, but Jewell chose to ignore him.

Jewell watched the wild animal as it seemed to contemplate its options. She could tell that it was weakened by its wounds and wondered how difficult it would be to carry it back to the mountain if it passed out.

"I know you came from Noah's Forest into this place," Jewell tried talking to the animal. "We don't kill each other in the forest. Don't kill Sam in here."

"Is that his name?" the animal hissed. "Sam?"

"That's me!" Sam said, trying to be perky in the face of danger.

"Sam or no Sam," the animal hissed, "I haven't eaten in days, maybe weeks for all I know. I need . . . I need. . . ."

Jewell saw it coming before it happened. The animal who had Sam pinned against the rocks fell over on its side and was suddenly unconscious.

"I guess it used up all of the energy it had left trying to catch me," Sam said. "Let's get it back to the mountain before it's too late."

"I found two birds on the other side of the mountain that are just barely alive," Jewell said as she lifted the unconscious animal up by its skin.

"I found a few wilted strawberries over there," Sam said pointing towards something that Jewell could hardly see. "I'm going to gather them up and bring them back to the pool. I'll be right behind you."

Jewell headed for the mountain while Sam went off to gather as many of the strawberries as he could pack into his cheeks. By the time Jewell reached the cave, Sam was right behind her and scurried on ahead.

At the pool, Jewell lay the wild animal, that she now recognized as being a very beat up cat, on the ground. She then went back to retrieve the birds she'd found as well.

"I'm going back out to search for more," Jewell said.

Sam looked quickly from Jewell to the beat up cat to the birds, then back to Jewell. "Do you think it's wise to leave a hungry cat in a room with two wounded birds?" He looked at the cat, still lying unconscious. "And me?" he added.

Jewell thought a second. "I'll put the birds on the far end of the pool, and I'll lay this cat right by the pile of fruit. If you put a pile of berries close by the birds, they'll be able to eat without disturbing the cat and the cat will be able to eat its fill before it realizes the birds are even here."

Sam looked at Jewell incredulously. "Hopefully," he said.

"Hopefully," Jewell echoed. "But we can't babysit them," she added. "Now that I know there really is life here, I have to find all those who are still alive before it's too late for them.

"I'm right behind you then," Sam said.

"Maybe you should concentrate on trying to find any sources of food that haven't gone bad yet," Jewell suggested. "I'll grab any creatures I find who are still alive and get them back here as quickly as I can."

"Good idea," Sam said as they started back down the tunnel. "I would never have been able to drag that cat here. That's for sure."

When they reached the entrance, Jewell stopped and looked at Sam. "By the way," she said. "You were right."

"About what?" Sam asked.

"About the kind of noise that your tiny, little body is able to make," Jewell replied. "It scared me half to death."

Sam chuckled. "I told you," he said. "Now let's get to it. There's still a lot to do."

Together, they started down the same side of the mountain this time.

"What are you doing?" Sam asked. "I thought we were splitting up."

"Not anymore," Jewell said. "I think we had better stay together this time. Especially if you're gathering food and I'm gathering whatever creatures we find."

"Agreed," Sam said. "It does make a lot more sense, doesn't it?"

Together, Jewell and Sam worked tirelessly through the remainder of the day, never seeing the Monster Shadow. By the time they were making their last trip to the mountain, they had found two more birds, a raccoon, and a creature that resembled Tolebit, but wasn't Tolebit, as well as a wealth of nearly dried berries and a walnut tree that still had enough walnuts on it to feed them and their new guests.

But, as they neared the mountain the rumbling began.

"It figures," Sam said exhausted. "When I had the strength to run the Monster Shadow was nowhere to be found. Now that I'm pooped it decides to come out."

"Forget about that," Jewell said. "Just get back to the cave as fast as you can. I'll be close behind with this. . . . aahh,..Tolebit looking thing."

"Stay close," Sam said as he took off as fast he could toward the mountain and up into the cave.

Jewell did her best to keep up, but even at his worst, Sam was still faster than any other creature she had ever seen. As Sam raced up the mountainside, Jewell was still on the shaking ground two hundred feet from the base of the mountain with the unconscious rescuee in her mouth. As she closed half the distance left to the mountain, she smelled the putrid smell and heard the angry roar. There was no need to look. She knew the beast was close and coming up on her fast.

Jewell did her best to get up the side of the mountain to the cave as fast as she could. Rocks were rolling down the mountain just as they had the first time she had run up its side to the cave. She was hit twice, but kept going.

Just as Jewell reached the cave, she felt the searing hand of the Monster Shadow as it lifted her off the mountain. Jewell dropped the creature from her mouth onto the lip of the cave, hoping it would land on something soft to break its fall.

She felt herself rising into the air, sensed an intense heat all around her, but the part of the beast that held her did not burn her fur as its previous swipe across her back had done. Jewell turned to get a good look at the thing who held her captive, and caught a glimpse of Tolebit in the Monster Shadow's other hand. He was still unconscious. Jewell could not tell if he was alive or not, but the mere sight of him in such a helpless state made her angry. Jewell began to bark fiercely at the evil creature who held her up, unconcerned whether it dropped her or not. She was too angry to care. She wanted this thing gone for good.

As she barked at the Monster Shadow, its grip tightened until Jewell could hardly breath. Her barking ceased, but her anger did not. Instinctively, she grabbed for the first thing she could reach and bit hard, then bit again, and again, and again. Suddenly, the Monster Shadow released her, but Jewell was high off the ground and falling fast.

Luckily, she fell toward the angry monster, landing on its lower sloping side that might have been some sort of leg. Sliding down the Monster Shadow's form toward the ground, Jewell managed to get a few more bites in before her fall was complete. She heard the Monster Shadow's angry roars each time she bit into it, but she was falling so fast that she had little time to think of anything else.

'*I'm going to die anyway*,' she thought as she inflicted bite after bite. '*I might as well do as much damage as I can before I go.*'

When Jewell finally hit the ground, she heard Sam's voice calling her from the cave in the mountain.

"Hurry!" he yelled. "Hurry!"

Jewell tried to get to her feet, but her back leg was riddled with pain.

"I can't!" she called back to Sam. "I hurt my leg. I can't climb."

"You have to!" Sam called. "I'll distract the beast while you climb."

"I can't, Sam!" Jewell yelled, insistent. "Just take care of the others."

"Shut up and climb!" Sam said as he began to yell at the Monster Shadow.

When Jewell realized the angry beast was truly distracted by Sam, she decided it was the only chance she had to get back to the cave. Standing up on her three good legs, she hobbled to the mountainside as quickly as she could.

"Keep coming!" Sam yelled to her without turning his gaze from the Monster Shadow. "You can do it!"

Jewell took one step up the mountainside, then another, then another, moving very slowly so as not to have to use her injured leg for balance. When she was almost at the cave, there was one last, steep incline to conquer, but Jewell knew she couldn't do it without the use of both back legs. She looked at Sam who now stood only a few steps away. "I can't do it," she said.

Sam took his eyes off the Monster Shadow and looked at Jewell. "You'd better do it," he said. "Because everyone we rounded up is going to need your help. Now move!"

As Sam finished speaking, they both realized the Monster Shadow was no longer distracted. By the time Sam tried to resume his efforts at holding its attention, it was too late. Both Sam and Jewell saw the swooping appendage begin to move under Jewell, but only Jewell saw the opportunity that it presented.

She waited for the right time when the Monster Shadow's arm was at the right angle and just about to touch her. The very moment she felt the heat from the awful beast, Jewell used her good leg to push off from the thing that lifted her from underneath. The momentum propelled her directly into the cave and right past a very surprised Sam who quickly followed her.

"Are you alright?" Sam asked.

"Except for my leg, I'm fine," Jewell replied.

"That was brilliant!!" Sam said, jumping up and down, then running back and forth. "Absolutely brilliant!!"

"Thanks," Jewell said, wincing. "How's the last little creature we found? I dropped it on the lip of the cave just as I was being lifted up by that thing."

"It's fine," Sam said. I saw it land on those dead leaves right at the edge. See where I mean?"

Jewel looked at the lip of the cave and saw the pile of leaves with the little sprite lying on them. A formation at the edge of the lip had held back the pile of leaves that had fallen or blown in from the dead trees. "Miracles do happen," Jewell said.

"All I can tell you," Sam said, "is that those leaves were not there yesterday. I think the Monster Shadow stirred them up when it sent all those trees crashing. They must've floated up and got caught there."

"However it happened," Jewell said, "at least it happened. Let's get that little creature out of the leaves and down to the pool."

"Can you move?" Sam asked.

"I can hobble along," Jewell replied. "As long as I don't have to do any more climbing for awhile."

Sam looked tentatively at her. "We'll work around it. It looks like the Monster Shadow has made another disappointed retreat. Why don't you grab that new little creature we found and meet me at the pool?"

"I'm right behind you," Jewell said as she limped over to the pile of leaves to retrieve her former passenger. Seeing that it was no worse-for-the-wear, but still unconscious, she lifted the creature up, then proceeded down the tunnel.

CHAPTER 20

"Well, will you look at that," Sam said as they entered the room in the mountain. "Who would've ever thought?"

Jewell looked around the room, ignoring the pain in her back leg. She was still holding the Tolebit-like creature in her mouth, but when she saw what was happening in front of her, she gently placed it on the ground and sat back, amazed.

All four birds they had rescued were gingerly nibbling on the berries that Sam left beside them. They were very weak, but they were eating. The cat and the raccoon lay on opposite sides of the pile of food Sam had collected. They too, were eating, though the cat seemed much stronger. The most amazing thing about the entire scene was that none of the animals who were nearly dead just hours ago had tried to harm any of the others.

"It's going to be alright," Jewell said softly to Sam. "It really is."

"I'm beginning to think so myself," Sam said. "Now let's see what condition that other little creature is in."

Jewell lifted the last creature they had saved and carried it over to the pool where she laid it back on the ground, and began to lick the ashes and dust from its body while Sam used an empty walnut shell to bring it water.

Together, they did what they could for the small sprite, but they were unable to revive it. Even the walnut shell, as small as it was, still seemed too clumsy to be of much use though they did their best with it. Once Jewell had the sprite all cleaned up, she could see that it was, in fact, just like Tolebit. This sprite, however, was a female.

"I don't know what else to do for her," Jewell said. "She hasn't come around the way the birds did."

"I can't even give her any water without getting her soaked and nearly drowning her," Sam said. "I'm at a lost myself."

While Jewell and Sam sat near the sleeping sprite, two of the birds they had rescued came forward.

"Maybe we can help," the first one said. "I've got an idea."

"What's your name?" Jewell asked as she inspected her hurt leg.

"I'm not sure I have a name," the bird said. "I've never had any use for one."

"Well, we have to call you something," Sam said. "How about if we call you Bird?"

"That won't do," the bird said. "There are four of us here and we're all birds."

"What kind of birds are you?" Jewell asked, leaving her leg alone to talk to them.

"I'm a robin," the bird said.

"Then we'll call you Robin," Jewell said. "What about the others?"

"My companion is also a robin," Robin said.

"Oh," Jewell replied as she thought to come up with an appropriate name.

"I've got it!" Sam said. "We'll call you Robin and your friend we'll call Sunny for his big orange chest."

"I like that!" Sunny chimed in. "I like it a lot!"

"Good," Jewell said. "Then it's settled. From now on we'll know you as Robin and Sunny. Now, why don't you tell us how you can help."

"Let us show you, instead," Robin said, glancing at her companion.

Together, the two robins lifted the female sprite into the air with their beaks. They flew over to the pool and slowly lowered her into the clean, clear water up to her shoulders where they each had their hold on her. Up and down they dipped her seven times before returning her to where Jewell and Sam sat and watched. As they lowered her to the ground, Jewell could see the sprite was coming to.

"Incredible," she said as she shook her head.

"The water is so refreshing," Robin said. "It helped wake us up after you left. We thought it might do the same for this little one. What is it, anyway?"

"She's a sprite," Jewell replied. "I came here to rescue a sprite that I know very well. His name is Tolebit."

As Jewell and Sam briefly relayed the story to Robin and Sunny, Jewell kept a watchful eye on the sprite who lay by her front paws. She could tell that the sprite was trying hard to listen to all that was being said.

"That's quite a story," Sunny said when they were finished telling them all that had happened. "What next?"

"What do you mean?" Jewell asked as she watched Sam scurry over to the pile of fruit and bring a raspberry back for the sprite.

"I mean, after we're all feeling better, what happens?" Sunny asked. "How will our renewed health help rescue your friend, Tolebit?"

"We're hoping that since this whole place is made of bad feelings and thoughts," Sam said, "maybe we can weaken it enough to rescue Tolebit by sending out our naturally good feelings and thoughts. Just by finding and saving all of you, we've done a caring thing. That kind of thoughfulness must be able to hurt the Black Place in some small way."

"Oh, I see," Robin joined in. "It's an energy thing. The world is full of good and bad energy. Creatures of the wild, like us, feel it more than others."

"More than people," Sunny added. "That has always struck me as strange, too, when you consider that so much of the energy of all kinds comes from them."

Just as Sunny finished speaking, he let out a loud scream and flew straight up to the ceiling with Robin close beside him.

"What's the matter?" Sam asked, startled.

"I think it's me," the cat who had tried to eat Sam said as he joined them by the pool. He looked up at the pair near the ceiling. "Don't worry. I'm not going to hurt you. You can come down."

Tentatively, Robin and Sunny drifted back to the ground beside Jewell.

"It's alright," Jewell assured them as she carefully stood up. "I think he's learned the value of friendship."

"I sure have," the cat said to her. "Thank you for saving my life. I don't know how I could ever repay you." He licked his paws, then walked between Jewell's legs and began to rub his head on her chest.

"What's your name?" Jewell asked, embarrassed by the sudden attention.

"Melvin," the cat replied. "That's what my family calls me."

"You have a family, too?" Jewell asked joyfully.

"Outside of this forest where I came from, I do," Melvin replied. "But I don't know how to get back home. I'm lost."

"We'll get you home," Sam said. "Don't you worry about a thing. But first, we have to rescue Tolebit. That's our priority."

"Didn't you have a guide who met you when you entered the forest?" Jewell asked, concerned.

"What do you mean?" Melvin asked. "I was only in the forest for a few minutes when I ended up in here."

Jewell looked at Sam, a worried expression on both their faces.

"What's the matter?" Robin asked.

"Well," Jewell began as she explained to them about the forest and how it works. "So you see," she concluded. "You weren't supposed to be able to enter the forest unless there was something you were looking for within yourselves."

"I felt drawn to the forest," the raccoon said as it wobbled up to the others. "It was almost as if it were pulling."

"So did I," the sprite said as she did her best to sit up.

"We all did," Jewell responded, limping to the pool to soak her back leg in the cool water. "What concerns me is that you had no one waiting for you as you entered. Noah sends out a guide to help you through the trials of the forest so that you can gain entrance to the garden. That's the way it's supposed to work."

"As soon as I entered the forest," the raccoon said, "I ran right into this place."

"Me, too," the sprite said.

"So did we," the last two birds echoed as they walked up to the group. "We thought we were flying through the trees, but before we knew it, we were here."

"Uh oh," Sam said suddenly. "I'm not liking this one bit."

"What are you thinking?" Jewell asked.

"I'm thinking that the Monster Shadow is so hungry, that it's calling in creatures from the Outside Place," Sam answered.

"Could it be that strong?" Jewell asked.

"Maybe, maybe not," Sam said, shaking his head. "I don't know."

"Well, if it's not the Monster Shadow," Jewell began, "then who could be calling these creatures in?"

"If not who," Sam said, "then what?"

Jewell lifted her head and pointed her ears toward Sam. "You don't mean the Black Place is calling these creatures in?" she asked, growing more disturbed by the minute.

"Why not?" Sam asked. "Don't all the mothers of the world have an instinctive concern for their babies?"

"Well, if that's the case," Melvin said. "Then we had better do something fast."

"What if we all go out on a massive rescue mission?" the raccoon asked. "We could round up an army to rescue your friend."

"That's a strong idea," Sam said. "Unfortunately, Jewell and I are in agreement that there's little or no time time left. The army we need is us."

"The question is," Jewell said, "are we all strong enough to go back out there?"

There was silence throughout the group by the pool. Finally, Sunny spoke up. "I don't think we have a choice," he said. "If this place is calling in others from outside of the forest, then the time to save your friend is right now so we can finish the job and destroy the Black Place before more creatures are trapped."

"I agree," Robin said. "We're going to have to do whatever we can with whatever strength we've been able to build up."

"I'm with you," Melvin said.

"Me, too," the raccoon added.

"Me, too," echoed the sprite who was now able to stand.

"I don't know about you being strong enough to go," Jewell said, pulling her leg out of the water. "What's your name, anyway?"

"Lipa," the sprite said. "It's my brother, Tolebit, that you came here to save."

"Tolebit is your brother?" Jewell asked, astonished.

"Yes," Lipa answered. "He's been missing for many, many years. I've been lonely without him around. He's my best friend in the world."

"Rest assured that we'll get him back," Jewell said. "I only wish I could promise you what condition he'll be in when he returns to us."

"Jewell," Lipa said as she placed her tiny hand on Jewell's paw. "I'm so thankful that you cared enough about my brother to even try to rescue him. I understand the situation that he's in. But can you see why I must go with you?"

"I can," Jewell said. "But I cannot guarantee your safety."

"I understand," Lipa replied. "Still, I'm bound to go."

"Alright, then," Jewell said. "You may ride on my neck the way your brother did during the days he traveled with Daffonia and me. No matter what happens, you will have to hold on as tight as you can."

"I will," Lipa promised. "I will not be your responsibility. I will be my own."

"Understood," Jewell turned to Sam. "What's the plan?"

"Well," Sam said. "It seems fairly simple to me. First we have to find the Monster Shadow. Once we do, we have to distract it, weaken it somehow if we can. Next, we have to sneak in and grab Tolebit from it."

"How can we help?" one of the last two birds asked.

"I think the birds may have to fly and grab Tolebit once the rest of us have done what we can to the beast," Jewell suggested. "I only wish I could do that part myself."

"You've done enough already," Lipa said. "My brother will be so proud of you."

"The biggest problem we're going to have," Melvin said, "is that none of us can last more than a few hours out there."

"I know we can't," Robin said.

"I might be able to last almost a day if I really push myself," the raccoon said.

Sam stepped up and put his little hand on his chin. "I have an idea," he said. "Let's go out in groups. One bird will go with each group so they can fly to the others as soon as the Monster Shadow has been located. It shouldn't take that long. That baby beast is too huge to miss."

"Yes, but we have no idea just how big the Black Place really is," Jewell said.

"And if it's growing as fast as you say it is," Lipa added, "then none of us know for sure how long this will take."

"That's true," Sam said. "So we have to work fast."

"How should we break up into groups?" the raccoon asked. "There's not many of us."

"How about this?" Jewell said. "I'll go with Melvin. Robin can ride on one of our backs until it's time to alert the rest. Sam. You go with. . . . ," Jewell began as she looked at the raccoon uncertainly. "What's your name?" she asked.

"I don't have one either," he said.

"Then I'll call you Burglar," Jewell said. "I remember the raccoons back home and how they used to steal any food that wasn't locked up."

The raccoon looked hurt for a few seconds, but cheered right up when Sam said, "How about Ringo? I like those rings around his eyes."

"You do?" the raccoon asked.

"Sure I do," Sam said. "It's unique, just like you."

Ringo beamed with pride at the uniqueness of his new name.

"Sunny can ride with you two," Jewell said, "until it's time for him to alert the rest."

"What about us?" the last two birds asked. "What can we do?"

"Do you need names as well?" Jewell asked, suspecting they did.

"Well, yes," the red bird admitted.

"Alright then," Jewell said. "For lack of more time, I'll call you by your colors. You will be called Red," she said to the red bird, then turned to the other one. "And you will be called Blue."

"No," Lipa said. "The red bird reminds me of a dress my aunt used to wear. Her name was Restia." Lipa smiled at the bird. "Would you like to be called Restia?"

The bird looked at her and ruffled her feathers. "It sounds very feminine," she said. "I like it."

Lipa reached her hand toward Restia and gently touched the side of her beak. "And I like you."

Sam stood up and crossed his arms in front of his chest. "And do you have a name for our blue bird friend as well?" he asked.

Lipa turned to look at him and smiled. "As a matter of fact I do, if that's alright."

"What is it?" Restia asked her.

"How about my favorite stone? Sapphire." Lipa watched as the blue bird jumped toward her. "You're the color of Sapphire stones," she said, her eyes sparkling as she touched his wing.

"That's good," Sam said. "Now there will be no mistaking who is who. Well, then."

"If I may make a suggestion," Lipa offered, sheepishly.

Sam turned to look at her, seemingly annoyed. "Sure," he said.

"Why don't we leave Restia and Sapphire behind to rest and stay strong," she said. "That way, when we finally find the beast who has my brother, they will be ready to fly out and help. Then all of us will not be weak and exhausted when the time comes to do battle."

"Not a bad idea."

"I'm in full agreement," Jewell said. She turned to the rest of the group. "Is everyone comfortable with this plan?"

They all shook their heads in agreement as they looked around at each other.

"What about your leg?" Sam asked. "Will you be able to walk."

"It feels much better since I soaked in the pool," Jewell said. "Is that some kind of magic water?"

"The magic is in its purity," Sam replied. "Nothing more."

"Well, whatever it is," Jewell said, "My leg still hurts, but not like it did when we first got back here. I can go with you."

"Well, then," Sam said as he scurried over to the tunnel that led back out of the mountain. "Let's go."

Together they filed through the tunnel on their way back to the heart of the Black Place. When they reached the place in the tunnel where the air usually begins to change, Jewell stopped and said to Restia and Sapphire, "This is as far as you can go without being affected by the nasty air out there. Stay here and wait to hear that we've located the beast. Then you may come out and join us in our mission."

"While we wait," Sapphire said, "I'm going to bring some of the food from the pool out here in case any of you need nourishment quickly."

"That's an excellent idea," Jewell said as she headed back down the tunnel. "We'll see you soon. Stay strong."

When the rest of the group had reached the cave, they stopped and looked around. In the distance they could see the flames that Jewell had seen when she first entered the Black Place to rescue Tolebit.

"You don't suppose?" she said to Sam who stood beside her.

"Nah," Sam said. "That would be too easy."

"Then, again," Jewell said, pausing. "It is just a baby."

"Maybe," Sam reminded her.

"Maybe," Jewell echoed. "But it's my first choice of where to look."

Sam watched the flames as they shot off their fiery arms in the distance before he spoke. "Mine too," he said.

"Hey!" Ringo said. "What is that?"

"What is what?" Melvin asked.

"That bright, angry thing in the distance."

"That, my friend," Sam said, "is our destination."

"The beast?" Melvin asked. "Are you sure?"

"Reasonably sure," Sam said. "That's where it was the day before yesterday when Jewell had her encounter with it."

"Then that's where we should look first," Melvin said.

"Even before we split up into our groups," Ringo added.

Jewell and Sam looked at each other in silence.

"What?" Lipa asked from atop Jewell's neck. "What's wrong?"

"Nothing," Jewell answered. "They read our minds, is all."

"They sure did," Sam said as he scurried down the mountainside, then waited for the others to catch up.

CHAPTER 21

As the rescuers approached the flames they had seen from the mountain, Jewell began to smell the awful, putrid smell that always seemed to indicate the presence of the Monster Shadow.

"It's here," she said to Sam, who passed the word among the others.

"Lucky for us," Melvin called back to Jewell. "I'm beginning to feel the effects of the dry heat already."

"Can you make it?" Jewell asked him.

"I will make it," Melvin answered with certainty.

"OK," Sam said. "When we approach it I'm going to try to distract it like I did before. I'm going to need everyone's help to take its attention away from Tolebit who should still be in its hand."

"We hope," Lipa added.

"That's right," Jewell said. "We hope."

"Sunny," Sam said. "As soon as I tell you, fly back to the cave and alert Restia and Sapphire that we've found the beast. Tell them to come as quickly as they can. It may take all four of you to fly up there and snatch Tolebit away."

"I'm with you," Sunny confirmed. "Just let me know."

They proceeded forward until they could all feel the heat of the flames, making the air they breathed even drier than before.

"I'd forgotten how draining this was," Jewell said.

"Hang in there," Ringo called to her. "You're stronger than the rest of us. If you can't make it, we don't have any hope."

"How does your leg feel?" Sam asked.

"It'll do," Jewell answered him. "That's the least of my worries."

"There it is!" Melvin yelled so loud that he startled Lipa, who jumped in her seat on Jewell's neck.

"That's your cue!" Sam called to Sunny, who immediately took flight and headed back to the mountain.

"Should we wait for Restia and Sapphire to get back with Sunny?" Ringo asked. "It shouldn't take them long at all."

"It's safer for all of us if we wait," Sam suggested. "We're right here, now. Another minute or two is not going to make that much difference."

"Then we'll wait," Jewell conceded even though she desparately wanted to have Tolebit safe and sound with her.

In no time at all, Restia and Sapphire arrived.

"Where's Sunny?" Robin asked sounding worried.

"The flight back was a bit tiring," Restia answered. "He's eating a few of the berries we had brought up from the pool and then he's going to join us."

"That's fine," Jewell said. "He knows where we are. Let's go in."

Together they continued their march toward the Monster Shadow who stood amongst the flames, arms raised as if worshipping their very presence.

"I think it sees us," Ringo said.

Just as the words left his mouth, the Monster Shadow let out the same, low-pitched, guttural growl as it had before. Once again, the ground shook with the thunderous noise of its anger. The few trees that were left standing from the day before began to fall, knocking down everything in their paths.

As if on cue, Jewell, Sam, Melvin, and Ringo ran toward the beast, while Robin, Restia, and Sapphire took to the air and headed for the height of the Monster Shadow.

"Surround it," Sam called at the top of his lungs.

"Can anyone see Tolebit?" Jewell called.

"I can't," Sam called back.

"What about you, Melvin?" Jewell asked him.

"Nothing," Melvin replied. "The beast's hands are too high. I can't see if there's anything in them or not."

Just then, Sapphire came flying back to Jewell.

"See anything?" Jewell asked feeling Lipa tense up on her neck.

"He's there," Sapphire shouted above the din of falling trees and shaking earth. "But he doesn't look good."

"At least he's there," Jewell yelled to him. "Which hand is he in."

"The far one from here," Sapphire yelled.

"We'll distract it from the other side, then," Jewell shouted, having seen the Monster Shadow take a step toward Sam.

"Go get him!"

"On our way!" Sapphire yelled as he turned and headed for Tolebit.

"He's there!" Jewell called to Sam, who sent word down the line. "We've got to keep the beast's attention on this side."

Sam spread the command to the other two and they all converged on the beast's right side. Sam chittered away in his chipmunk voice as he scurried back and forth. Jewell barked her angry bark, jumping at the Monster Shadow, but never getting so close as to burn her own fur. Melvin hissed and spit, swiping his claws across the beast's lowest parts as he lunged, then ran, lunged, than ran.

Ringo took an entirely different approach. He found a high cluster of very large boulders that stood immediately behind the Monster Shadow. Climbing to the highest point of the rocks, he called to the birds who hovered over the Monster Shadow's left hand.

"If you can, grab Tolebit," he yelled. "Bring him down to me, then head back to the cave."

"It's too hot up here," Restia called back. "Our feathers are being singed. We can't get in close enough to get him."

"One of you is going to have to take the chance and go in," Ringo called back. "There's no other way."

Just as he said that, Restia dropped out of the air and hit the ground near the Monster Shadow's feet. Immediately, Ringo ran down from the rocks over to where Restia landed. He scooped her

up, then ran back to the shelter that he'd seen between the boulders on which he stood.

"Robin, Sapphire!" he called. "One of you has to do it. It
doesn't look like Sunny is going to make it back to us."

"What's happening over there?" Jewell called out to them as
she continued her efforts at drawing the beast's attention away
from Tolebit.

"Restia is down!" Ringo called back. "The other two say it's
too hot up there. Their feathers are burning."

"So are my lungs!" Jewell yelled.

"Where's Sunny?" Sam shouted.

"He isn't back yet!" Melvin answered, forgetting not to hiss at
the same time.

"What should we do?" Ringo called to Jewell. "The birds are
not going to make it!"

"Neither am I!" Melvin shouted. "I'm burning up!"

"This isn't going to work!" Sam hollered as loud as his parched
voice would allow.

"Oh yes it is," Sunny shouted as he came swooping out of the
sky with a trail of multi-colored lights behind him.

"The Eyes of the Forest!!" Jewell called. "They made it!!"

"Robin! Sapphire!" Sunny called. "Get out of there! I've got
him!!"

Both birds who had been working so hard to reach Tolebit,
veered out of the way just as Sunny swooped down over him, grabbed
the sprite in his beak and flew him over to Ringo who immediately
headed for the safety of the mountain with Tolebit in his mouth.

"Only a thief could think that fast," Sam called to Jewell as
they watched many of the Eyes of the Forest surround the Monster Shadow. "Maybe you were right to name him the first one you
thought of."

Jewell smiled but was interrupted before she could say a word.

"Get away from here!" a familiar voice called to them. "We'll
take care of this. Daffonia told us your idea. You saved my sister.
Now it's my turn to save you. Now go!"

"Sprig!" Jewell shouted happily.

"Not now, Jewell," Sprig said. "Go back to the mountain. You'll know when it's safe to come out."

"Thank you," Jewell said, but she knew that Sprig hadn't heard her. He had already disappeared amongst the many colors that had taken over the entire Black Place.

"Let's go!" Jewell called to Melvin who was pulling Restia out of the safety of the rocks.

"I'm right behind you!" Melvin shouted back as he ran to catch up with Jewell on her way back to the mountain.

Colored lights of every hue imaginable surrounded them, lighting up the incredible darkness of the Black Place and revealing the awful devastation that was everywhere.

"Look!" Sam called back to Jewell when they were almost to the mountain. "Over there!"

Jewell looked to her right where Sam had pointed. She could see that the trees were turning green.

"Melvin! Look!" Jewell called to the cat who trailed her by a few feet. "Look at the trees!"

"Is that from the Eyes of the Forest?" Melvin asked as they reached the base of the mountain and began to climb.

"That's what they can do, alright," Jewell answered him.

"Let's get to the pool," Melvin said. "Restia needs help. We can come back out here and see what happens once she's safe."

Sam was the first one to reach the cave, followed by Jewell who was stopped dead in her tracks when she reached the lip of the entrance and stood to wait for Melvin.

"Daffonia!!" Jewell called in a raspy voice. "I'm so glad to see you!"

"As I am to see you," the deer responded, nuzzling the dog in a motherly fashion. "I'm sorry it took so long. Glory had taken a turn for the worse and I couldn't get to Noah right away to tell him the rest of your plan."

"I understand," Jewell said. "We're all OK, except for Tolebit. I don't know how he is at all. But I have his sister with me."

"Tolebit's sister?" Daffonia asked, surprised.

"I sure do," Jewell said. "Daffonia meet Lipa."

Lipa stood on Jewell's neck, weakly holding onto her ear for support. "I'm so pleased to meet you," Lipa said. "Jewell told me all about your journey with my brother. I thank you for putting up with him."

Daffonia laughed. "He was no trouble," she said. "Not really."

"Let's go see how he is," Sam urged. "Ringo is the only one who knows."

"Where are the birds?" Melvin asked.

"They're inside already," Daffonia said. "Where you should all be. Let the Eyes do their work out here. Amethyst is with them. So is Tempo, but just to observe."

Melvin was the first to head down the tunnel with Restia in his mouth. When they reached the pool, the other birds took care of Restia, while Jewell took Lipa to where Ringo had laid her brother along the water's edge.

"How is he?" Lipa asked.

"Badly damaged," Ringo answered. "I got him back here as fast as I could."

"You did well," Daffonia said to him. "You all did very well. Noah is so proud of you."

"What about Tolebit?" Jewell asked.

"I'll take care of him," Lipa answered as she went to the pile of fruit and looked it over. "Sam," she said, "where's that walnut shell that was lying near me when I awoke?"

Sam found the walnut shell and ran it right over to her.

"Thank you," she said politely as she went about choosing certain pieces of fruit to mix together in the nutshell with a tiny stem that she'd broken off a pear.

"What is she doing?" Sunny asked as he birdwalked over to the rest of the group.

"Saving the rest of her brother's life," Daffonia answered. "I suggest all of you eat, drink, and wash yourselves. When you feel strong again, come outside to see the work of the Eyes of the Forest."

Everyone washed and ate quickly. They were unconcerned with their aches and pains now that their mission had been accomplished. Restia had begun to come around, though it would be a long time before she could fly again. Lipa was gently feeding Tolebit and washing him with the water that Jewell had brought back on her fur after she dove in the water just like the first time she'd come in from the Black Place.

When Tolebit began to awaken, he saw his sister first. "Lipa," he said weakly.

Lipa leaned over Tolebit and kissed him on the forehead. "It's alright now," she said. "You're alright. Jewell is here and Daffonia, too."

"Jewell?" he asked, trying to lift his head. "Where is she?"

"Right here," Jewell said as she walked over to Tolebit, then lay her head down beside his little body.

"Jewell got everyone together to rescue you," Lipa told him. "She wouldn't leave until you were safe."

"She almost got herself killed trying," Sam chimed in. "And more than once."

Tolebit smiled. "And I thought you didn't like me," he said, patting her nose.

"I didn't," Jewell replied. "But I do, now."

When everyone was fed and cleaned up, Sunny flew both Lipa and Tolebit up on to Jewell's neck. Restia rode on Melvin's back with Robin and Sapphire who were both suffering from burnt feathers, though not nearly as bad as Restia's. Sunny soared through the tunnel under his own strength, even ahead of Sam, who scurried along as fast as his little, chipmunk body would go.

When they were halfway to the opening, they all noticed how the air had not changed into the dry, hot air they had come to expect. Instead, the air stayed cool and refreshing all the way to the cave.

"Oh my!" Lipa said as they reached the opening that led out of the mountain.

"How beautiful!" Ringo said.

"Isn't it, though?" Jewell sighed as she stood at the edge of the cave and looked out around the forest that had reappeared in place of the Black Place they had left only a short time ago.

"So this is what we were supposed to fly into," Robin said.

"This is Noah's Forest," Daffonia said. "I think Jewell understood it better than the rest of us."

"Nah," Jewell said, turning her head sideways in embarrassment.

"Regardless," Daffonia said to her. "Are you ready to go to Noah's Garden?"

Jewell looked startled. "Don't I get a day or two to rest after this?" she asked. "I'm not sure that I'm ready to pick up on my journey to the garden, again."

"There's no more journey, Jewell," Daffonia said. "There's only the garden, now." She looked around at all the good friends Jewell had made. "For all of you," she added.

"Do you mean I can go to the garden, now?" Tolebit piped in. "Is this what I had to go through to get past the Day Lilies? What kind of a. . . . "

"Ssshhh," Lipa said, trying to sooth him. "None of us were supposed to go through this. Just relax."

Jewell looked at Daffonia with a tear in her eye. "Really?" she asked her dear friend.

"Really," Daffonia said as she took a step forward. "Just follow me and I'll take you there."

"Let's go!" Sam said, scurrying ahead. "What is everyone waiting for?"

Jewell laughed even as she shed a few tears of joy for having come through Tolebit's rescue with her tiny friend alive, and the Black Place gone.

As she followed Daffonia through what used to be the Black Place, she could see the trees that had fallen from the beast's angry yell, but they were now covered with moss and vines. Flowers of every shape and color stood clustered in beautiful masses as far as the eye could see. In the distance, Amethyst bowed to them before turning to walk among the trees. Jewell breathed in the crystal clean air of renewal and prepared herself to see a place even more beautiful than where she was right now.

CHAPTER 22

Jewell knew they were near Noah's Garden after only a few minutes. Huge, colorful Day Lilies grew in great masses everywhere she looked. Tolebit made a point of bringing Jewell's attention to them.

"So that's what they are," Jewell sighed in amazement. "They're beautiful."

"They are," Daffonia agreed.

"Will we see the garden after we pass through these?" Jewell asked Daffonia.

"Not exactly," Sam said as he scurried along.

"When then?" Jewell asked, but she didn't have to wait for an answer. At that exact moment they were approaching the edge of the mass of Day Lilies, and although Jewell could still see many clusters of them scattered about in all the brightly lit places ahead, she also saw and smelled the most beautiful flowers she could ever remember seeing.

"Aren't they just gorgeous?" Lipa asked excitedly. "Look at all the roses. I've never seen so many different kinds of roses in one place."

"Every kind of rose that exists," Daffonia explained, "is right here on the borders of Noah's Garden."

"Are there roses in the garden, too?" Lipa asked.

"Oh yes," Daffonia said. "Just wait until you see."

The group of travelers walked down a path that cut through the center of the hundreds of rose bushes that were strewn naturally about.

"There's so much to take care of," Jewell said. "Who does it all?"

"The Eyes of the Forest, of course," Daffonia answered. "They take care of everything."

Jewell could not help but be mesmerized by the multitude of roses. The smell of them was sweet and hypnotic. Mixed in between them were more of the Day Lilies they had fought so hard to find along with purple campanula.

"Look up ahead," Sunny said as he swooped low over their heads.

As the travelers all did what he said, a great gasp went out among them. Straight ahead they saw a golden shimmer that seemed to cover a huge section of the forest. It arced upward as if to cover something beneath it. Right at the innermost part of the arc was a magnificent rainbow, the likes of which no one else on earth had ever seen. The colors were brilliant and glimmering with specks of gold throughout every part of it.

"Incredible!" Tolebit said as he looked up weakly from his place on Jewell's neck. "That's what I've spent all these years looking for."

"That is Noah's Garden," Daffonia said. "If your heart is fully open to all the good that exists, then you will be able to see it from anywhere."

"Even from the Outside Place?" Robin asked.

"Even from the Outside Place," Daffonia confirmed as they walked the hundred yards to the edge of the field of roses.

"Now what?" Melvin asked.

"Keep walking," Daffonia said. "You will all walk right into it."

They did as they were told. Jewell went first with Tolebit and Lipa riding her neck. After only seven steps, Jewell entered a misty veil. Four steps later she walked out of it into an entirely different world.

"Tolebit," Jewell said in awe.

"I see it," he answered.

"It's paradise," Lipa sighed.

"I believe you're right," Melvin said as he walked through the misty veil with the rest of the travelers and stood beside Jewell.

Sam was still scurrying back and forth ahead of them, seemingly oblivious to what they were experiencing.

As they watched Sam, they suddenly realized the path directly before them over which he ran was covered in a shimmering golden substance. On either side of the pathway stood rose bushes with flowers in a color none of them had ever seen before.

"Blue?" Lipa asked. "Blue roses? Why, they're as blue as the sky on a clear summer day."

"Real blue roses only exist in Noah's Garden," Daffonia explained. "In the Outside Place you'll find lavendar ones, but the real blue roses can only be found here."

Jewell walked up to the roses and breathed in their fragrance. "Heavenly," she said with her eyes closed as if she were dreaming.

"Exactly," Daffonia said contentedly. "Exactly."

"Come on!" Sam shouted in his chipmunk voice. "What are you all waiting for? There's more to see. Follow me." And with that, he scurried further up the path and around a bend.

The others began to follow, but they were constantly distracted by the incredible sights that surrounded them. Clusters of gleaming white birch could be seen everywhere they looked. Tall Pampas Grass bordered the edges of sunny spots, but even that was different from what any of them had ever seen.

"Lavendar?" Tolebit asked, bending one of the stems down toward him "Why that stuff grows along the roads that people in the Outside Place use to travel on. I've never seen it in such colors, though."

"Actually," Daffonia said, "the pink and white Pampas Grass varieties do exist in the Outside Place, but the lavendar can only be found here. There's even a small cluster of blue Pampas Grass further ahead in the garden."

"It's like a dream," Restia said from her perch on Melvin's back. "It doesn't seem as if any of this could really exist."

"Everything exists somewhere," Daffonia said. "But the world doesn't deserve to have it all. Not yet, at least."

"What do you mean?" Ringo asked as they proceeded down the golden path.

"There will come a time when the Outside Place is ready for these splendors," Daffonia explained, "but that time has not arrived yet."

"When will it arrive?" Sapphire asked from his place next to Restia.

"Quite soon, actually," Daffonia said. "But only Abba knows for sure."

"Who's Abba?" Melvin asked.

"Do you mean to tell us that you don't know who Abba is?" Sunny asked, surprised.

"Why, everyone knows who Abba is," Restia chimed in.

"Well, I don't," Melvin said feeling silly. Then to Ringo he asked, "Do you know about Abba?"

"All animals who live in the wild know of Abba," Ringo answered.

"Don't worry, Mel," Jewell said comfortingly as they proceeded down the path. "I didn't know who Abba was either, until I entered the forest."

"Who is it?" Melvin asked, sounding disturbed.

"Let me explain," Jewell said as the others listened. "Abba is a good and powerful force. He exists through the love and care we give to each other. Where there is love, there is Abba. Where there is understanding, there is Abba. Where there is mercy, there is Abba."

"How do you know this?" Melvin asked.

"Because I feel it deep inside of me, now," Jewell answered. "As I traveled through the forest I learned about Abba along the way. Now I understand it all so much more."

"What else do you understand?" Daffonia asked.

"I understand that Abba is in every one of us," Jewell replied. "I understand that any time we do something good, something loving, we invite Abba to be a larger part of us."

"That's beautiful," a voice said from a little way down the path.

Together, the travelers all looked toward the direction from which the voice had come. They saw a figure walking toward them, a man dressed in draped clothing of such incredible whiteness that it made it difficult to look at him without hurting their eyes. As he came closer, however, their eyes seemed to adjust to it, making it easy for them to see the sparkles of gold that seemed to surround him and to lay on his garments. He carried a large walking stick that curved at the topmost part where it was higher than the man was tall.

In silence, they all watched as he approached, followed by pairs of animals of every kind. The line of animals behind the man seemed to go on forever.

Finally, Daffonia took a few steps forward, meeting him half way between the weary travelers and the entourage that had come to greet them. She turned sideways between the man and Jewell who stood in front of the travelers.

"Jewell?" Daffonia questioned to get her attention. "Jewell, this is Noah."

Jewell stepped up to Noah until she stood a foot away from him. She'd never been able to talk to a person before and she didn't know what to do.

But Noah seemed to understand.

"Jewell," he said, leaning over to pet her on the head. "I'm so glad you finally arrived."

Not knowing how to answer, Jewell licked Noah's face, making him laugh delightedly.

"You may speak to me the way you've been able to speak to all the other animals with whom you've kept company," Noah explained. "All creatures here understand each other without question."

"I'm happy to be here, finally," Jewell said to Noah. "It's so beautiful!"

"Thanks to God," Noah said. "He created all of this as He did the entire universe."

"God?" Jewell asked in confusion. I thought Abba created all things."

Noah let out a deep chuckle. "God is Abba."

"I don't undertstand," Jewell said.

"Abba is a nickname, of sorts that a group of people used to call the creator of all things a long time ago," Noah explained. "But the being they were referring to is the only god there is. Even back in my days on earth, we called our creator by other names. But since He is the only true God, we simply know Him as God, now."

Jewell nodded her head in understanding. "I think I understand," she said. "It's like my family named me Jewell, but they call me a lot of other names at different times. Like Sweety and Honey and things like that."

"I believe you do understand," Noah replied.

"How's Glory?" Jewell asked, changing the subject and making Tolebit sit upright hoping for word of Poppy.

"Glory is going to be fine," Noah said. "I'll take you to see her. She's been worried about you."

"I'm anxious to see her, too" Jewell replied. "But first I think you should meet the bravest bunch I've ever known."

Jewell introduced every one of the group to Noah who had something pleasant to say about each of them. When she was finished, she said to Noah, "I'm proud to know them all."

"And I'm sure that Abba is proud of all of you," Noah replied. He turned and pointed his arm toward the walkway. "Shall we go see the others?"

"Yes," Tolebit agreed. "Let's go see the others."

Noah began to walk back the way he'd come while all the pairs of animals that had followed him, parted to create their own lines for the travelers to pass through and be welcomed into the garden.

"Noah?" Jewell asked

"Yes, Jewell?" Noah responded.

"Is the Black Place really gone?" she asked.

"For now," Noah said almost sadly.

"What do you mean?" Jewell asked nervously.

"It should never have gotten that powerful, Jewell," he replied. "For now, the Faeries, or Eyes of the Forest, as you've come to know them, have managed to rid the forest of its evil. That was a very smart idea you had, Jewell. It worked perfectly."

"Didn't you know that it would?" Jewell asked, amazed. "Hadn't anyone been able to figure it out before?"

"Oh yes," Noah said. "But you see, we cannot stop it from happening again. Every thousand years, it grows strong enough to cause trouble. The only way to prevent it from ever happening again is for everyone on the earth to stop fighting, stop hating, stop killing, stop antagonizing, and stop destroying each other."

"Only people do that," Lipa said.

"Not true," Noah replied. "Is it Jewell?"

"No," Jewell conceded. "It's not true at all. I was a terror in my own way in the Outside Place. I disobeyed everything my family said and I antagonized their neighbors by making the other dogs run with me and tear up lawns and garbage and. . . . gardens," she finished sheepishly.

"So, you see," Noah said. "There's room for improvement everywhere. Not only in the people, but in all creatures, great and small. Tolebit can tell you all about his own shortcomings once he's feeling stronger." Noah winked at Tolebit.

"But if all living creatures stopped doing wrong, then there'd be no need for Noah's Forest," Melvin chimed in.

"On the contrary, my feline friend," Noah said. "If all living creatures became the good and wonderful beings Abba intended, then this forest Abba gave to me for refuge and to take care of, would be able to spread out across the entire world."

"Wouldn't that be wonderful?" Lipa asked, a dreamy expression on her face.

"Just imagine," Sapphire said. "I could sit on a blue rose and blend right in."

"You can do that while you're here," Daffonia said. "Enjoy this garden for as long as you like."

"We're almost there," Noah said as the golden path began to

widen dramatically, ending in a large circle covered with the same substance.

"Where are we?" Tolebit asked as he looked around in awe.

"This is the center of the garden," Daffonia explained. "It's where you'll find Noah if you ever decide to come back to visit."

"It is also where Astilbe lives," Noah said, indicating a tall, white structure in the center of the golden circle. It looked like a four foot tall castle made entirely of white marble. Surrounding its base, grew a foot tall plant nearly covered from top to bottom with tiny, blue flowers that gave it a fuzzy appearance.

"I've never seen anything like that before," Jewell said as she tried to breath in their aroma, then began to sneeze.

"Those are blue Astilbe," Daffonia explained.

"That's Astilbe?" Tolebit asked as Jewell completed her last sneeze.

"That is a flower called Astilbe," Noah explained. "Once again, they exist in the Outside Place in different colors, none of which are blue. Astilbe, herself, created them with Abba's help."

"Why is blue such a nonexistent color in the Outside Place?" Jewell asked.

"Oh, blue does exist in many parts of nature in the Outside Place," Noah explained. "But there are many kinds of flowers that cannot be found in blue."

"There's so much of it here," Sapphire said. "I like it."

"I would expect that you would," Noah said, chuckling. "Blue is a soothing color. It's pleasing to look at. It has a calming effect."

"That's why you'll find so much of it here, in the garden," Daffonia explained. "But you'll see many other colors as well. Every living thing that exists all over the world can be found right here."

"Greetings," a tiny voice said from an opening high up in the marble castle.

"Hello, Astilbe," Noah said. "How is Glory feeling today?"

"Almost new," Astilbe answered as she stepped further out where everyone could see her.

"You're beautiful!" Jewell gasped as she watched Astilbe's gentle, flowing movements. The tiny mother of the Eyes of the Forest glimmered in shades of pale blue and pure white with the same sparkling gold all around her. She wore a garment that was long enough to hide her little feet and her wings dropped gold dust every time she moved.

"The garden is paved with the goodness that comes from Astilbe's wings," Noah said.

"You're so beautiful," Jewell said again as she sighed at the awe inspiring sight.

"Thank you," Astilbe said graciously, bowing her head. "But there's someone else who is very anxious to see you, Jewell."

Astilbe turned sideways and extended her right hand into the marble castle. A glimmer of deep red could be seen as a tiny hand reached out to take hers. Through the little doorway, high up in the castle, emerged Glory. She was radiant in glowing red with gold specks all over her.

Immediately upon seeing Jewell, Glory took to the air and flew to her, landing on her nose. She wrapped both of her arms as far around Jewell's nose as she could make them stretch and hugged her until she turned away from the rest of the group, embarrassed.

"I love you, Jewell," Glory said as she continued to hug the dog who had found her in the forest. Finally, Glory released her grip on Jewell's nose and sat upright on her nose.

"I only did what anyone else would have done," Jewell said.

"Anyone else might not have bothered," Glory said. "But you did."

"Awww, it was nothing," Jewell said, feeling deeply touched by Glory's intense gratitude.

"To me," Astilbe said, "it was everything. These Eyes are all my children, born of pure love. Each one of them means the world to me. To lose even one of them would be to lose a part of myself. By saving Glory, you've also saved me. And for that, I too, am deeply grateful."

Jewell was at a loss. She was surprised that they were making such a big deal out of a simple deed.

"And for you Tolebit," Astilbe said. "I know someone who has waited a long time for you to reach the garden."

As the travelers watched the small castle, Poppy emerged from a different opening in the little castle. Her brilliant, light, sunny color, also sparkled with bits of gold dust, causing her to be flagrantly displayed against the backdrop of white marble.

"Poppy!" Tolebit shouted as he watched her flutter down to his side.

"I've waited so long for you to get here," she said to him. "I'm so happy that you finally made it."

"Me, too," Tolebit said, mesmerized by her presence.

"Hhm, Hhm," Lipa sounded from her brother's side, releasing him from his reverie.

"Oh, I'm so sorry," he apologized. "Poppy, this is my sister, Lipa."

The two exchanged greetings and began to become acquainted as they moved down to Jewell's back, away from her ears, so as not to disturb her with their tiny chattering.

"We still have a few things to attend to," Noah said. "First of all, these poor birds have really taken a beating from their attempts to rescue Tolebit."

As Noah said that, fourteen white doves descended from the skies and landed all around them. Two landed on the marble castle, two landed on Noah's shoulders. Seven of them landed on the ground near Melvin and Ringo where the four injured birds stood perched, two on each of their backs. The remaining three perched themselves on Noah's right arm that held his walking stick.

"These doves will take Robin, Restia, Sunny, and Sapphire," Noah said. "They will clean you up and start the healing process that will make you whole again."

With that, the four weakened birds were invited to nestle on the backs of four of the doves who had stood on the ground nearby.

As soon as they were comfortably settled, all fourteen doves took flight with the four traveling birds as their passengers.

"Wow," Ringo said. "That was different."

"That was as it should always be," Noah responded. "As for the rest of you. We have places set up for each of you to rest and be attended to."

"Tolebit and Lipa will stay with me," Astilbe said. "We would like to take care of them here in my home."

"Very well," Noah said, smiling in a pleased manner.

As they all watched, Tolebit and Lipa were carried to the castle by four Eyes of the Forest who had emerged from the blue Astilbe growing nearby.

"The rest of you may follow me," Noah added.

"Hey," Jewell said, suddenly. "Where did Sam go?"

There was a rustling among the bushes to their left, after which Sam proudly emerged. "A chipmunk is always close by," Sam said, puffing up his little chest.

Together, Jewell, Daffonia, Melvin, Ringo, and Noah laughed as they headed down another golden path on the other side of the circle that surrounded Astilbe's marble castle.

CHAPTER 23

After they had walked only a short time, a young man appeared on the golden path.

"Jewell," Noah said. "This is Jacob. If you like, Jacob will take care of your wounds and get you something to eat."

Jewell looked at the young adult and was saddened as she remembered the family back home she had grown to miss so terribly. He looked friendly as he bent down on one knee in front of her and smiled. Jewell could feel his loving nature pour out of him as she slowly approached him.

"That's a good girl," Jacob said as he rubbed Jewell's head and ran a gentle hand down her back.

"I like him. I'll go with him," Jewell said to Noah.

"Good," Noah replied. "When you're rested and fed, feel free to join us back at Astilbe's castle if you'd like." Then to Melvin and Ringo, Noah said, "You two may follow me and we'll get you cleaned up and feeling better as well."

Jewell watched Noah and her friends continue down the path.

"They'll be taken care of just fine," Jacob said to her as he stood up and started to walk toward a small clearing just off the golden path.

"I know they will," Jewell replied. "I was just thinking about how short a time I've known them, yet I feel like they're part of me."

"That happens when new friends go through the kind of experience together that you went through with them," Jacob explained. "That was a major crisis you all took care of. Your lives were at stake, as well as all the life in the forest. The evil you destroyed may even have been able to get into the garden for all we know."

Jewell shuddered at the reminder of what had happened mere hours ago.

"It's over now," Jacob said, noticing her discomfort. "Just relax and forget about it for now."

Jewell watched as Jacob walked over to a wooden table that was set under a huge elm tree with sparkling, green leaves that shimmered with golden specks.

"This is for you," Jacob said as he set a large plate on the ground in front of her. "Eat first to regain your strength. Then we'll see to your wounds."

Jewell looked at him curiously. "Who else besides you is going to take care of me?" she asked.

"We are!!" came the tiny voices from out of the nearby bluebells.

Jewell looked to her right and saw the familiar show of colors that the Eyes of the Forest make as they flutter through the air.

"Verbena!" Jewell yelled happily. "Sprig!! Oh, and Twain!! I'm so happy to see you. Oh, it was awful. I felt like I had just made friends with you and then the thing with Glory happened and I didn't see you anymore and. . . . "

"Relax, Jewell," Sprig said as he flew up to great her. "Sometimes these things happen. But I'll always remember how you helped my sister. Always."

"Us too," Verbena said shyly. "You were very brave, Jewell."

"Yes, you were," Twain said as he flittered forward. "We're all very proud of you, Jewell. You certainly have come a long way from your first day in the forest."

Jewell thought about it for a few seconds. "I have, haven't I?" she replied, realizing the full extent of the changes that had taken place in her.

"How does it feel?" Sprig asked.

"It feels. . . . like I grew up," Jewell said quite seriously. "It feels like I really didn't know what life was about until now. I was always playing around and having fun. I never took anything seriously. I hurt those around me and made everyone angry and all the time I thought it was funny. I thought it was alright to be that way. I thought anything goes just because I say so. I had no idea there were things that were good and things that were bad. Now I know how the bad things have such a terrible effect on those who come in contact with them. Just think what an awful influence I've been on the other dogs in my neighborhood. I've got to fix that."

"In due time," Jacob said. "In due time."

"Besides," Twain said. "Do you remember your friend, Sheldon, from your neighborhood? Well, he's on his way through the forest right now. His journey won't be nearly as hectic or frightening as yours was. He only needs to break the bad habits you taught him."

"Does he have a guide?" Jewell asked.

"Yes, he does," Verbena answered. "Your little friend, Sam, went out to greet him."

"Oh." Jewell sounded disappointed. "So, I won't see Sam again before I leave."

"You never know," Verbena said. "Anything is possible."

"But for now," Jacob interrupted, "we've got to get you fed and cleaned."

"Why don't you just lay down and munch your food," Sprig said, "while the rest of us work on your wounds."

"Will it hurt?" Jewell asked tentatively.

Twain chuckled as his lavendar wings grew brighter.

"You won't feel a thing, Jewell," he said. "Honestly, you won't."

"I trust you," Jewell said as she walked back to her plate of food and began to nibble on the grains and fruit that were on it.

"You'll need something to wash it down," Jacob said as he placed a bowl of water beside the plate.

"Thank you," Jewell said to him, then sniffed the sweet-smelling water before she started to drink.

"Oh, you're welcome," he replied.

As Jewell drank from the water bowl and ate the food that was given to her, Sprig, Verbena, Twain and Jacob inspected the cuts and bruises that riddled her body. Jewell barely felt a thing as they worked to clean and dress them.

"What about that back leg of yours?" Twain asked after the smaller cuts had been attended to.

"It hurts a little," Jewell said. "I'm not sure what happened to it."

"There's only a small cut below the joint," Verbena said. "I think the worst of the damage is inside the leg."

"Is that bad?" Jewell asked.

"That depends on what happened inside," Jacob said. "It's obviously not broken because you're able to walk just fine. I only noticed a slight limp when you walked up to me."

"Does it feel warm?" Sprig asked.

Jewell thought about it.

"No," she said. "Just achy."

"I think it's a simple sprain," Twain said. "Maybe even a pulled muscle. Nothing that some of Astilbe's golden healing dust won't fix."

Jewell watched as Jacob gathered gold dust from the path on which they had walked, and brought it to where she lay. Twain took handfuls of the dust from Jacob's open palm and rubbed it deep through Jewell's fur into her skin. It felt cool and tingly. In no time, the pain in her leg began to fade until it was completely gone.

"It works that fast?" Jewell asked, amazed.

"It sure does," Sprig said. "Your leg is feeling better, I presume."

"It is," Jewell said. "It feels wonderful."

"Good," Sprig said. "Next then, you'll need a bath."

"What?" Jewell asked, alarmed. The idea of a bath with all the hot, soapy water that cools off so quickly, and the feeling of weighing twenty pounds more, did not appeal to her in the least. "I don't think a bath is really necessary."

"It is," Jacob said. "It will make you feel so much better."

"Hhmmmm," Jewell replied, laying her head between her paws.

"Don't worry," Verbena whispered in her ear. "You'll enjoy this bath."

Jewell did not respond, nor did she move. She was sure they meant well. Maybe it wouldn't be that bad. She watched Jacob mix more of the golden dust in a large, stone container with a small amount of water that he had drawn from a nearby well. Into the mixture, he added tiny pieces of leaves that the Eyes had picked from a sweet smelling plant that grew in a neat patch by the walk way. Verbena added many heaping handfuls of pure, white sand that she had gathered from a garden to their left. Jewell was intrigued as she watched them create this concoction that was supposed to clean her fur. It made no sense to her at all.

"Ready for your bath?" Jacob asked as he carried the stone bowl to where Jewell still lay.

"As ready as I'll ever be," Jewell replied.

"Good," Jacob said. "Then we'll all pitch in and clean you right up."

They each took turns grabbing handfuls of the strange mixture in the bowl and Jewell found that she was enjoying the aroma of the unusual substance. It had a minty lemon scent.

"What is all that stuff you put in there?" she asked no one in particular.

"The gold dust is for general healing of your skin," Jacob said.

"The white sand is an abrasive to break up the clumbs of mud and grime that are stuck to your fur," Verbena added.

"The leaves are from the peppermint and lemon grass," Twain said. "They will make you smell nice."

"And the water is there to hold it all on to your fur until it's time to rinse it off," Sprig said, completing the recipe.

Jewell looked around for the source of water they would use to wash the strange concoction from her fur, but she found none. The well certainly wasn't large enough, unless they were planning to carry buckets of water to dump on her. The idea did not appeal to her in the least. "How are you going to rinse it off?" she asked finally.

"We're not," Jacob said. "You are."

"But how?" Jewell asked growing concerned.

Jacob smiled. "You'll see," he said playfully. "We're almost done."

Jewell waited patiently. Her skin actually felt terrific and the smell that surrounded her was so pleasing that she wasn't minding this bath at all. She felt pampered and she was thoroughly enjoying it.

"Ready?" Jacob asked as he walked the bowl back to the wooden table and left it there.

"For what?" Jewell asked.

"To rinse off," Sprig said.

"I guess," Jewell said uncertainly.

"Then follow us," Twain said as he started to flutter away through the sparkling, white birch trees that surrounded them.

"Come on," Jacob said. "There's a little path right here. You're going to love this."

Jewell stood up and began to follow Jacob. She was surprised to find that she didn't feel any extra weight.

"Don't shake off," Jacob warned.

"I won't," Jewell replied, although the urge to do just that was strong.

They walked a short way through huge, green ferns and deep red lilies. Jewell began to hear the sound of falling water and her curiousity grew. Up ahead she could see the colors of the Eyes of the Forest as they twinkled excitedly. Twain's soft lavendar, Verbena's deep yellow and Sprig's shiny green. She even thought she saw Tempo fluttering around in the sun.

"Here we are," Jacob said, walking through the last tall fern and into a clearing that surrounded a crystal, clear pool of spring water. A thin water fall emptied into it from one hundred feet up the side of a rocky cliff that was covered with dense, green foliage and brilliantly colored flowers. And, as was the case everywhere else in Noah's Garden, there was a golden sheen over all of it.

"It's beautiful," Jewell sighed in disbelief.

"Isn't is, though?" Sprig commented as he fluttered up beside her.

"Well," Jacob said as he walked to the edge of the pool. "Ready to rinse Jewell?" With that he dove in, head first and came up for air directly in front of the waterfall.

Jewell couldn't resist. She took a running start toward the pool and jumped right in without hesitation. The cool, spring water felt invigorating. She couldn't remember ever feeling this good about herself or as healthy and strong as she felt at that moment.

"Awesome!" she said to Jacob as she came up for air and began to swim for shore. Jacob swam right behind her.

After climbing out of the water, Jacob climbed on to a small cliff and dove in to the water, again. Jewell followed right behind him, loving the feel of the fresh, pure water on every part of her body.

For over an hour, Jacob and Jewell played in the pool while Sprig, Verbena, and Twain watched from their perches in the centers of the lilies. The Eyes of the Forest laughed at the antics of Jacob and Jewell as they found new ways to dive into the water. Sometimes they dove in together. Once they jumped in while Jacob had Jewell in his arms. They splashed and played, enjoying every moment of the time together.

Finally, the sun seemed about to set and Jacob stopped playing in the water and let himself begin to dry off.

"What's the matter?" Jewell asked him.

"Nothing's the matter," Jacob said, smiling. "We should be going to Astilbe's castle soon to meet the others. They should all be feeling pretty much the way you are."

"That's right," Jewell said. "Noah did mention that we could meet back there once we were feeling rested. But I have to say, that we've been playing here for quite a while now, and I don't feel all that tired."

"The water gives us energy," Jacob said. "So do the trees and flowers and everything that surrounds us. It's a gift from Abba so that we never get sick or angry. We never age the way those in the Outside Place do."

"But Noah is old," Jewell said.

"Noah was old before he was given this place to care for," Jacob said. "The way he looks now is the way he's looked for thousands of years."

"Wow," was all Jewell could think to say.

"Where is his family?" she asked after some thought.

"With God," Jacob replied. "Sometimes they come here to see him, but that doesn't happen that often. I've only seen his wife once."

"Doesn't he miss her?" Jewell asked.

"The way Noah explains it is that he doesn't miss her because he never feels empty," Jacob replied. "God keeps him company and Abba keeps his wife and his children company so Noah feels their presence at all times through Abba."

"Abba is mighty powerful," Jewell remarked. "I mean God."

"It's alright for you to call him Abba," Jacob reassured her. "The name means 'Daddy' or 'Father' in another language called Hebrew." He paused for Jewell to acknowledge that she understood. When she nodded her head, he continued. "God is everything," Jacob said lovingly as he stood up and started to walk back the way they'd come to reach the pool.

"Can I meet God here?" Jewell asked.

"You already have," Jacob replied.

"What do you mean?" Jewell asked. "I only saw you and Noah and Astilbe."

"And all the animals that came to welcome you to the garden," Sprig said as he fluttered up to Jewell and landed on her nose.

"And all the different plants that are only found here," Twain added.

"Not to mention at least one of every kind of plant that exists in the world," Verbena said.

"Then what are you saying?" Jewell asked. "I don't understand."

"What we're saying," Sprig began to explain, "is that God is everything because God made everything. His love abounds in everything you see. It's in you and me and this tree and in Noah and just everywhere. God is all around you and part of you at all times."

"No wonder Noah never feels lonely without his family around him," Jewell said. "We're all his family because we're all part of God."

"You couldn't be more correct," Jacob said as they reached the golden path and headed back toward the center of the garden and to Astible's castle.

CHAPTER 24

"Hello, everyone!" Jewell called as she raced to the golden circle that surrounded Astilbe's castle. "Did anyone miss me?"

"We all did," Glory replied from her perch on the little balcony that extended from one of the many entrances to the castle. "Most of all, I did," she finished, smiling.

"Jewell!" Ringo exclaimed as he came toward her. "Why, just look at you, all shiny and clean. Your hair is so fluffy. You look beautiful!"

"Ahh,. . . . thanks, Ringo," Jewell replied, embarrassed. She hadn't taken the time to consider how she looked. She had only thought about how good she felt since going with Jacob.

"You look pretty good yourself, you know," she said to Ringo, then looked around at the others. "You all look good."

"Look at me," Restia said as she came forward to show off her new feathers.

"How did you grow new feathers so fast?" Jewell asked her, amazed.

"The Eyes of the Forest gave them to me," Restia replied. "I'm as good as new, now."

"You sure are," Noah said as he slowly approached the group, followed by two tigers and a pair of giraffes. "You should all be feeling as good as new." Then to Jewell he said, "What about you, Jewell? How are you feeling?"

"Much better," Jewell replied as she stared in awe at the size of the giraffes. "Jacob and I went swimming in the pool with the waterfall," she continued. "It felt terrific!"

"Ah, I'm glad to hear it," Noah replied. "And what do you think of the garden?"

"Oh, it's beautiful," Jewell sighed. "I've never seen anything like this in my whole life. I wish the whole world was like this."

"With God's help it might be one day," Noah said. "For now, however, this is all there is."

"You make it sound like it's a small place," Melvin said. "I think your garden is huge."

Noah laughed. "It is quite large," he said, "but you have to understand that the whole world used to be like this at one time . . . at its beginning."

"What happened to it?" Robin asked.

"Oh, people built things," Noah began. "Then they built bigger things. Their own two feet weren't good enough to get them around. They started using horses, camels, mules, any animal that would carry them, but that wasn't good enough or fast enough. So, they built cars, then trucks, then airplanes and before they knew it they had invented pollution along with all the rest of their inventions."

Noah shook his head sadly as he looked off into the forest surrounding the golden path.

"Not to mention the factories," Verbena said as she fluttered around to the front of Astilbe's castle.

"And all the garbage they throw around," Jacob added from his place beside Jewell.

Silently, they all sat, lost in their individual thoughts about an entire world as beautiful as Noah's Garden.

Suddenly, Jewell remembered Tolebit.

"Hey," she said, laughing, "where's the little troublemaker we rescued?"

"Do you mean Tolebit?" Noah asked.

"Yes. Where is he?" Jewell asked. "How is he?"

"See for yourself," Noah said, pointing to Astilbe's castle.

Jewell turned toward the castle in time to see Poppy flutter out of the upper doorway, then stop in mid-air to wait for someone else. Tolebit emerged slowly with his sister, Lipa, by his side.

"Tolebit," Jewell said. "Are you OK?"

"I'm fine," Tolebit said. "Thanks to you I'm fine."

"Don't forget about these folks," Jewell said. "They had as much to do with getting you away from the Monster Shadow as I did."

"Thank you. All of you," Tolebit said. "I can't thank you enough."

"You're alive," Melvin said. "That's all the thanks any of us need."

Tolebit nodded his head to show he understood.

"There is one more creature who was part of your rescue," Jewell said. "He's not here right now, but I thought you should know about him, too."

"Oh yes," Tolebit said. "The chipmunk. I remember seeing him running back and forth all over the place."

"That was him, alright," Jewell said. She turned to Noah to ask him a few questions that had been bothering her. "Noah," she said.

"Yes Jewell."

"Can you tell me why Tolebit got stuck at the Day Lilies for so long?" she asked.

"Wasn't that obvious?" Noah questioned her with a gentle smile on his face. "He had to learn a little humility and a lot of kindness."

"I guess I knew that," Jewell said sheepishly.

"Then what's really on your mind, Jewell?" Noah asked as he walked to her side and knelt down beside her. "Ask me the question you really want an answer to."

Jewell licked the back of Noah's hand timidly before she spoke.

"Why couldn't Tolebit find the Day Lilies again when he was with me?" she asked.

"What do you think, Jewell?" Noah challenged.

Jewell thought about it for quite a while before she replied.

"I guess I needed to learn what it was to make the ultimate sacrifice for someone you love," she answered. "Like I might have to do for my family back home someday."

"More than that," Noah said. "You may not remember this, but when you were still a puppy, you ran away. You didn't get very far because you were still so small. The man in your family was chasing you. He saw you run out into the middle of the street. You ran right in front of a car and never knew the danger you were in. But he did. He risked his own life to jump out in front of the car to make the driver stop before it hit you. You, of course, just kept running. They found you later, but you were alive and well."

Jewell put her head on the ground between her paws.

"Do you understand?" Noah asked.

"I understand," Jewell replied.

"Why is it that the rest of us were able to enter the garden so quickly?" Ringo asked. "We didn't have to go through the journey that Jewell went through."

"Because you were all willing to work together and to make the ultimate sacrifice for another," Noah answered. "Think about it. What more could you have given to save Tolebit's life than your own?"

The newcomers to the garden all shook their heads as they began to realize what Noah meant.

"No matter what else you do with the rest of your lives," Noah began, "remember just one rule to live."

"What's that rule?" Tolebit asked.

"Do unto others as you would have them do unto you," Noah answered. "If you live by that one, simple rule, you'll find that you have very few troubles and always a very clear conscience."

"I like it," Melvin said.

"I love it," Jewell said, sniffling back the tears as she thought about her family.

"What's the matter?" Noah asked as he stroked Jewell's head.

"I miss my family," she answered between quiet sobs. "I miss my family an awful lot."

"You may return to them whenever you like," Noah said. "You know all that you need to know now in order to fulfill the purpose God gave you."

"I wish I could bring my family here," Jewell said.

"I wish you could, too," Noah said. "But this garden is here only for those who find that something is missing in themselves. Until they have exhausted all possibilities in the Outside Place to find what they're looking for, neither the garden nor its surrounding forest is open to them."

Jewell looked around the garden, marvelling again at its splendor.

"Is that why there are more animals here than people?" Jewell asked.

"Yes," Noah answered. "People have a multitude of ways to find what they're looking for, many of which they created themselves. Some go to others to talk about things. They talk to doctors and friends and those who are in various religious fields. They take up hobbies and fight for causes. Many of them turn to God right away and find their peace there."

"Do the people know about Abba, too?" Jewell asked.

"Sure they do," Noah replied. "They call Him by many different names, but they all mean the same person. There is only one God no matter what you may choose to call him."

"Wow," Jewell said. "I feel peaceful just talking about him. He is very good indeed, if his very name can make me feel this way."

"He is very good," Noah said. "Look around you and see what He created. Look at your friends. Look at the flowers. Look up at the stars at night and see Him there, too. God is everywhere."

Jewell looked up at the daytime sky and, for a moment, thought she saw a loving, smiling face in the clouds. She smiled back just in case.

"So more animals end up here," she said when the face was gone.

"That's true," Noah said. "Because animals are spiritual, too, but no one seems to know it except for other animals. And me."

"And me," Jacob added.

"And us," the Eyes who were present chimed in.

"But rest assured, Jewell," Noah said as he stood up beside

her. "You are welcome to come visit any time you want to. You know the way, now."

"But I'm not sure that I do," Jewell said. "I could never remember how I actually got here."

"Sure you do," Noah said. "Don't ever forget the things you learned here and you'll never forget the way to Abba's garden."

"What about the rest of you?" Jewell asked. "What are you going to do?"

"I'm staying here," Ringo said. "It's too beautiful to leave."

"I'm staying here too," Restia echoed. "For a little while, at least."

"I'm going home," Melvin said. "I miss my family, too. They're probably worried sick about me."

"What about you two?" Jewell asked Robin and Sunny.

"We've decided to stay for a little while before we head back to our own forest," Robin replied.

Then Jewell turned slowly toward the castle. "What about you Tolebit?" she asked. "What are you going to do?"

Tolebit looked lovingly at Poppy as she fluttered up along his side. He put one arm around Lipa and the other around Poppy.

"I'm staying for good," he said. "I could never bear to live without Poppy near me.

"I'm going to stay for a little while," Lipa said, looking at her brother, then giving him a big hug around his middle. "Then I'll go home and take word that Tolebit is alive and well."

"Always remember," Noah said. "Those of you who leave are always welcome back as long as you remember what you've learned here."

Daffonia, who had lain a body length behind Jewell, stood up and walked to her. "I think I'm going to miss you most of all the newcomers I have accompanied to the garden," she said to Jewell as a tear rolled down her cheek. "I've never met anyone quite like you."

"Oh, Daffonia," Jewell said as she stood up and nuzzled her. "I gave you such a hard time, didn't I?"

"Oh, but it all worked out for the best," Daffonia answered.

"I love you, Daffy," Jewell said.

"I love you too, Jewell."

Turning to Noah, Jewell said, "I have another question."

"What is it?" Noah asked as he stroked the head of the tiger who stood by his side.

"What took you so long to send the Eyes of the Forest to help us in the Black Place?" she asked. "I don't mean any disrespect in asking, but it seemed like you didn't really care about us."

"Never think that I don't care about any of you," Noah said. "I care about all of you more than you could know. Daffonia delivered your message to me almost immediately," he explained. "Abba would never have allowed me to let any serious harm come to any of you. You were all here to learn something and become more than what you were. None of you were here to die. But sometimes you learn more about yourself by pushing beyond your self-imposed limits than you do in any other way. All of you did more than you ever thought you'd be able to. You went further in trying to save Tolebit than anyone could have ever expected you to. You learned about working together. You learned about trusting each other. You learned how strong the power of love and caring for each other really is. It had to be the most dramatic event that I've ever seen in all the years I've been caretaker of the garden. I'm so proud of all of you that I can't even find the right words to describe my feelings. Had you given up, then I would have sent the Eyes in much sooner, but you didn't. And so, I let you learn as much about yourselves as there was time to safely allow without losing a single one of you." He paused as he looked at each of them. "I learned to let each one learn in their own time, at their own pace, and the lesson will not be forgotten."

There was silence all around as Noah's explanation sunk in. Finally, Jewell sat up. "I'm glad you did what you did," she said. "I learned what I'm really capable of and I don't think I would have learned it any other way."

"I'm glad you understand," Noah replied.

"There's just one more thing," Jewell added.

"What's that?" Noah asked.

"I really wanted to see Sam before I left," she said, "but Jacob told me that he's in the forest with a friend of mine from home."

"If you want to wait just a little bit," Noah said, "they'll be arriving shortly. Sheldon had very little to learn except to break the bad habits that you taught him," Noah finished with a wink.

Jewell lowered her head because she felt embarrassed by the bad things she had taught her friends. "I'm sorry," she said.

"I know you are," Noah replied. "But rest assured that all is forgiven. God always forgives an honest heart."

"I wish I could talk to Him," Jewell said, hopefully.

"You can talk to him with your heart," Noah said. "He hears everything you say and He knows everything you feel."

Jewell just stared at Noah, dumbfounded by the incredible power of such a being as Abba.

"Where does he get his name?" she asked Noah out of the blue.

Noah laughed. "Abba means 'father' or 'daddy,' as I believe Jacob has already explained to you," he replied. "But as I told you, there are many names for him. It all depends on the culture of the people who name him."

"Who named him Abba?" Jewell asked.

"All of the creatures he created," Noah replied. "That name was given to him a very long time ago."

"The Hebrew people?" Jewell asked.

"Even before them, actually," Noah replied.

"Oh," Jewell sighed, not really understanding.

"Hey! Jewell!" a tiny voice called from behind her as she stood, contemplating Noah's words. She quickly turned around when she recognized the voice.

"Sam!" she called. "I'm so glad to see you. Melvin and I are getting ready to go home."

"I thought you would," Sam said as he stopped scurrying and stood before her. "It's the reason you came here in the first place.

You're needed at home, but you had to be stronger and wiser in order to fulfill your purpose."

"I know," Jewell replied. "I understand now."

"There you are!" Sheldon said as his short-haired, chestnut colored body came trotting down the golden path. "I thought I was going to be lost," he continued as he approached the group, but stopped short when he saw Jewell.

"Hi, Sheldon," Jewell said when Sheldon continued to stare at her without saying a word. "How have you been?"

"Why, I've been worried about you and missing you," he replied. "And wondering what the heck you had gotten yourself into this time."

"Didn't you know I was here?" Jewell asked him.

"No, I didn't," Sheldon replied. "Sam never told me."

"He had his own lessons to learn first," Sam said without explaining what they were. "But Noah also felt that if you ever wanted to come back for a visit, you'd have Sheldon to accompany you all the way. You two could visit together."

"That's right," Jewell said. "We could."

"For right now, you and Melvin will have each other's company to travel home," Sam said.

"Yeah," Sheldon added. "I need to stay a day or so, but I'll be home soon and we can start planning our trip back here to visit."

"And you might even want to be a guide like Daffonia every now and again," Noah suggested.

"You know," Jewell said. "I like the sound of that. But first, I have to get home and make sure my family is taken care of. They're the most important thing to me right now."

"As they should be," Noah replied.

"Well," Jewell said uncomfortably, "I guess this is it. Are you ready to go, Melvin?"

"Whenever you are," Melvin replied.

Jewell looked around at all of her new friends and at the wonders of Noah's Garden before she spoke. With a tear in her eye, she turned first to Daffonia. "Thank you for everything," she said.

"I'm really going to miss you. Who is going to answer all my questions?"

"You'll find the answers inside yourself, now," Daffonia replied. "But remember, I'm only a thought away."

"And Sam," Jewell said, looking down at the chipmunk who stood by her front paws. "You saved my life in that awful Black Place. How could I ever thank you for that?"

"You already have," Sam said. "You thanked me when you saved all the other lives that were at stake there, including Tolebit's. That's the way it works. You do something good for someone and hope that they do something nice for someone else in return."

"I'm going to miss you," Jewell said to him.

"Oh, you'll see me running around your neighborhood," Sam said. "Just remember not to chase every chipmunk you see until you're certain who it is."

"I'll remember," Jewell said, laughing.

Then Jewell walked over to Astilbe's castle.

"Tolebit," she began, but was quickly choked up with emotion.

"Don't even start with me," Tolebit joked. "You did much more for me than I was able to do for you. I owe you everything."

"You're alive," Jewell said. "As long as you stay that way, you don't owe me a thing."

"It's a deal," Tolebit said, laughing, but Jewell did not miss the tiny teardrop that rolled down his cheek.

"Noah," she said finally. "Thank you so much for letting me come here."

"Don't thank me," Noah said. "Thank God. He chose you, not me."

Jewell wasn't sure what Noah meant or how she could thank someone she couldn't talk to. Then she remembered seeing the face in the clouds. She looked up toward the sky and there it was again. "Thank you, Abba," she said. As she did so, she saw the face in the clouds smile at her. She smiled back once again.

"I guess it's time to go," she said as she looked at everyone around her. "But I'll be back soon."

"I think we all know you will," Noah said. "Because there will come a time when we'll need you, too."

"And I'll be there," she said, turning toward Melvin. "I guess we should get going."

"I guess so," Melvin agreed reluctantly as he began his good-byes to everyone.

When he was finished, Jewell began to walk toward the golden path that led away from the castle and back into the forest. She felt something tap her on the top of her head and she stopped walking.

"What?" she asked the air around her.

Sprig flew from her head to her nose and stood there.

"What is it?" Jewell asked him.

"I just want to say 'thank you' for giving me back my sister," he said timidly. "That's all I wanted to say."

"Forget about it, Sprig," Jewell said.

Sprig looked her right in one eye and said very seriously, "I never will." With that, he fluttered back to the center of the garden.

"He's a bit unusual," Melvin said to Jewell as they headed down the golden path back to the forest.

"Who isn't?" Jewell asked, and they both laughed.

CPSIA information can be obtained
at www.ICGtesting.com
Printed in the USA
BVHW030102200219
540716BV00001B/1/P

9 780738 818382